THE RUTHLESS LAND

A B Endacott

Book Title Copyright © 2018 by Alice Boer-Endacott.

Cover designed by Marcus Moltzer
Cover illustration by Nicole Sizer
Map illustration by Ellen Liu

This book is a work of fiction. Names, characters, places, and incidents either are products of the author's imagination or are used fictitiously.
Any resemblance to actual persons,
living or dead, events, or locales is entirely coincidental.

ISBN-978-0-6481875-5-4

Books in the Legends of the Godskissed Continent

Queendom of the Seven Lakes

King of the Seven Lakes

The Ruthless Land

Coming soon

Dark Intent

Dark Purpose

Dark Heart

Untitled (First Country)

For Jess
One of the most true friends I could possibly have.
And the person who I'd want by my side if I were crossing a hostile country.
Because she knows karate.

None of it's my fault.
It's the fault of the earth
And of that perfume
That comes off your breasts and your hair

-*Frederico Garcia Lorca, Blood Wedding*

The Fourth Country

BEFORE THE FALL

ONE

Passing through the lightning storm made her skin tingle and raised the hair on the back of her neck. But Lexana barely noticed, thanks to the forget-me-not. She lifted the long holder to her lips and inhaled, feeling the smoke coalesce in the back of her throat. She stared out the window at the sparse landscape of the mountainside and watched the forks of lightning streak down to kiss the ground. It was beautiful in a terrifying way. The mountain was free of lush foliage. The tallest things which grew were shrubs that stubbornly clung to the earth. Beyond the end of the lightning storm, she could see the other mountains stretching away and out of sight. The winter she was to spend up in the mountains would be unforgiving. It was an intimidating thought.

She felt the fear that the magnificent sight of the lightning storm inspired, but it was as though she was experiencing it from a distance, like she was feeling the memory of that fear. Forget-me-not, when drunk in the forgetting dens by those whose purses, heavy with worthless coins, did not permit them the safer inhaled version, could be crippling. However, when smoked, it was far less dangerous, offering a respite from fear or sadness, but not complete oblivion for which someone had ironically named the drug.

Lexa let her head rest against the cushioned wall of the carriage with a sigh. The smoke on her breath clouded the window and the streaks of lightning became hazy. Her free hand clutched the letters which had been waiting for her when they arrived at the small village at the foot of the mountain the previous evening. She had just finished reading them, only able to muster the courage to open them once she had sunk into the embrace of forget-me-not. Even the drug could not entirely dispel the emotions that swirled within her, roused by their contents.

She had read the letter from her mother first, knowing that whatever it contained, she would likely find it the most off-putting. She had been correct. Her mother, Tanita, had told her in the direct brusqueness that she reserved for her immediate family that once Lexa returned from the Academy she was to take her first slave-husband. The prospect of such intimacy with another person left Lexa unsettled. She was already worried enough about what the Academy might have in store for her without the nervous anticipation of taking a husband hovering above her. Once more, she brought the holder to her lips and inhaled in a bid to calm her nerves. Her mother had deliberately waited until she was on her way to tell her of this. Tanita entrusted many of her plans to her daughter and heir, but she kept a great many more to herself. Lexa chastised herself for not having suspected this particular plan. The gentle way her father had held her as they said goodbye, his voice soothing and warm through his veil, should have been a giveaway that her mother had chosen a first husband for her quiet daughter and heir. At the time, though, Lexa had assumed that her father was going to miss her. She certainly was going to miss him.

The second letter had been barely any better than her mother's, despite Lexa's hopes. One of her closest friends, Emi, had written to express her excitement at the news that her brother was to be Lexa's husband. Perhaps her mother had thought this a kindness, but Lexa could only see it as further cause for anxiousness. *Elui* – slave-husbands – were bound to the will of their wife. Lexa knew as well as anyone that while one could care for their husband, they must nevertheless be treated with a firm hand. After all, the primary function of men was to serve the interests of women. She did not feel entirely comfortable with the idea of commanding the life of her friend's brother.

Perhaps she had been travelling for too long. The meandering route to get to the Enclave – the building which housed the institution of the Academy – had taken more than four of the five day-long day-cycles. It had been dictated by visits to her family's publicly known friends and allies. She had spoken with merchants openly known to be in the employ of the Farwan family's massive trade network, also overseeing a few important shipments and handoffs. She had dutifully reported to her mother that all appeared to be going well, detailing anything that might require closer scrutiny. Nobody would ever accuse the Farwans of being lax, and the intimate knowledge of their various enterprises was a not insignificant reason that their businesses were among the most prosperous – and far-reaching – in the Fourth Country, and beyond. Being personally present to speak with business partners and inspect operations was crucial. But the one thing Lexa looked forward to when she eventually replaced her mother as head of the family was that she would no longer have to undertake such tasks – it would be somebody else's chore. Speaking with so many people left her exhausted, as did the careful observation for any hint of treachery. Life in the Fourth Country was characterised by families invading one another. Indeed, the route she had taken to the Academy needed to be altered twice in response to attempted takeovers. While the Farwan family was entrenched within the Fourth Country thanks to its wealth and trade network, it did not mean that there weren't individuals who would seek to take advantage of any perceived weakness. There had been times, speaking to women who had appraised her with calculating eyes, when Lexa had wanted to scurry away and hide. But she had stood straight-backed and stared those women down, letting them know that house Farwan was a force that would crush anyone who tried to hurt it. Only when she had been back in her lodgings had she reached for the forget-me-not, inhaling it with trembling fingers that stilled once the drug had coiled itself around her with soothing smoky tendrils.

Indeed, Lexa's true talent lay in her natural aptitude for figures. It meant she loved the aspects of her family's business that many others loathed. To her, there was nothing more calming than the mundane task of balancing a ledger, or of doing more complicated sums that tracked the costs and rewards of certain trade routes or goods. Her mother had always encouraged this, recognising it as a skill that could uniquely advantage the Farwan family and their business, securing their status as one of a handful of families everybody knew it was madness to attack. But as her mother's heir, she could not seclude herself away and balance account books. She had to be publicly seen, recognised as the girl who would succeed Tanita, and would be just as competent as her mother before her. Hence, the meetings she had been forced to endure.

She consoled herself now with the thought that she had several months at the Academy before she would be forced to think with any seriousness about the prospect of having to speak once more with the many merchants and so-called friends of her family, or indeed her marriage. Her previous fears about what the Academy would be like seemed trivial now when faced with the threat of marriage. Tanita had been tight-lipped about what her daughter should expect, merely promising her heir would come back more ready than ever to flourish in the world of trade and takeovers.

Lexa took a final drag of the forget-me-not, then extinguished the little flame. Her eyes needed time to return to their normal brown hue. The vibrant violet shade that gave away the fact that an individual was deep in the throes of the drug's embrace would not be a good first impression to make on her teachers, or any of the other students.

As the carriage continued its ascent, she glanced out the window at the lightning, still forking down around her carriage. She wondered how the monks managed to maintain the storm. It ran in a full circle around the mountaintop on which the Enclave was situated, ensuring that entry or exit could only be undertaken on the road. That way, nobody could approach without the monks being aware of it. Although, Lexa reflected, anybody who tried to ascend the mountainside would probably arrive at the Enclave desperately fatigued even without the barrier of the lightning storm, thanks to the harsh terrain. Still, it was an interesting mathematical problem to consider. For how long could any one monk sustain the lightning, and how much could they conjure at any given time? To ensure that the lightning was around the entirety of the mountain, the measurement of the area would need to be known, too. She successfully passed a few minutes contemplating all the ways the area could be measured. Losing herself in the task meant she almost didn't notice the warmth that left her as the forget-me-not seeped from her body. The maths was not particularly challenging, but it occupied her thoughts, and she was content with that.

From there, she turned her attention to contemplating how many carts would have been needed to haul away the parts of the mountain to build the road. She made several different calculations, varying the amount that a given cart could take and the weight of the soil. Factoring in the probability that several carts would likely break in some way, she then determined how much time it would have taken to complete the path, assuming that the dirt and rocks were deposited somewhere within a half day's travel. That was more difficult to calculate as she did not note any of her sums down, keeping the figures in her head. It was a pleasant stretching of her mind.

She was startled from her thoughts by the carriage coming to a stop. In fact, they had long since passed through the lightning storm and broken back into terrain under clear skies, just in time to see a magnificent sunset. There were some advantages to living on the top of a mountain, it seemed. The driver opened the door for her and she stepped out. She saw the briefest flash of her reflection in the window of the carriage door. The violet was gone from her eyes, the irises returned to their normal deep brown.

After the long journey it felt strange to be fully stretched out. She reached her arms wide, enjoying the space. "Thank you," she said to the driver. He nodded, a pillar of cloth with a human form. He had served her well on the journey. Her mother's fifteenth *elui*, he was well accustomed to tasks such as this and often took Tanita on business journeys.

"You're welcome, mistress Lexana. I wish you all the best during your time here," he replied, his voice clear despite the veil. If Lexana remembered correctly, he was nearing his fortieth year. He had been given plenty of practice speaking through the fabric.

"Will you be safe on your return?"

"You are too kind to worry, mistress. I'll be fine," he reassured her.

She offered him a smile and rested a hand briefly on his arm in a gesture of thanks and farewell. He was family, after all.

"I'll see to the luggage," he said, nodding over her shoulder. A greeting party had appeared in the cleared area which served as an entrance yard. Lexa's eye was immediately drawn to the natural stone of the mountain which continued to climb toward the sky. She could see the glint of a few windows reflecting the setting sun, all seemingly set into the face of the mountain itself. It was common knowledge that the Enclave was actually carved into the mountain itself, but that was very different to seeing it in person. For the winter months, she would actually be in the heart of a mountain. She cut off staring in amazement at the feat of construction that built such a vast complex inside the grey stone of the mountain and returned her gaze to the three women who had come to greet her. What appeared to be a natural cave in the mountain had been made into the entranceway. Impressive wooden doors perfectly fitted the space, carved with an inscription to the goddess Mawani. Unusually, one of the women was hooded. They all remained silent until the driver steered the carriage back down the mountainside. No man was permitted to stay in the Enclave unless they were swearing themselves to the order, or in the very rare case that a family's only child was male and he was a student at the Academy.

"Lexana Farwan. Welcome." The woman's voice carried through the still mountain air.

Lexa pulled herself up straight, tilted her chin slightly skyward, the very picture of a daughter of wealth and power. "Thank you. It is an honour to be accepted to the Academy."

The third figure pushed back their hood and Lexa realised the error of her assumption. In front of her were not three women, but two women and one man whose naked face was now on display for the world to see. She gasped at the sight of the unveiled man. Except for those times he was alone with her and her mother, Lexa's father had always worn some form of shroud. Even her two younger brothers would have always seen her father with some kind of covering. The only men they would have ever seen without any form of veil would be their own fathers.

She felt a blush work its way up her throat and cheeks as she all too slowly averted her gaze from the man's bare face. In the time that she had gazed upon him, she noticed he was most attractive. That fact alone intensified the blush and left her struggling to speak.

The man gave a warm chuckle, but she remained looking steadfastly at her feet, saying nothing as she fought her profound embarrassment on behalf of this unveiled man. She wondered what he had done to be so shamed.

"You'll get accustomed to seeing Jaxen's face," the women who had first spoken told her, amusement in her voice.

Lexa raised her gaze to look at the women, refusing to look at the man's face, even out of the corner of her eye. "Yes," she whispered. The mortification at seeing an unveiled man still robbed her of the ability to speak normally.

"Come, let us show you to your room," the woman said, green eyes crinkling with mirth at Lexa's obvious discomfort. The three walked back through the open door. Lexa hesitated, unable to dismiss the silly fear that if she went inside the mountain structure, she would be swallowed by the very earth itself.

"My trunks?" Lexa had to struggle to ask the question. The presence of an unveiled man was so off-putting.

To her discomfort, it was he who answered. "Will be brought." He gave her a wink that sent the crimson flying back up her face.

Mutely, Lexa followed the three figures into the Academy, wondering to what exactly her mother had sent her.

TWO

Despite the fact that Lexa was given the freedom to roam the Enclave in the days before the arrival of the final two students, she kept mostly to herself, staying in her room and reading. She caught glimpses of the students alongside whom she would be attending the Academy, but it was mostly in the traces of their presence rather than actual sightings: in the kitchens a dish not yet cleared away, or water clinging to the tiles of the sunken tubs in the washing rooms. The peace was enjoyable, while it lasted.

The Enclave itself was an enigmatic place. Silence reigned in the stone corridors. The monks who inhabited the Enclave spoke almost exclusively to one other, only speaking to Lexa in response to her questions. In her isolation, she found an affinity with the curious structure which was half built into the mountainside. Despite the severe grey-black mountain stone walls, reaching up to flow into ceilings of the same material, there was a sense of peace and serenity to the Enclave.

Two days after her arrival, she was summoned to the library. A bookworm all her life, she had found the library on her first morning; she easily navigated her way there, passing through corridors exposed to the sunshine as well as passages which never saw any daylight. Because it was cut directly into the mountainside, the Enclave was an odd mixture of beautiful workmanship and design born purely of utility that arbitrarily varied from room to room. Lexa delighted in the sudden burst of light as she passed a corridor where one side was the mountain itself, and the other was only windows, letting in the view of the land and it dropped away, and the other mountains in the distance. She had even come to appreciate the terrain, although that was easy to do when safely nestled in the warm corridors of the Enclave, rather than outside in the biting air.

As she entered the library, two monks were weaving their way through the shelves, talking quietly. Placed at various intervals, glass globes containing lightning storms illuminated the library so that even at night it was easy to read. The globes were creations of the Enclave, containing small versions of the lightning storm that surrounded the mountaintop. Every house of the powerful was illuminated by a lightning storm, demonstrating their power through the placement of the fiendishly expensive globes within their halls. As a child, Lexa had been fascinated by the flashes of contained lightning in the spheres which were found throughout the Farwan houses. An echo of that fascination flickered inside her now as she looked at the huge globe – larger than any she'd ever seen – suspended above the area where seven chairs were arranged in clear invitation. The cool illumination of the lightning was a curious counterpoint to the warmth of the light provided by the fire burning in a huge fireplace. The shadows of the two light sources danced with one another.

Lexa sat in a chair at the end of the line, looking cautiously at the students who were already there. Of the four, she knew two by sight. One was the daughter of a family in exile from the Second Country. Their arrival almost two years earlier had been quite the talking point. Serenah, she was called. Lexa had seen her at several events over the years; the social circle of those who were in the very upper echelons of power was reasonably small, if often changing in composition. Serenah had transformed from a quiet, timid girl into a startlingly lovely young woman over the time her family had been in the Fourth Country. Lexa had often watched from an unobtrusive corner as Serenah commanded the attention and admiration of those who orbited her with a reverential fascination. Her status as an exile seemed only to heighten her allure.

The other girl Lexa knew was named Kaitlen. She came from a family that had only recently gained power in an exceptionally bloody attack. Lexa had only seen her once or twice, but she had been struck by the girl's haughty arrogance. For someone who had not been born into a family of any meaningful position, she certainly acted as though wealth, power, and all associated trappings, were her birthright. Lexa did not like her. To Kaitlen's left sat a young man. He was lightly veiled, not wearing the full face covering that a man who had formally entered his adulthood was required to wear. As such, Lexa could see a distinctly uncomfortable expression on his face. She felt a stab of pity for him, especially as he was broad of stature, which made him particularly conspicuous. If he was here, it meant that he was the only child of his family and as such, they had to elevate him into the world of women and rule. Once he was married off to the daughter of a good family, she would likely take over much of the day-to-day activities of his family's affairs, taking no *elui* in deference to her husband's status. Looking at the young man, Lexa thought perhaps she did recognise him, but she was unlikely to have seen him more than once. Families shamed by the absence of daughters were unlikely to parade that shame among their peers.

Lexa did not recognise the third girl. Her hair was streaked with magenta, the vibrant colour standing out amongst the rich brown tresses. Putting such colours in one's hair had recently become fashionable, although Lexa had abstained, knowing that she was going to be visiting her mother's business associates on her journey to the Academy. She did not think that women who managed swordpower and money in dangerous amounts on a daily basis would take a girl with frivolous colours in her hair particularly seriously. She looked with envy at the bright streaks in the unknown girl's hair.

The final two girls entered the room. Lexa recognised both.

One was called Veleth, and she was the daughter of the Lord Protector. Despite the fact that she was the same age as Lexa, Lexa hadn't considered the possibility that they might be at the Academy together. She swallowed nervously as Veleth strode into the room and took a seat somewhere in the middle of the line. The other girl glanced at her and gave her a nod of acknowledgement. They had never spoken often, but the Farwan family's position meant they had met on many occasions. Lexa returned the gesture of greeting. The other girl was from one of the major families, too. Their wealth lay in agriculture, so they had loosely worked with the Farwans to carry their goods across the Fourth Country and beyond. Yet that was a partnership Tanita had overseen, not Lexa. The girl's name was Kirrith and her reputation preceded her. For her sixteenth birthday, her mother had given her a small farm. She had surprised everyone by not selling the fruit it produced but making them into liquor. The first batch had come out two years previously and was absolutely delightful. Everyone agreed Kirrith's first foray into business was a resounding success. Having never really had much reason to speak with Kirrith, Lexa did not know her well, and they exchanged a polite murmured greeting with one another before Kirrith settled in a chair. Lexa felt decidedly unaccomplished in the presence of Veleth, Kirrith, and Serenah. She consoled herself that at least her status would never be as lowly as that of the boy, nor Kaitlen, despite the haughty air with which the other girl surrounded herself.

Once Veleth and Kirrith had settled themselves, the seven students looked at one another in silent appraisal. They would learn together, be tested against one another, and ultimately be offered or rejected the Academy's certification, which should make anybody who considered attacking their families think again. It would be a very intense winter, to say the least.

Serenah gave a wry smile. "Maybe it's all a grand hoax. Perhaps there's no lessons at all." She addressed the entire room with an enviably easy charm.

"Unfortunately, there are lessons. Many of them." Three people stepped into the room, coming to stand in the middle of the semicircle.

Rather than blush and mutter an apology as Lexa would have – had she even been bold enough to make such a comment in the first place – Serenah tilted her head back and laughed. "Can't blame me for hoping," she said cheerfully.

The three were the same who had greeted Lexa on her arrival. She immediately averted her gaze from the naked face of the man. From the corner of her eye, she saw him staring at her, his lips curled in a smirk.

The woman who had spoken to Serenah said, "Now that you have all arrived, we may begin." She was of average height, wearing trousers brought in at the ankle to draw attention to a shapely leg. Yet the way she carried herself made her seem taller than she actually was and dispelled any suggestion of frivolity that her clothes may have inferred. "I am Laskana. I will be teaching you how to make people willing to die for you. To my right is Leyana. She will be teaching you how to buy people. And to my left," she gestured to the unveiled man, "is Jaxen. He will teach you how to bend people to your will. We are the Academy's teachers, and if you pay attention in our lessons, you will leave with skills that are likely to secure your family's fortunes."

Kaitlen spoke. "I won't be taught by a man who dares show his face. It's unnatural and immodest, and I won't have it."

Laskana's face was quite unlined, although Lexa suspected it gave her a deceptively youthful appearance. Her response to Kaitlen's declaration was only a look that gave away nothing of what she really might have thought of the girl's words.

Jaxen spoke, not bothering to ask for permission. His brazenness made Lexa wince. "If you do not wish to be taught by me, that is fine. But you will fail, and your time and coin invested here will be for nothing." His amused voice was a deep melody that for reasons she attributed to the strangeness of seeing an unveiled man so comfortable despite his immodesty, made shivers run up and down Lexa's spine.

When Kaitlen did not answer, his smile broadened. "I do encourage any and all concerns to be raised directly with me." He let his gaze rove along the students, resting long enough on each face to be certain that none of them was going to voice a similar objection to Kaitlen's. When he got to Lexa, she met his gaze with an effort of will. His cool grey eyes made her feel as though she was the one improperly dressed, not him.

"Excellent." He clapped his hands softly as though the matter was resolved.

Laskana spoke once more. "Every day you will have lessons, except on the Day of Sorrows. You may go anywhere within the Enclave, as some of you have already done. However, it should be obvious that if an area is marked off-limits, you will not enter it.

"It is unfortunate that I must also say this on our first day, and I will say this once and once only. This morning we intercepted a letter from someone to their contact in the Capital. The contents of that letter detailed information about the Enclave that could only have been acquired by intruding somewhere they should not have been. Spying on us in the Enclave is strictly prohibited and will be met with harsh consequences." Her pale violet eyes scanned the seven students, the promise of an unpleasant reprisal within them if her warning went unheeded.

The caution left Lexa deeply uncomfortable. Someone among her six fellow students was spying on the goings-on in the Enclave. It was understandable. The supernatural power that the monks wielded offered any who hired their services a considerable advantage in battle. To know more about how they mastered this power would give whoever possessed that knowledge freedom from the backbreaking fees of the monks, and a tactical advantage. To try to discover the knowledge possessed by the monks while attending the Academy was certainly daring, but foolish, too.

"The same will ensue if we learn that one of you is spying on the others. This is not a place for such things to occur," Laskana added.

Lexa had not even considered the possibility that the students may spy on one another to find weaknesses that could be exploited at a later date. Now, she thought herself foolish for having failed to realise how treacherous her time at the Academy might in fact be. A sense of dread crept into her bones as she surveyed the six faces before her. Each of them would have their own motivations to spy on their fellow students. Her mother had sent her with the advice to observe the other students, but with no specific direction to spy on them. Perhaps she had known that Lexa would have balked at such a request.

"Please follow Leyana. Your first lesson will begin now," Laskana said, the severity of her warning melting away with the mundane prospect of lessons. Lexa's sense of barely contained panic felt almost surreal.

Without waiting for her students, Leyana walked down the central aisle of the library. Lexa scrambled to her feet and followed, hastily adjusting the loose-fitting top that she wore so that it was less revealing. It was perfectly acceptable for men to gaze upon women, but there was something particularly off-putting about knowing that Jaxen was watching her as she passed by him. Being able to see the appreciative look that he gave her did odd things to her stomach. Lexa silently cursed her mother for failing to tell her of all the perils that she might encounter at the Academy.

Leyana's class might have been about the art of how to buy people, but it was more concerned with the art of numbers. The room into which she led them was cut into the depths of the mountain. It had no windows, and the illumination came completely from the lightning spheres lining the room. The sparse decoration, and bare stone from which the walls, floor, and ceiling were cut, should have made it an uninviting room in which to be, but as soon as she saw the sums written up on the board which took up nearly an entire wall, Lexa felt comfortable. She loved numbers. They had always made sense to her, requiring very little effort on her part to resolve them into satisfying solutions. Sums were an important skill to know - especially given that she was the daughter of a trade family. However, judging from the expressions of her fellow students, Lexa's aptitude with numbers was quite unusual. Kaitlen was frowning at the wall with a look that suggested she had not the slightest idea what the equations were. The boy was also staring at the board, his face a rictus of utter panic. It seemed impossible, when looking at their frank expressions, that one of the six students had tried to prise out the secrets of the Enclave, but Lexa reminded herself that all of them came from families who had waded through blood to acquire or maintain their position.

The students stood uncertainly as Leyana wrote on the slate with a piece of chalk. Once she finished, she turned to them and shook her head in obvious bemusement.

"Well, sit down," she said, straightening the pleats of her trousers while she waited. Unlike Laskana's, her trousers were not brought in at the ankles, but merely hung from her waist in deep pleats. It was a good choice – Laskana had a bit of curve to her that was worth emphasising, but Leyana was so thin that Lexa feared a strong wind would snap her. The simple line of her trousers added to her narrow height, making her an even more imposing figure. The students sat in the chair nearest them. They were arrayed around a long table at the head of which Leyana now stood, the board at her back.

"It is a truth of our world that coin speaks more powerfully than anything else, in most instances." Leyana had a beautiful voice; she caressed each syllable. Seemingly from nowhere, she procured two coins and began to play with them as she looked around at her students. "Thus, the ability to use and to make money is invaluable." She smiled a little at her wordplay. "I will be teaching this to you. Copy down the sums I've written."

She gestured and notebooks flew from the stack at the end of the table and gently landing in front of each student. Lightning flickered to life in several more glass globes around the room. Lexa was not alone in giving a little gasp at this display. It was known throughout the Fourth Country that the monks of the Enclave had some form of elemental power. Lexa had witnessed the effect of those powers during several land grabs, but always from afar. The Academy was an opportunity for the monks to demonstrate their powers up close so that the next generation of those who would lead a family were assured of the benefit to hiring one of the monks. Certainly, there was an enormous difference between hearing about this fabulous power and seeing the wind controlled with such finesse that books could be placed in front of seven people, and lightning summoned into an empty glass globe. Lexa wondered whether Leyana was one of the monks or simply a teacher hired by them for the Academy, but especially after the warning that someone was spying on the monks, she did not feel it would be viewed well if she asked.

Mastering herself, Lexa opened the soft leather cover of the journal. As was the case with almost all books found within the Fourth Country, it had been bound by hand, the creamy blank linen pages a testament to the wealth that had brought her here and how high the stakes of her education truly were. Paper sheets, let alone notebooks, were prized possessions.

She picked up the pencil and began to dutifully write down the sums. To her left, the boy stared in dismay at the board for a moment before laboriously copying the equations.

"Now solve them," Leyana said when everybody had completed her first instruction.

Lexa got to work immediately, her pencil flying across the

page as she completed each line with ease. Within only a few minutes she had finished, putting the pencil down and looking around her cautiously. She was the first to put her head up. Everybody else was still bent over their pages in various postures of concentration. The boy had yet to write anything. An expression that was caught somewhere between panic and profound unhappiness had settled itself across his face. Lexa glanced at Leyana. The teacher stood by the board regarding her new students. She caught Lexa's eye and smiled in a manner that could have meant anything, but she did not move.

Finally, Lexa could take no more of the boy's distress. He had started softly whispering to himself, although it sounded more like whimpering. Possible spy or no, the despair was profoundly uncomfortable to witness. She slid her chair over and began to softly step him through the first equation. He glanced at her warily, but she ignored the look and continued to direct him, giving him instructions on how to complete each equation. She could feel Leyana's eyes boring into her, but she dared not look up to meet the woman's gaze. There was something disconcerting about Leyana's dark eyes, especially given the way they blended into her dark skin and tightly curled black hair. Lexa couldn't say why, but she got the sense that Leyana enjoyed watching her students suffer.

"But why?" the boy whispered to her as she corrected an error he had made.

"You forgot to carry the one here," Lexa said, feeling impatience creep around her. The boy wanted to understand everything rather than accept that she was giving him a way out of his torment.

He tapped his head gently with his free hand in self-recrimination, dislodging his head covering. A rust-brown curl escaped and he tried to tuck it back in.

"Leave that, just do what I'm telling you," Lexa snapped softly, immediately feeling bad for the harshness of her tone.

Obediently, the boy let his hand fall.

Finally, all the equations were completed. Lexa straightened herself and realised Leyana and the other five students were silently regarding her. Her eyes went wide in alarm at the attention she was receiving. Leyana strode over and looked down at Lexa's work. Saying nothing, she stepped across to the boy's work and examined it.

"You're very lucky that your neighbour is both good and graceful," she told the boy who was staring at her with trepidation. Only once Leyana said that did Lexa realise she might have incorrectly solved the sums.

Leyana took her time going along the other students. She said nothing about anybody else's solutions. Once she had finished, she began to explain how each of the sums should have been solved, at some points offering variations in method. Most of it Lexa was familiar with, although there were one or two methods she had not considered. She dutifully wrote them down, bored for the most part, but staying perfectly attentive as though this was all new information.

Once Leyana had gone through all of the equations, she told them to go back to the library. There was an economy to her words and movements that Lexa couldn't help but appreciate, even if she found the woman terribly intimidating.

The boy Lexa had helped came up to her, shyness clouding his face. "Thank you," he said. There was something so earnest about him that she couldn't help but smile. If he was the person responsible for the discovered note, she would be very surprised.

"You're welcome. Sums can be unpleasant if you aren't familiar with them," she said, feeling bad for her earlier impatience.

"I'm Aravand. Family Lengathan."

Lexa knew the Lengathan family. They were of medium status, holding land in a remote part of the Fourth Country. That remoteness gave them a certain security – few had sufficient capital or inclination to muster people to march that far in an attempt to claim land that was also naturally easy to defend. The Lengathan family's fortunes came from grain. She should have at least been able to guess his origin. The Lengathan family had not been seen in the Capital for quite some time, and now she knew why: the desire to not advertise that their heir was the wrong gender.

"Lexa Farwan."

"Oh, I know." His eagerness was a little forward, but she forgave him the lack of decorous restraint. He had never really been into the Capital and thus exposed to proper society, after all.

"Did her explanations make sense to you?" Lexa asked.

"Not really." He looked down at his feet, which peeked out from the hem of his loose-fitting trousers as he walked. The obvious dismay was somehow touching, even though he should have known better than to parade his feelings for all to see.

"If you'd like, I can try to help you," she offered.

His reply was cut off by a huff of derisive laughter from Kaitlen. Evidently the girl had been walking close enough to overhear. Lexa turned to her and raised an eyebrow, not daring to actually say anything.

"If he can't learn it on his own, he shouldn't get extra help. Same with any of us," Kaitlen said, the venom in her voice giving it unexpected nastiness.

"I can help you if you find you need it, too," Lexa said, widening her eyes in apparent innocence.

The girl's face turned an unpleasant shade of pink. "Just what exactly are you suggesting?" she hissed, walking closer to Lexa than was strictly necessary.

"That if you need help, I'm happy to offer it," Lexa said. "Unless you understood everything perfectly," she added after a beat had elapsed.

The pink in Kaitlen's cheeks deepened to become a shade of crimson. Apparently not able to conjure a sufficient reply, she moved away. As the students reached the library, Serenah met Lexa's eye and motioned applause.

Lexa sat in the same chair she had initially chosen and looked across at the six other people. Kaitlen had sat in the chair at the other end – as far away from Lexa as possible. She glowered at the rug just in front of her feet. Now there was someone who Lexa would not be at all surprised to learn was trying to discover secrets that were not hers to know.

Lexa bit her lip as she considered what had just transpired. She did not like to make enemies where possible and yet it seemed she had just done exactly that.

THREE

Despite the aptitude she demonstrated in Leyana's class, Lexa did not find herself at an advantage in the following two classes. She wasn't entirely terrible at the strategy game that Laskana made them do, but she was merely competent while Veleth excelled at it, earning Laskana's praise. Lexa found her less intimidating than Leyana, although the two women shared a severity that made them both extraordinarily intimidating. Nevertheless, the two were both obviously masters of their discipline, and Lexa knew she could learn a great deal from them.

However, it was in Jaxen's class where she truly floundered. The last class of the day, he led them from the library into a room completely bereft of furniture. The walls were severe stone, but the floors were timber. Windows entirely lined one side, offering a view of a brilliant expanse of sky. By the time his lesson began, the sky was streaked with the beginnings of sunset, filling the room with a beautiful yellow glow. The unusual absence of any light spheres made the stillness of the light and shadow almost unsettling in its serenity. Jaxen stood before them, the warmth of the light making his skin look lustrous, setting fire to the grey-green of his eyes. He looked over each of the students with obvious appraisal, a half smile tugging at his mouth. Lexa tried to meet his gaze but found herself unable to hold it, looking down at the floor after only a moment. He chuckled at that.

"I am here to teach you the art of seduction." He spoke softly, but his voice rolled off the bare stone and timber. "Seduction comes easily to some, and less easy to others. The trick—" he began to pace, "—is to understand that there is more than one type of seduction."

He came closer to the line of students. "For some, the most alluring thing is boldness." He tugged on a purple lock of hair of the girl whose name Lexa had learned was Karra. In reply to Jaxen, Karra arched an eyebrow and cocked one of her hips. He smiled and continued. "For some, it is the ability to charm." He paused in front of Serenah, who smiled openly at him. He gave her a little nod and continued walking. "Competence and assurance also have a certain appeal," he noted, pausing in front of Veleth. "But of course, many forget that sometimes being demure and shy can be especially and unexpectedly beguiling." He came to a halt then in front of Lexa and brushed a finger along her cheek. She felt fire bloom at the contact, despite the lightness of his touch. Practically trembling, she looked up at him. He winked at her, then returned to where he had originally stood. "My role here is to teach you this. Coin and the promise of a perfectly-planned attack are all well and good, but capturing the heart of someone can get you further than you might ever have imagined." He spoke with a deliberateness that ensured everything he said settled into the minds of his audience. Lexa enjoyed listening to him speak, finding the depth and modulation of his voice delightful, even as his assured manner unsettled her.

"Sometimes in order to seduce, you must conceal." He slipped his hands into his pockets and rocked back onto his heels. "Today I am going to pair you up and ask both of you to tell each other one truth and one lie."

Everybody immediately turned to their neighbour. Because she had once again chosen to place herself on the end of the line, Lexa turned straight into Kaitlen's back. Jaxen appeared by her side. "It seems I am fortunate enough to be paired with you." The crinkling of his eyes suggested he was amused by some internal joke.

With no small amount of awkwardness, she followed him to a space by the window. He sat cross-legged on the floor and looked up at her expectantly. She sat opposite him, wondering how he managed to look so comfortable.

"Lexana, am I correct?" he asked. She nodded, uncomfortable with the naked amusement in his eyes.

"How about you go first," he offered.

"May I have a moment to think?"

"Of course you may. I can spend the time admiring your lovely face."

She looked at him, her eyes wide at his boldness. The memory of his finger brushing her cheek made her furiously bashful and any retort she may have had lodged in her throat.

He laughed. "Are you thinking?" His voice was playful, teasing.

She bit her lip as she cast through the fragments of her life, trying to find a truth that would sound like a lie and a lie that would sound like a truth. She did not look at him but instead at the floor between them. Eventually she felt that she had been deliberating too long, despite his patience.

"I—" He cut her off before she could say anything else.

"Look at me." He put a finger under her chin and tipped her face upward so that she was looking directly at him. She felt a blush threatening to make its way along her face again. Something about his confidence despite the lack of any shroud left her deeply uncomfortable. Especially when he seemed to take such delight in being so terribly intimate with her. It was shameful. She should have rebuked him for such impropriety but found herself unable to form the words of recrimination.

"You have such deep eyes, Lexana. Anyone fortunate enough to look into them would just about fall to the bottom of your heart. You should not avert them," he murmured.

Lexa swallowed. "Is there anything in particular that I should tell you?" she asked, ignoring his comment.

He shook his head. "You can tell me anything you like provided one thing is true and one thing is a lie."

"All right then." She moistened her bottom lip slightly with the tip of her tongue. "The first thing I have to tell you is that I was born in the middle of a thunderstorm and took my first breath exactly at the same time that a flash of lightning hit just outside the window. The second is that I have a younger sister."

"You don't have a younger sister," he said almost immediately.

Her mouth fell open. "Surely my truth sounded far less plausible than my lie," she protested.

"That's why I knew it was the truth."

She crossed her arms. She was unable to stop her frown. "Fine then, your turn."

He put his hands on the floor behind him and leaned back, regarding her from below half-closed lids. A hint of a smirk stained his mouth. A cascade of Serenah's laughter rang across the room during the silence between them, making Lexa uncomfortably aware of that quietude.

"I never saw my mother after my tenth summer, and I once kissed Leyana." He raised an eyebrow in challenge.

"So you've kissed Leyana?" She couldn't envisage Leyana kissing anyone, but she was certain that he would not reveal something as intensely personal about his family to someone he had only just met.

"No."

Her mouth fell open. "You've not seen your mother since you were ten?"

He nodded.

"But why would you share something like that with me?"

He leaned forward, resting his forearms on his knees. "Because you weren't going to believe it. Sometimes the truth is the best deception."

"Jaxen, I'm ... I'm sorry," she said softly.

His smile was amiable. "Hardly something for which you need to apologise. Come on, lie to me again." There was something completely enchanting about the way he said it. She leaned forward in response despite her reservation.

"I've always wanted purple streaks in my hair like Karra, and I have never been drunk."

"You know, I wouldn't have picked you the sort to put pretty colours in your hair. Although I would admit that it would look mighty fine among those beautiful dark tresses of yours." He shifted his gaze from her face to look at the hair she had casually pulled back into a plait during the wargame lesson.

"But surely it sounds so absurd, that I've never been drunk, it would have to be true," she objected.

"It was too personal."

"That's not fair, you're anticipating what I'm going to say off your own teachings." Outrage entered her voice.

"Of course it's not fair. How else will you learn?" He tilted his head. It seemed as though the afternoon rays were soaking into the darkness of his hair.

"Perhaps you could just teach me," she snapped, blushing almost immediately at the fact that she had let her temper get control of her.

"And here I was thinking you had no fire in you at all." His voice was low, seductive.

She stared at him in mortification, no idea what she could say in response to that.

"I think it's my turn," he said, breaking the moment that had stretched between them.

Her gaze slid away from him but she forced herself to look at him properly to try and see if he had a tell when he lied.

"You remind me of the last woman I was with. I don't really like the colour purple." He easily held her gaze as he spoke. Something about it made her extraordinarily conscious of her limbs. She felt she was holding them awkwardly rather than naturally letting them arrange themselves, as he appeared to have done.

"You like the colour purple," she said, fighting to keep her voice level.

He shook his head. "It reminds me of the colour of bruises. But if you were wondering, I don't think I've ever been with a woman quite like you," he added.

At this, she had no choice but to avert her gaze. Men did not speak openly of their sexual encounters. It was considered inappropriate given that they existed to serve at the pleasure of women.

"Have I shocked you?" He sounded almost delighted at the prospect.

She kept her eyes averted and shook her head.

"Another lie." There was something so intimate about the way he accused her.

"Why say something like that?" she asked. The chatter of the other six students filled her ears.

"Why not? I knew it would make you uncomfortable. People shy away from something that makes them uneasy, looking instead to anything else."

She nodded, still not wanting to look directly at him. It wasn't right that a man should be so comfortable flouting everything that was proper. "I don't see how this has anything to do with seduction," she snapped, anger rescuing her from the silence of her discomfort.

"You're terrible at this," he said, the sting of the comment entirely removed by the gentle way in which he said it. Yet that served to make it somehow more insulting.

He stood up. The movement immediately captured the attention of the students. "My partner, the lovely Lexana, has asked me what the art of telling a lie has to do with the art of seduction." He padded across the room as he spoke, arresting in the trousers and shirt that were too bold and too tight.

"Seduction is not simply about bringing someone to your bed. It is about making someone want you, making someone believe that you can offer what they desire. Sometimes, the stars align, and the mere fact of who you are is enough. But sometimes, being pretty, or clever, or demure, is insufficient. Lying is not simply about telling a plausible story, it's about being able to tell what someone will want to believe."

Jaxen looked slowly at his students, seated on the ground and looking up at him expectantly. Then he gave a little laugh. "I promise this will make sense in time. There is a beautiful book of histories in the library that I recommend you all read, *Fabiane's Wishes*. The writing is quite lovely and the stories – well, the stories are all very satisfying to read. Some of them are even true. That book is perhaps the best example that I can give you of someone knowing what their audience wants to be told. I think we'll leave it there for today."

Lexa sat in her room, quietly wishing that she was back at the Farwan home in the Capital. There, she would not be looking in suspicion at her fellow students, wondering if they were trying to learn something about her to use to take her family's lands. If she were home, she could be doing any number of useful things, perhaps even playing with her younger brothers. Soon they would be too old for it to be proper for them to play with her. She was sad she was spending that fleeting time at the Academy.

A knock at the door startled her from her melancholic reverie. "Yes?"

The door opened and Serenah's blonde head appeared around the corner. "Do you mind if I come in?"

"Of course not." Lexa sat up straighter on the bed.

"You have a window," Serenah exclaimed, closing the door behind her.

"You don't?"

"No. My room is cut directly out of the rock. It's cosy, I suppose, and they've given me an extra light sphere. But seeing the sky as I wake up would be nice," the other girl said with a shrug.

Lexa had nothing to say to that, so she remained silent, wondering why Serenah had come to her. They might have attended the same parties in the Capital, but they had barely shared one conversation. Rather than ask, she waited for the blonde girl to volunteer the information. She wondered if this was the spy of whom Laskana had spoken that morning. If she were, and she had come to see what she could learn about Lexa, it would be a bold move indeed.

"How did you find the first day of classes?" Serenah asked.

"Leyana's class was fine, although I don't know that I like her too much," Lexa replied. "I did not enjoy Jaxen's class," she added dourly.

Serenah laughed. "Nobody can be good at everything." She had a slight accent that clipped her vowels short. Lexa had never noticed it before.

"I think Kirrith may prove you wrong there," Lexa said with a slight gloominess, her thoughts going to the liquor Kirrith's farm produced.

Serenah laughed, a beautiful arpeggio of amused sound. "I'm sure you're wondering why I'm here," she said presently.

Lexa blinked slowly in an affirmation that was more restrained than a nod.

"I was wondering if you had any forget-me-not."

Lexa raised her eyebrows in surprise. "Would you like some?"

"If you have any, yes."

"What makes you think I have any?" Lexa asked, more curious than cautious. This was definitely not how she would have expected a spy to behave. Although, she had no idea how a spy was supposed to behave, so perhaps this was exactly how someone who was spying conducted themselves.

"I heard from a friend that I should ask you." Serenah smiled mischievously.

Lexa saw no point in being coy. She went to her trunk and pulled out the little box in which she kept the holder and dried leaves. Wordlessly, she placed the tiniest pinch of leaves in the small hollow at the thin pipe's base, struck a flint, and lit the leaves. "It'll take a moment," she told Serenah.

"Thank you," the foreign girl said. "Do you mind?" she asked, gesturing to the bed.

Aside from a small writing table, which had the least comfortable chair Lexa had ever encountered, the room had barely enough space for the bed and her trunks.

"Of course not." Carefully holding the pipe in one hand, Lexa resumed her seat on the bed and leaned over to crack open the window. Forget-me-not was not strictly an illegal drug, but she did not want her room to reek of it.

Judging that the leaves had smouldered enough, she passed the holder to Serenah, who took it with a word of thanks and inhaled deeply. At the end of her breath, she passed the holder back to Lexa to take a breath of her own. The simple ritual caused the knot of misery and anxiety that had grown inside her after the day of classes to loosen.

Serenah exhaled, the mauve-tinted smoke streaking from her slightly parted lips in a long, thin stream. "I must say, today was curious," she commented.

"Oh?" Lexa passed her back the holder.

"Mm. I didn't expect the classes to be, well, what they were," Serenah admitted, taking the holder and inhaling. Already her eyes were looking more vibrant. She was lucky. The light blue of her eyes would make the drug's violet hue less obvious. "Did you have any idea what you were in for?"

Lexa shook her head, beginning to feel more distant from the emotions that swirled within her. She was glad Serenah had come to find her. She had been so distracted by the events of the day that she hadn't even thought of smoking forget-me-not to offer herself some respite from the worry and homesickness that had engulfed her. "My mother came to the Academy, but all she told me was that the classes change over the years."

"I've never done any of the things my mother did." Serenah's admission was dreamy, the distant curiosity with which she said it almost certainly the doing of the drug.

Lexa looked at her. Her bright blonde hair and clear blue eyes – made more purple at the moment thanks to the drug – marked her out from the more dark-haired and dark-eyed inhabitants of the Fourth Country. Lexa had always assumed Serenah appreciated her difference and used it to her advantage, but she had never stopped to consider that the girl might yearn for her home. "Do you miss the Second Country?"

Serenah shook her head, then took a breath from the pipe Lexa had just passed to her. "There wasn't really anything left for us after my grandfather lost the battle for Herran. The idea of going back there after that is too embarrassing for me to think of missing it."

"Your cousin is on the throne?" Lexa confirmed. She delicately avoided the fact that Serenah's cousin was a man. She inwardly shuddered at the thought of a man on the throne. Such a thing was unnatural.

"Yes. It was generous of Gidyon to spare our lives, I suppose," Serenah said.

"Did you want to be queen?" The question slipped out before Lexa could stop it. Something about Serenah made her feel able to say anything.

If she was bothered by Lexa's probing, Serenah did not show it. She tilted her head to one side, staring at the wall as though there was a pattern on it she was trying to discern. "I think I thought I wanted to be queen. My grandfather told me so often that I was the rightful ruler I never really questioned it. But no, I never actually wanted to rule."

"Your grandfather was behind everything?" This was news to Lexa. The story of Serenah's family that had been passed between idle tongues was merely one of a failed coup which would have put Serenah on the throne when she had been just a girl.

Serenah nodded.

"And he failed. So your exile here is because of him?" Lexa realised only after she spoke that she could have been more tactful. The forget-me-not was doing away with her worry of such impoliteness, loosening her tongue before she had time to properly weigh her words.

However, Serenah did not seem to mind. "Yes."

"Does that make it hard to be around him now?" She fought to choose her words with more care this time.

"At times. My mother wouldn't really let me hear much of the discussion surrounding what happened. But from what I've been able to understand, he did some very bad things," Serenah said. "But he's my grandfather. I love him despite what happened."

Lexa stared at the girl in surprise.

"And even though his actions meant our family was exiled, he did look after us. He had enough money and interests here to ensure that when we were exiled, we were able to be comfortable here," Serenah continued.

"But he's a man," Lexa blurted out. Shock at the brazenness of Serenah's grandfather cut through the veil of the forget-me-not.

"Yes. He still runs our family, you know. Although my mother is the public face. It used to be my grandmother, but she said last year she didn't want to anymore."

"He must find it hard to see everything run through his daughter," Lexa said eventually.

Serenah nodded. "Very much so. He's a very strong man and used to being listened to."

"Thank you – for telling me that," Lexa said after another

pause had drifted between them, broken only by sighs as they breathed in and out, passing the pipe between one another. She could not see any way that this foreign girl who smoked forget-me-not or revealed such scandalous truths about herself was possibly someone who would go sneaking about the Enclave in a bid to discover the monks' secrets. She found herself liking Serenah immensely.

The other girl turned to her and smiled. "I've always thought you were a person to be trusted, Lexana, even though we've not spoken much. You tend to hide yourself away at all the parties where I've seen you."

"Please, call me Lexa. I'm not really one for parties, so I don't like to be anywhere near the centre of attention," she replied.

"I can understand that. I sometimes get very tired of them, especially if I just want to be with one particular person. Generally, whenever I've tried to slip away with her, you've already occupied the most secluded spot," Serenah admitted.

Lexa looked at Serenah in surprise. She had never thought that Serenah wanted to be anywhere other than where she was – at the centre of a large group of noisy people. She looked at the girl, thinking. "Kellen Aranjay."

"How could you tell? I thought we hid it well."

"She's always the person you talk to least. I would have thought you barely know who she is," Lexa said.

Apparently, she had learned something from Jaxen that day, after all

FOUR

"The Enclave is not as I expected. While some of the students are unex-pectedly lovely – you'll never believe that I seem to have befriended Serenah Katan – others leave me feeling as though they're watching my every move to find out some secret that can be used against me and my family. The teachers are both more and less formal than I anticipat-ed. I definitely did not expect there to be a male teacher, especially not one who walks around without any form of covering. You know me, Kel, so it would come as little surprise that I could barely speak in his pres-ence when I first met him. However, it has been over a day-cycle now, and I cannot help but find him...," Lexa hesitated, the nib of her quill hovering over the page as she sought the right word. A drop of ink splattered onto the paper and she swore.

A chuckle from behind her made her startle, spilling yet more ink across the page.

"You know I really didn't expect you to be improper enough to swear," Jaxen said, appearing from behind a bookshelf.

Lexa purged her quill of any remaining ink and put it down to one side, glancing ruefully at the ruined page. She would defi-nitely have to rewrite it. "I didn't think anyone was around."

"So you're only improper when nobody's around? Interest-ing." He smirked and sat in the empty chair next to her.

She had chosen one of the little round desks in the middle of the library, at least five minutes' walk from the main entrance. Surrounded by bookshelves, she had assumed herself safe from anyone's intrusion. "Can I help you?"

He shrugged. "I was just wandering through the bookshelves and spied you. Thought I'd say hello."

She looked at him warily. The day-cycle's worth of his classes could only have been described as torture. Each exercise he had given them had been some form of interaction, and she had been hopeless at each one. The previous day he had made everyone dance. Lexa had never considered herself a dancer, possessing neither the coordination nor the desire to be conspicuous the way dancing made one. She had stumbled through the steps he called out, contorting herself in vague time with the beat he clapped. It had been awful, and only made worse when he had come to correct her, placing his hands on her waist and pulling her this way and that. The worst part was how unexpectedly pleasant the firmness of his touch had been. She was sure he had seen that in her face somewhere, too.

"What are you doing?" he asked when she said nothing.

"I'm writing a letter to one of my friends," she said. She moved the light sphere she had been using to illuminate the page a little farther away. She would not be needing it, given the devastation her spilled ink had wrought on the page.

"What about that would cause you to curse with such violence?" he asked.

"I spilled some ink." Her tone was more curt than she intended. To give herself something to do rather than look directly at him, she took the ruined page and folded it carefully so the ink was contained, then tucked it back into her satchel.

"Ah." He seemed irritatingly content to sit next to her, despite her awkwardness.

Vexation with him and his obvious enjoyment at her clear discomfort in his presence prompted her to say, "I read the histories you recommended, *Fabiane's Wishes*. I don't agree with what you said about them being what people want."

He raised an eyebrow. "Oh?"

"Some of the stories are not what people would want to hear

at all."

"Are you sure about that?" He crossed his arms and leaned back in his chair, looking outrageously comfortable. His eyes darkened to a grey akin to charcoal. Lexa had not noticed how lean he was until he stretched himself out like that. Unlike Aravand, whose discomfort with his broad shoulders and height made them even more prominent, Jaxen's narrow stature was barely noticeable given the certain manner with which he carried himself.

"Yes."

"Can you elaborate?" he asked.

She thought for a moment. "Well, the first one tells the familiar story of why men must be veiled." She paused, wondering if he would feel she was making a comment about his own lack of covering. He did not seem to have taken it as amiss at all and was merely looking at her expectantly.

"Well, the story in the histories is that the gods made mortals as playthings for themselves, almost like children's dolls. The goddess Mawani saw her sister, Addene, playing with men she had created, and Mawani's eye was caught by the most beautiful of those creations. Mawani took herself down to the mortal, took on a physical form, and wooed him. Of course, no mortal man can resist the charm or beauty of a goddess, and he fell deeply in love with her. They lived together for many years. She made the moon in the night sky so that he could gaze upon something beautiful even in darkness. She adored him.

"Then one day, she realised he had grown old while she remained unchanged. But she did not worry about that, for she had stopped loving him for his beauty and instead loved him for his heart. And then he died, like all mortals do. Her grief was so profound that she shattered the moon because it reminded her too much of how much she had loved him, and it became the thousand twinkling stars in the sky endlessly trying to form one whole again, succeeding for the briefest of instants before falling

back apart. Then, she declared that men were too frail to be loved
by women, and so to protect the hearts of women, all men must
cover themselves, lest they tempt women to fall too deeply in
love." Lexa had bent the truth when she said to Jaxen she had
read the histories just that day-cycle past. She was well ac-
quainted with them, having read them many times over the
years. This was one of her favourites, and as always when she
read or told this story, she felt a certain melancholy pass over her
at the fact that someone so many years ago had written about an
experience so profound, so human, that it was able to resonate
with her despite the fact that she was living in a completely different era.

This story, entrenched in myth and religion, was particularly famous, and had heavily influenced many of the Fourth Country's customs, including the practice of covering men, as well as
the names ascribed to days.

"Yes, I know the story well," Jaxen said. It was difficult to
tell what exactly he meant by that. The changing shadows from
the light sphere's captured lightning danced across his face. "I'm
curious to know why you claim it hasn't been written to be what
someone wants to hear, though."

"We all know the story, and depending on where you go,
there are many different versions of it. This one, though, it emphasises the relationship between Mawani and her lover far more
than many of the others," she replied.

"And how is that not what people want to hear?" He narrowed his eyes as he looked at her, his curiosity obviously piqued.

She chose her words with care. "The idea of a woman – especially a goddess – falling so passionately in love with a man
makes people uncomfortable."

"You think that people don't like the idea of falling in love
with someone?"

"True love between men and women is very rare," she said.
"And not often spoken of. Especially given the place of men in

our society. Most men," she corrected herself.

"And why do you think that is?" He leaned back even farther, regarding her in an almost lazy fashion.

"Men do not exist for women to love in that way. They live in different worlds."

"So you prefer women, then?" His question was blunt but not rude. Many women formed romantic relationships with one another, using their *elui* for procreation more than physical pleasure.

Lexa blushed. "I don't know that's relevant."

He smirked. "That depends on your perspective."

Uncomfortable, she pressed on with her initial point. "Anyway, the idea of love between a man and woman in the way the story describes, it's not what we consider particularly desirable. The idea that a woman would be so totally undone by her love for a man is," she hesitated, "unwise. "I don't think that anybody wants to hear that kind of ruinous tale."

"Ruinous tale?" he repeated, sounding amused.

She nodded, feeling the threat of a blush on her cheeks, even though she wasn't exactly certain for what she should feel embarrassed.

"You really don't think a woman should love a man in a way that consumes her?" he asked.

She shook her head. "It is unwise. Begging your pardon, Jaxen, but the place of a man is not by a woman's side."

"What about the Third Country where men and women are equals in everything they do?" he asked.

She gave an uncomfortable shrug. "They do things differently there. They are a different people."

"And the Second Country? They are ruled by a man," he pointed out.

"Who is only on the throne because he had no sisters. And it nearly tore the country apart," she retorted, mentally glossing over the role of Serenah's family in that part of recent history.

Jaxen let out a theatrical sigh. "You know, for someone with as sharp a mind as you, you keep it so curiously closed."

Lexa dropped her eyes to look at the fabric of her trousers. "I wouldn't necessarily say I have a sharp mind."

"But you would say that you have a closed mind?"

Now the blush did make its way along her cheeks. "Why do you care anyway?" she snapped, looking up at him.

The smirk returned, accompanied by a slight dimple. "Because you are interesting."

"I'm not interesting. I'm doing badly in your class and you pick on me for it. Leyana picks on me in her class because I do well in it. And I came here to be by myself and you've come and made fun of me." At the end of her tolerance, Lexa made to sweep the rest of her things into the satchel, only to knock over the unsealed jar of ink and spill it across the table. It was the final humiliation and Lexa closed her eyes, willing the rush of tears to remain unshed. To be embarrassed in such a manner, in front of and by a man, too.

It was almost too much.

Jaxen's hands on hers stilled their frantic movement. "Lexana." He said her name softly but with such intensity that he may as well have shouted it.

She reluctantly looked at him. She was terribly conscious of the way his hand felt on hers.

"I'm sorry. I did not seek to upset you." He squeezed her hand in emphasis. "I enjoy your presence. Forgive me for not expressing that better."

He had no reason to lie, but she could not see why he would want to seek her out in particular. Among the students there were women who were far more interesting or impressive than her. That thought must have shown itself on her face, for he pulled her ink-stained hands from the table so that she was facing him properly now.

"You seem so innocent, Lexana. It's not something I've seen

40

in the longest of times. It's a nice thing to be around," he said.

She pulled her hands from his. "I'm not innocent," she said. She tentatively reached into her satchel and pulled out the ruined page from her letter and used it to wipe the excess ink off her fingers. The dark green of the ink left sticky, ugly smears on the paper.

He made no move to retake her hands or to touch her. "You may not think that, but before I came here I worked in a pleasure house. Many of the clients I served there were less cynical and cruel than the students who I've seen here over the last few years. You are nothing like any of your fellow students."

At his revelation, she stopped and looked at him. "You worked in a pleasure house?"

He nodded. "From the time I was eleven years."

Normally found near the Fourth Country's port, Ketter, or in any area frequented by many travellers, pleasure houses catered to all manner of people and all manner of tastes. They were one of few establishments in the Fourth Country that did not take issue with foreign males who went improperly covered and openly spoke of desires they wished to sate. Few worked in pleasure houses by choice, often servicing a debt that they or someone close to them had accrued. justification for allowing them to remain was that at least regulations could ensure nobody under the age of fifteen years worked to satisfy the demands of those who came craving release. True, such establishments would always exist in some form or another. But the taxes they paid to the holder of the land on which they happened to be found were a reason most found more compelling to allow them to stay. As such, the law's prohibition on anyone younger than fifteen working there was a very loosely interpreted one, and even less strictly enforced. Lexa wondered what torment had been forced upon an eleven-year-old Jaxen.

"How did you leave?" she asked.

"Leyana found me. Said she saw something in me that

would be of use to the Enclave, so she paid out my service and brought me here." He spoke so casually of it that he could have been speaking about the evening meal.

"Leyana ... visits pleasure houses?" The idea of the stern woman in a pleasure house was impossible to consider.

Jaxen chuckled. "Only when seeking replacements for my position."

"So she hired you?"

"Bought me," he corrected her.

Even though such things were completely normal, Lexa could not help but feel uncomfortable. It did not seem fair that he was forced to work at the Academy after he had been forced into the service of a pleasure house. He must have seen the sentiment on her face.

"I live a comfortable life here," he assured her. "I do not have to cover myself, and I am free to roam the Enclave when I am not teaching."

"Why did she pick you?" Lexa asked.

"When I was in the pleasure house, I was smart. I worked hard to make sure that I was very good at whatever I needed to do. Someone who's that good is valuable, is wanted. I promised myself the day I stepped through that door that I would do anything I needed to survive. And it seems that exact approach was what singled me out to Leyana. I knew better than anyone in that house how to find out what someone wanted and give it to them." Something akin to pride settled across his features. "It's what we're trying to teach you here. How to survive when everything is against you."

The cramps started later that day. Lexa was fortunate that mostly she suffered only a little discomfort. When she was going through her bleeding days, only occasionally would the pain wind its way around her and not let go. But this looked like being one of those times.

She lay on her bed staring at the ceiling and trying to count the number of breaths in between each wave of pain. It was a technique her mother had taught her, advising to push through the agony. Tanita was a tough woman, that was certain.

A knock on the door had her calling out an invitation to enter even as she stayed still so as to not anger her writhing abdomen.

Serenah poked her head in. "Are you all right? You weren't at lunch."

"Bleeding day," Lexa answered.

Serenah's eyes widened in empathetic understanding. "I have some sweet-tea among my things," she offered.

"I can't take it. But thank you," Lexa replied. Many women used sweet-tea, a painkilling drug, to relieve the pain, but Lexa had discovered an allergy to it on her first bleeding days when she was fourteen.

"Did you want some food? It might help."

Lexa shook her head. "I feel like throwing up already, I don't think I need to add to it."

"I'll be right back," Serenah said.

Lexa remained staring at the ceiling as she waited for Serenah to return. She distracted herself from the pain by thinking back to the conversation between her and Jaxen that morning. It amazed her that he was so willing to discuss his past. She would have assumed anyone who had endured life in a pleasure house would not want to talk about something so dark and unpleasant. She could not understand why he seemed so carefree and amused by the world around him when he knew all too well the least pleasant aspects of humanity. He had appeared so sincere when he said he liked her for her innocence. It displeased her to find that a large part of her wanted to believe it. He was nothing more than a man, and yet she was as put off by him as any woman she had ever encountered. His comments about love continued to prey upon her thoughts. Love was not something highly prized by members of the Fourth Country. The near-constant invasions made forming strong and stable relationships often difficult. Lexa considered herself fortunate to have found firm friends in Emi and Kellen – a different Kellen to Serenah's lover. However, Lexa knew that even those friendships were not impervious to the politics of invasion. And love? Love was a luxury in a world that destroyed the weak.

Serenah returned with a bundle of letters and a blanket with something folded inside it. "Mail came," she explained. "I brought yours."

"Thank you."

Serenah passed her the bundle of letters and placed the blanket across Lexa's pelvis. Something inside it was deliciously warm and made Lexa sigh with the relief that it brought. After a minute, she felt good enough to prop herself up. "A heated stone?"

Serenah nodded. "My mother uses them if there isn't any sweet-tea available. This one was infused directly with warmth by one of the monks in the kitchen rather than placing it near an open fire. It was quite interesting to watch, and much faster than the normal way." She spoke idly as she began to pick through the letters and separated her letters from Lexa's. One in particular caught her interest and she opened it quickly, beginning to read with obvious anticipation and delight.

Lexa had just started reading a letter from her mother which came in reply to something trivial she had sent while she had still been making her way to the Enclave. Suddenly, Serenah flung the correspondence she had been reading away. It fluttered up and then fell to the floor.

"What's wrong?" she asked, looking up from her mother's detailed preparations for her upcoming wedding ceremony. Truth be told, whatever had upset Serenah was a welcome relief from thoughts of taking her first slave-husband. Tears filled Serenah's bright blue eyes.

"Kellen just wrote to me. She's ending things." Despite the distress across her face, Serenah's voice was impressively steady.

"What?" Lexa propped herself up further. It felt somehow an insufficient display of support to remain half lying down.

"I'd need to re-read her letter, but I think she met someone else."

"Oh." Lexa wasn't sure exactly what she should say. "I'm sorry." She squeezed Serenah's shoulder.

"I can't believe it," Serenah whispered, a tear breaking free and trailing down her cheek.

"Did you love her?" Lexa asked, her thoughts returning to Jaxen's comments about love.

The blonde girl shrugged. "I suppose I did. Do. Divine One, I don't know." She brushed away the tear. Her vowels were noticeably more clipped, her accent beginning to slip in the face of her distress.

Lexa could offer no comfort other than the gentle pressure of her hand on Serenah's arm. As they sat together, she thought about love and the way it twisted people around. As much as she was afraid of taking her slave-husband, there was a certain comfort to be had in knowing that she would be bound to someone who would carry out her every request and never leave her side, even if she would never love him.

FIVE

The letter Lexa received from her mother a few days later was a blistering response to a cautious letter of her own in which she expressed her hesitance about taking a husband. Clearly her mother had paid an exorbitant amount to send it by the messengers who crossed the country virtually without ceasing to deliver important or time-sensitive documents. In addition to her words, the action made clear to her daughter such doubts were unacceptable. Such was the force of Tanita's wrath that even through the medium of the written word, Lexa had been forced to read the letter in two sittings. Mentions of 'family honour', 'duty', and 'outrageous' were liberally sprinkled throughout the four pages of recrimination.

Seeking refuge from the tempest in her mind that her mother's words had stirred, Lexa's first response was to sink into the distant haze evoked by forget-me-not. It was the first time since her arrival at the Academy she had smoked the drug without Serenah. She had come to enjoy the companionship of sharing the drug with the foreign girl. But she did not know where her newfound friend was, and the swirling emotions too urgently required attention for her to wait for Serenah.

Once Lexa was safely ensconced in the drug's embrace, she re-read her mother's letter, allowing her emotions to slip by like a river far below her. Tanita laid out very clearly for her daughter the fact that Lexa had no choice in the matter. This was her duty to the Farwan family, to secure its position with marriages of alliance. Taking an *elui* was her responsibility, as she had been told for years.

Her mother was correct. Lexa knew that. But Tanita's words nevertheless were like stinging barbs. She knew some girls her age took part in the process of choosing who would become their *elui*. The fact that she had not even been warned her mother was contemplating her heir's first marriage was what she found truly upsetting.

She reached the end of her forget-me-not. With reluctance, she returned the pipe to its box and sat on her bed while she waited for the drug to drain from her body. The vibrancy of her emotions crept slowly back until she could feel the anger and hurt pulsing inside her, demanding to be expressed. But the drug's respite had its intended effect, and those sentiments were once more controlled.

After checking in her hand mirror to ensure the violet had faded from her eyes, Lexa wandered aimlessly through the corridors. It was the fifth day of the week, the Day of Sorrows, and no lessons were scheduled. She would have rather had lessons – even the torment of Jaxen's classes – than be left to ponder her mother's words. Lexa found herself in the Enclave's prayer room. Windowless, and cut directly into the rock of the mountain, the long, narrow space was devoid of any ornamentation or furnishing other than the altar in the farthest part of the room, and the rows of plain stone benches. It was illuminated only by two light spheres. Their noiseless flickering made the space at once eerie and soothing.

She had never considered herself overly religious. Certainly, she believed in the goddess Mawani, the patron deity of the Fourth Country. One would be a fool not to believe in the existence of the gods. But unlike some who sought to live their lives in exact accordance with the worship of Mawani, Lexa had never found the mere existence of a god a compelling reason to determine every aspect of her life. Yet there was comfort to be had in the little room. It was almost as though the prayers of others had somehow imbued the room with a sense of tranquillity, like the presence of the goddess were here in some way, and she were listening for the troubles of her worshippers.

As custom dictated, Lexa picked up a long-stemmed pellen flower from the offering tray at the door. Its citric fragrance curled up to caress her senses. Idly, she wondered how the monks sourced the flowers, which normally grew at a different time of year. She hadn't seen a greenhouse in the Enclave – the manner in which the wealthy procured fresh flowers for their worship. Those who were unable to access such wealth had to make do with cloth replicas, or the pellen's less well-regarded cousin, a jeyan, which bloomed all through the year. Rather than one flower with seven perfect, oval petals at the end of its long stem, the jeyan had a number of smaller blooms along the length of its stem.

Lexa approached the altar and brought the flower up to her lips. A burst of the citrus flooded her nose, evoking a mild impulse to sneeze. She laid the flower on top of the small pile on the altar. She plucked a single petal from the bloom and placed it on her tongue as she regarded the dark stone wall. The taste took her back to her childhood when her father would take her to the temple in the Capital to pray to Mawani. Tanita's time was always occupied with matters of business, so it had been Lexa's father who had ensured her religious education. He was a true believer, unlike many of the Farwan household, Tanita included. The Farwan matriarch granted him permission to take Lexa to the temple every other day, and to instruct her in the myths and teachings that surrounded the deity, which in turn informed how the Fourth Country's society had unfolded through history. Her father had read her the stories from *Fabiane's Wishes* when she had been too young to read them herself. For her seventh birthday, he had given her a copy of the book. It had beautiful illustrations on several pages, which had been drawn by one of the Capital's finest painters.

Yet Lexa had proved to be more like her mother than her father when it came to religion, and she had thought the stories more interesting than instructive. Whatever disappointment he might have felt that his daughter did not share the extent of his belief, he did not show it, merely enfolding her in his soft embrace when she told him she did not consider religion to be that important. It was an acceptance of her divergence that she had not properly appreciated at the time.

For a long time, she sat in the dark room, reflecting upon her father – an *elui*. There was a responsibility to being in charge of someone's life like that. It served as a reminder that she would be responsible for a great many things one day. Yet her mother refrained from telling her so much that she felt she would never be able to manage a house and a slave-husband, let alone her family's trade network. This more than anything was at the core of Lexa's discomfort, yet when had she tried to tell her mother this, Tanita either refused or failed to acknowledge what her daughter was saying.

Perhaps Tanita truly couldn't understand what her daughter was trying to tell her. She was the sort of woman who wouldn't have been afraid of anything in her youth, merely eager to adopt more responsibility and acquire more power. When her own mother had died unexpectedly, she had assumed the position of family leader and ensured its continued prosperity, all while bearing three children. By contrast, Lexa had always needed to be ordered to participate in anything that did not possess an equation for her to solve.

The pellen petal slowly dissolved on her tongue, the bright acidic sweetness a contrast against the dark of the room. Lexa sighed. As always, her attempt at prayer had brought her no solace. She could not clear her mind enough to allow Mawani access to her heart.

As she exited the room, she found Jaxen in the corridor outside.

"Prayer, Lexana?" Jaxen's voice held that customary faint amusement.

"Not really," she replied, restraining her reflexive shock at seeing him without any covering. That response was less profound each time she saw him, but it was still there.

"I didn't take you for the type to be particularly devout."

"Nor I you," she replied.

"Oh, I wasn't heading to the altar." Derision edged his voice.

"Don't you believe?"

He regarded her with those cool grey eyes. "Of course I believe in Mawani. Given her influence here, she has to be acknowledged, and respected."

"But?"

"But I can't say I choose to worship her."

"Why not?" Lexa asked.

"Worship is a curious thing, Lexana." He caressed her name in that intimate way which made her fight to suppress a shiver in reply.

"Is it?" She folded her arms across her chest to conceal the fact that she was so affected by the mixture of interest and amusement with which he looked at her.

"The monks here claim their power comes from their worship."

"They do?" Her curiosity quelled her discomfort. She had never heard that before.

He leaned against the wall, his eyes never leaving her. This part of the Enclave was deep in the mountain, and the corridor was illuminated by lighting sphere rather than natural light. The dancing light added a sense of mystery to his silent reply.

"Is that possible?"

He shrugged.

"I suppose it could be – perhaps not the prayer itself, but the way it focuses the mind," she said. "Have you asked if they know how prayer gives them power over the elements?"

He smirked. "They're very secretive, in case you hadn't noticed. I only found out about the way they regard prayer by accidentally overhearing a conversation."

"You mean eavesdropping."

His teeth flashed as he grinned. "If they weren't going to check to ensure nobody was listening, it's not my responsibility to make my presence known."

Her lips tightened in disapproval at his impudence, but she supposed she couldn't exactly blame him.

"You look troubled," he said. "Isn't prayer supposed to alleviate worries?"

For a moment, her discussion with him had chased the thought of her marriage and family from her mind. They returned now. "I did not receive divine instruction on my concerns. Thus, they remain."

"Is there anything I might be able to help with?"

"I doubt it."

"Oh?" His eyes turned light grey, humour and curiosity dancing in them like sunlight on water.

"Just a strongly worded letter from my mother," she mumbled.

"Is she rebuking you for some mischief you conducted?" The seductive tone that affected her in ways she didn't quite understand was back in his voice.

"No."

He waited, as comfortable with the silence following her reply as she was not. Finally, she could take it no longer. "She's decided I'm to take my first *elui*."

His eyebrows raised. "You're the right age. Why the problem? Do you not want to get married?"

She looked away, unwilling to meet his gaze. "It's not that

simple."

"Have you ever been with someone?"

"That's none of your business," she snapped. "Besides, that's irrelevant."

"Is it?" He appeared unrattled by her anger.

"Yes," she said, the bite still in her voice.

"Well, what is the problem then?"

She debated telling him to mind his own business, but telling him what troubled her was less daunting than the prospect of facing his speculation if she refused, especially given his curiosity about her romantic history. It felt wrong to conduct this conversation in the corridor, so Lexa led the way back into the serenity of the prayer room. They sat on one of the benches near the doorway.

"Do you know who my mother is?" she asked.

"I've some idea." It was hard to see his face in the soft light, but easy to tell from his tone that he was amused.

"Then you'll know the idea of me replacing her one day is a laughable one."

His silence was disparaging. She felt compelled to speak into it. "My mother is brilliant. she ordered that all crates containing goods sold by family-associated distributors be stamped with our family motto, 'quality is the secret to success'." As a result of Tanita's initiative, the Farwan name subsequently became synonymous with high-quality products, even while some sneered that Tanita's initiative had merely created a false perception of the quality of products branded under the Farwan trade house. While not all families had a motto, those who did and were involved in trade followed her lead. The effect of branding their wares worked less well when sayings were things like 'coins come to those who work', as such expressions did little to encourage people to buy the related products.

When did reply, his voice was gentle, seeming to fill every part of the near-dark space. "I think you undervalue yourself,

Lexana."

She wished she could see his face properly. "You don't know me."

"I know enough."

"You're always comfortable. You can't understand." The room echoed with the petulance in her voice, eliciting contrition for being so childish. She wished she could have expressed herself better.

"It's not about simply being comfortable. It's about appearing comfortable for long enough that it becomes true."

"I'm not good at that," she said.

"You may surprise yourself. You are Tanita Farwan's daughter, after all. If the secret to success truly is quality, then there is very little chance you cannot succeed in your chosen endeavours."

She had nothing to say in reply to that. She would not have thought this gentleness lurked behind the mild amusement with which Jaxen met almost everything.

"Perhaps you might do well to avoid telling too many people about your concerns," he suggested.

"I was hardly planning to share them with the other students," she retorted.

His laugh rolled around the room. "I'd go so far as to advise you to go to great lengths to conceal them. As well we know, someone here is interested in secrets that might be found within the Enclave. The knowledge of your sentiments toward your marriage and familial obligations may be unexpectedly useful to those who wish to do you and your family harm."

She looked at in the darkness of the room. His words, like him, left her with a sense of discomfort. "But I can trust you?"

"You shouldn't. You don't know me."

In the distance, the gong which marked the hour sounded.

"I promised Aravand I'd help him with something Leyana showed us yesterday," she said.

"You aren't running away from me, are you, Lexana?" Back was the lighthearted flirtatiousness, as though their conversation had never occurred.

"No, Jaxen." She sighed the words out, wary of what she had just told him as much as she was of his warning to her.

"Lexa." His hand caught hers as she made to rise. It was the second time his hands had captured hers, and she was just as unprepared for it as the first time. In the darkened room, it felt even more intimate. The familiarity of her nickname was like a physical blow that sent her heart racing.

For a moment, her throat refused to work, then she regained some mastery of herself. "Yes, Jaxen?"

He stood, pulling her closer to him with the movement. She could see his face almost perfectly now as her face neared to his. Looking into his eyes while so close to him was unsettling. For the moment, they were still. Intense. She wondered how many people before her had been so captivated by that grey gaze.

"Perhaps you should consider your own worth when it comes to matters of your family affairs." His eyes never left hers as he spoke. "I believe you are stronger than you realise."

Abruptly, he released her hand and looked away. She stayed where she was for a moment, inhaling the memory of the way his hand had felt, and the way his eyes had looked. Then she left with only a whispered "thank you" that she was uncertain how she managed to actually force out.

Aravand was waiting for her, the familiar haunted expression of someone being somewhere they are not supposed to be chasing his features. She sat next to him, trying to marshal her mind, which Jaxen had so effectively disordered.

Aravand opened his notebook. Unlike Lexa's, which was neatly filled with lines of ordered equations, interrupted only by the occasional note, his was a mess of crossed-out lines. It hurt

Lexa's eyes to regard it for too long.

She explained what they had looked at in Leyana's class, breaking down the ideas piece by piece. Aravand nodded obligingly each time she spoke, but it was clear that he was barely following. After a few minutes, she stopped and asked him, "How can you find the unknown number I've written here, then?"

The expression of being caught should have frustrated her, but instead she felt bad for him. If she felt unworthy of taking her mother's place, she couldn't imagine how he must feel. She began to explain the principle again, using an even simpler explanation. She could see that he was beginning to slowly understand. A small smile tucked itself into the corner of his mouth as the mystery of the problem was revealed.

They had to pause when one of his unruly russet curls freed itself from his veil and he had to adjust the garment. Because his status meant he did not have to cover his face, the garment he wore was actually more intricate than most veils.

"Does it bother you, wearing it?" Lexa asked, her thoughts on Jaxen and his lack of decorum in refusing to wear a veil.

Aravand looked at her in clear incomprehension. "I've always worn it."

"Do you ever wish you didn't have to wear it?" She had never considered that the garment might actually be uncomfortable to wear.

Aravand paused fiddling with his veil, his brown eyes wide at the suggestion. "It would be indecent," he all but hissed at her. The mere thought called forth panic to his face.

"What about Jaxen, then?"

"It's not decent for him to go about the way he does." The boy's disapproval tightened his features, making him look older than he actually was. "But it's not for me to say that to anyone. That's something for you and the other girls to say."

"Well, Kaitlen did say something on our first day, and she was told off for it," Lexa pointed out.

Aravand shrugged, evidently uncomfortable with the conversation. "If Jaxen is allowed to go about half-dressed, that's for him to do. But it doesn't mean the rest of us should."

She let the subject lie. Aravand was not going to change his mind, and there was little point in her pushing him on it. Besides, he was correct. Jaxen's state of dress was indecent. It was only the confidence with which he carried himself that stopped it from being outright embarrassing for himself and everybody around him. But he had told her that confidence had to be faked until it became true. She wondered if from time to time, he still had to throw up a pretence of that assurance in order to feel he truly belonged.

SIX

Something had changed between her and Jaxen, and she couldn't quite identify what it was. She was still hopeless in his classes, but it no longer felt that he was singling her out in the way he had before. Sometimes she would ask if he could recommend anything that she could read to try to better understand that day's lesson. He initially laughed at her apparent belief that anything she might read in a book would make her a grand seductress, but she pointed out that she was so terrible that it certainly couldn't make her less effective. Sometimes he would accompany her to the library. On those times, they would chat about any number of inconsequential things. He made no further mention of their conversation in the prayer room, nor his past. She often wondered if he thought about the life that he had escaped.

Two day-cycles after that day in the prayer room, they left the classroom together, in the way that had become a habit for them. It was a beautiful afternoon. The sunlight coming through the windows had the hazy depth that accompanied mid-autumn. On top of the mountain, the clear, clean air made that light even more radiant.

"I see you and Serenah are becoming close friends," he commented.

"No more than I and Aravand, or her and Kirrith," she countered. She had grown comfortable speaking with him, contradicting him. She had even almost become accustomed to the discomfort that the sight of his bare head created each time she saw him.

"You are being kind to Aravand in helping him with his sums. Serenah and Kirrith, well..."

His smirk was suggestive.

"Really?" she asked, caught between exasperation and amusement that he would infer such a thing.

"I'm a master of seduction. I think I can see it going on between my students," he said.

She snorted. "Master of seduction. Is that your official title, then?"

"Yes. We have the master of coin, the master of strategy and the master of seduction here," he said. For all his smooth delivery, it could have been true, too. "Speaking of which, you rarely speak of how you find Laskana's classes."

She gave a courteous nod to a monk who passed by them, using the interruption to consider her answer. The monks were a silent, mysterious presence within the Enclave. They spoke as rarely as possible to the students, and when they had to, it was with as few words as necessary. Lexa had seen no further demonstration of any elemental powers. The mystery of their power intrigued her.

"Laskana's classes are difficult but make sense. I don't think I'll ever be the most brilliant tactician, but I'll be able to hold my own," she said.

"Do you plan on getting into any battles?" he asked casually. The semblance of passing interest didn't fool her. It was a question with quite some weight behind it. She or her mother may wish to expand their enterprises and their land. The best way to do that in the Fourth Country was by force. Such things went on every day.

"Only battles of coin," she answered truthfully. She had no stomach for warfare, despite the world in which she had been raised. Her mother was willing to shed blood – she had seen as much when rival families had tried to cut off Farwan trade routes once when she was four, and again when she was seven – but Tanita did not seek to take any more lives than was necessary. It was an approach that had been passed down to Lexa.

"Might I offer a piece of advice?" Jaxen said. They had reached the library. Lexa spent much of her time in the extensive space, preferring it to her tiny room.

"You may always offer."

He smiled at that. "Having a friend like Serenah may not ultimately benefit you. She is an exile. That will always hang over her."

Lexa looked at him in bewilderment. "I don't spend time with her because I think she might be a useful friend to have one day. I spend time with her because I enjoy her company."

His smile could have been deemed patronising. "I know. It's one of the reasons I like you." His slight emphasis on the word 'like' left her wondering what exactly he meant by that.

She looked directly into his eyes, something she would never have done a few day-cycles ago. The intensity of his gaze made her feel that she was as inappropriately dressed as him.

"Thank you for the advice, even though I won't take it," she said.

He laughed, then stepped close to her and murmured, "One other thing..."

"Yes?" She leaned toward him in response to his lowered tone.

He also leaned forward, in an almost conspiratorial manner. She could feel the heat from his body.

"Perhaps you should consider not smoking forget-me-not."

She pulled back, shock making her go rigid. The intimacy of the moment was lost in the face of her horror that he somehow knew of her clandestine habit.

"Don't worry, nobody else would know," he reassured her, looking more amused than anything else.

"How do you know, then?"

"I used to work in a pleasure house. I know what it looks like when someone takes forget-me-not." He said it so casually, as if it were a recommendation for a book, or a comment about the weather, that it was almost possible to not quite realise what he was saying.

"Jaxen, I–" Lexa faltered, uncertain what exactly to say.

"Perhaps just something for you to consider, then," he said. "I'll see you tomorrow in class."

With that, he left. Lexa watched him walk away, mesmerised by the easy roll of his hips. There was something incredibly sensuous about the way he walked.

"Are you sleeping with him?"

Kirrith's question made her jump. Lexa hadn't realised that she and Jaxen were being observed. Lexa made her way to where Kirrith sat in one of the deep armchairs in the space designated for reading and quiet chatter.

"Don't worry, you were too far away and talking too quietly for me to hear anything," Kirrith reassured her.

"We aren't. It's not like that," Lexa protested.

The other girl threw her an amused look. She had a sea of papers in her lap, and several sheets fanned out in her hand. "I mean, I doubt it would be favourably looked upon, but I'm also certain that such things have happened before." She selected a page from one of the multitude in her lap and tucked it behind another in her hand. "I've let these records for the farm be unordered for far too long," she muttered, half to herself. She juggled the papers in her hands so she could pick up a small light sphere and bring it closer to one of the pages.

"There's nothing romantic between us," Lexa insisted.

"If you say so," Kirrith said distractedly as she scanned another page, a slight frown on her face. "Does this make sense to you?" She held out a page.

Lexa ran her eye over the neatly written figures – an inventory, by the look. The girl's willingness to show her information such as this surprised her. Especially with the warning of a spy in their midst. Perhaps everybody else had forgotten Laskana's comment on the first day. Lexa certainly hadn't.

"Without any other information, it looks more or less correct. Oh, wait, it doesn't quite add up. It's three off." Lexa handed it back.

"Mawani curse this. I knew it." Kirrith folded the corner of the page and placed it back on the complicated system in her lap.

Lexa cautiously sat in the adjacent chair, watching as Kirrith sorted her papers until they became a neat stack. There was a fierceness to her demeanour that Lexa couldn't decide if she liked or found offputting. It certainly made conventional beauty impossible. But there was something nevertheless arresting about her appearance. Her black hair was tightly tied back, emphasising high cheekbones, the straight line of her nose, and the fullness of her mouth. Lexa had occasionally seen her practising weaponscraft with Laskana or Kaitlen in the early mornings, adding to her toned physique that radiated competence and warned off any confrontation. Apparently, Kirrith, unlike her, was willing to fight keep what was hers, or to take what she wanted. Lexa had refused to undertake any weapons training, to her mother's chagrin.

"Kaitlen doesn't like you, you know," Kirrith commented once she was finished. She looked over what she had done to check for any errors.

"What did I do to her?" Lexa asked. The news did not particularly surprise her. She had not forgotten Kaitlen's comment after she had helped Aravand on the first day. In the intervening day-cycles, the other girl had been clear enough with expressing her contempt for Lexa. She pointedly refused to speak with Lexa and would often roll her eyes or pull a face in classes if Lexa spoke. The childishness of the other girl was amusing, if not also frustrating.

"I think your existence is reason enough," Kirrith said.

"Wonderful," Lexa muttered.

"I'm not sure she could do anything against you here, but she may try something once we leave the Academy," Kirrith noted.

"Why would she do that?"

"Her family is new to power. People who don't come from families that have held their positions for generations like you or I often feel the need to prove themselves, often at the expense of a powerful family. Of course, they most often fail given that they lack resources and skill, but occasionally they do succeed." Kirrith put her stack of papers into a leather folder and stretched in her chair. "Anyway, I'd best be off. Do you know where I could find Serenah?" Her tone was utterly casual, but after Jaxen's remark about the two, Lexa looked intently at Kirrith's face. Sure enough, she saw the practised nonchalance that inferred emotional investment.

"I think she was going to bathe," Lexa said. The Enclave was built over a series of warm springs. Several rooms offered a variety of options for luxuriating in the waters. Some pools were even large enough to swim in. Lexa had never learned to swim, so she limited herself to the shallow pools. Serenah, however, had apparently learned to swim from the time she was a small child. The Second Country was also known as the Queendom of the Seven Lakes – although with a man on the throne, Lexa was not sure how appropriate that name was. True to its name, seven great lakes were spread around the country. Serenah had told Lexa with great relish how nice it was to be able to swim up here on the mountain.

"Bathing, you say?" A slight smile settled across Kirrith's face. "Thanks," she said, and departed at a swift walk.

Lexa hated to admit that Jaxen could have been correct, but now that he had planted the thought in her head she couldn't help but wonder about the exact nature of the relationship between Serenah and Kirrith. They had been together quite a bit over the past few days, although Serenah had never mentioned anything about Kirrith to her. Lexa settled into the chair and withdrew a book from her satchel. It was enjoyable having access to such an extensive number of books. Given how difficult paper was to make, the construction of an entire book was very expensive. The Farwan family library consisted of a respectable number of books, but it was nothing compared to the Enclave.

She had read only a few pages when low laughter broke through her concentration. Curious and vaguely irritated at the interruption, she peered around the corner of her chair. At one of the tables several paces away, she saw Jaxen sitting with Karra. Something he said had evidently amused her greatly. She leaned forward flirtatiously, invitation imbued in the way she curved toward him. He tugged on one of her purple streaks, the picture of cheekiness. She laughed harder as she looked up at him. Lexa retreated around the corner of her chair and sank into its embrace. She could not deny that she felt jealousy hotly surging through her at the idea that Jaxen might be close with another student. She had thought she was his favourite, although now that she contemplated it, she had little on which to base that assumption.

She replaced the book and slunk away, all but running into Leyana in the corridor outside.

"My pardon," she stammered, looking up into the severe woman's face.

Leyana did not seem to be overly bothered by the near collision. "You should probably be more vigilant in looking at what's in front of you," she said mildly.

"I know. Jaxen and Karra were making a lot of noise and it was bothering me," Lexa said, realising as soon as the words left her lips that she sounded jealous.

Leyana's eyebrows rose. "Walk with me."

Lexa obliged, wondering why the terrifying woman had requested that she accompany her.

"You are a very fine student," Leyana told her. The comment was surprising. She had never given Lexa any hint of a compliment during her classes. She merely watched her with that impervious gaze.

"Thank you," Lexa said.

"And you are very generous in helping Aravand," Leyana noted.

Lexa glanced at her. Leyana did not seem to walk so much as glide. Lexa wondered how the woman's night-black hair remained in such perfect ringlets, hovering around her face and down her back when she walked so quickly.

"I feel bad for him. He is in a woman's world," Lexa said when she realised Leyana was awaiting a response.

"He is fortunate that you are willing to help him. Although I note your charity does not extend to Kaitlen." A smile flash across the woman's face.

"I'm not sure what I should say to that," she said honestly.

"Kaitlen has not treated you in any way that merits your generosity," Leyana told her. Lexa wondered what that was supposed to mean. Certainly, she and Kaitlen had kept a distance from each other since that first day, but aside from the girl's efforts to make it clear she disliked Lexa, she had done nothing specific that Lexa could recall. Yet it was the second time in one day that someone had commented on Kaitlen's acrimonious feelings toward Lexa. Perhaps Leyana and Kirrith were hinting at something that Lexa did not know. She wondered once more who among the students was responsible for trying to discover information about the Enclave.

"Were there any important secrets in the message you found?" Lexa blurted out, realising too late that a question like that could make her look like a spy.

Leyana threw her a look of cool amusement. "Are you sure it's wise to ask such questions?"

"I'm sorry, I would never..." Lexa stammered her apology,

looking away from the formidable woman in an attempt to hide her growing blush.

"Don't worry, none of us think that you are behind such a thing," Leyana said after a moment had passed, in which the sound of their steps on the timber floor had sounded unbearably loud to Lexa.

Lexa swung her head back to regard the taller woman.

"You do not have the heart for such things."

Lexa was not sure if she was being insulted or complimented.

"Here we are," Leyana said, stopping in front of a wooden door. She turned the handle and pushed, but nothing happened. To Lexa's amusement, she cursed. "I keep asking them to plane down the door, but they just won't do it. Stand back."

Lexa obliged, watching as Leyana gestured toward the door. Lexa felt her hair suddenly ruffled by a silent rush of wind that swirled around her before almost pulling her toward the door. Of course, Leyana remained perfectly still, her hand outstretched. For a moment, nothing happened, then the door abruptly snapped open. "That was incredible," Lexa said, following Leyana into the stone-walled room. While she was reasonably certain Leyana was part of the Enclave's order of monks, she had not verified this. There was no way she could think to sate her curiosity without looking like the spy about whom they had been warned on the first day.

"A worthless trick," Leyana said, waving her hand dismissively, with the same motion bringing lightning to the dormant spheres. Most people had to cover their light spheres with a thick cloth to dull them. Leyana paid no heed to what others would have regarded as a miracle. "Now, where was it?" she muttered.

Lexa looked around the room, marvelling at the fact that it appeared she was inside Leyana's private residence. She would not have expected the woman to have such a penchant for the colour orange, nor for any decoration, yet paintings adorned the walls, and an orange throw and several orange pillows were placed on the chairs. The room was clearly devoted to personal work and relaxation. A large wooden desk sat immediately opposite the door, occupied only by several pieces of neatly stacked paper and two books. Lexa presumed quills, ink and anything else that Leyana might need were stored in the desk's drawers. A screen was mostly drawn across an archway leading into another room. The screen was painted with a pastoral scene where birds and animals were drawn in painstaking detail. The glimpse offered of the room beyond showed a large bed with the covers (orange, of course) neatly arranged. The room was cosy – almost too cosy with the preponderance of orange.

"Sit," Leyana said distractedly as she rifled through the papers on her desk.

Lexa obeyed. As she watched her teacher, she wondered why exactly she had been brought here.

"Ah." Leyana pulled out a paper. "Look at this."

Dutifully, Lexa accepted the page and scanned it, noting the drawing of an arch and annotations surrounding the image.

"Do you understand it?" Leyana asked.

"Yes. It's the principle of force. If the keystone is the right shape and inserted in the correct place, then it will put enough pressure on the surrounding stones that they will remain together in the right shape without any glue or mortar," Lexa replied. "There isn't much information on this sort of method in the Capital, but I've read bits and pieces."

Leyana snorted. "It's a wonder you learned to read and write. You did have tutors, I assume?"

Lexa nodded, unwilling to point out that her mother had paid some of the finest tutors in the Fourth Country to provide Lexa with an education.

"You are perhaps one of the most competent students I have encountered. Your mind is wasted on the trivialities of accounts and storage capacities." Leyana's bluntness was almost frightening.

Lexa looked at her in surprise.

"You could calculate the rate of interest for a loan standing on your head. You may as well practise standing on your head in my classes, given how far ahead of everybody else you are."

Lexa stifled a laugh at the image of her doing headstands while the severe Leyana laboured through basic sums with everybody else.

"Have you ever considered learning different kinds of mathematics?" Leyana asked.

Lexa shook her head. "I've only ever needed to know formulae related to accounts and trade."

"Such a waste," Leyana said, more to herself than Lexa. "You could be put to use refining the designs of catapults or unpicking the trajectory of the stars."

"But the use of catapults was outlawed a year ago," was all Lexa found herself able to say. It had been decided that catapults were too destructive, both to the territory in the line of fire and the attackers. Things often went wrong when it came to catapults.

Leyana raised an eyebrow. "What about the aqueducts of the Third Country? Oranis sits in the middle of a plain devoid of any significant river or stream, and the city's water is fed from a great distance away by aqueducts. Aside from questions about how the city itself was founded without a large source of water, how were its aqueducts constructed so that water flows across such a great distance, and to each of the city's houses no less? Can the design be improved? Aren't you the least bit curious to understand the mathematics behind such things?"

Lexa's curiosity was piqued by the suggestion that she could learn the kind of maths that would teach her about the construction of enormous and complex things. A whole new world had been tantalisingly dangled in front of her, and she wanted to see more of it. "How much can I learn?" she asked.

"Builders use a string and weight in order to calculate how much force is pressing on an arch, or on certain areas of a building. I believe that there is a better way, but thus far, every time I think I have it, the numbers fail to work," Leyana said. "I would be interested to see what you could do with this problem of mine."

Lexa frowned. "I'm not sure that I'm good enough—"

"If you read the books that I give you, you will easily be good enough. What I did with the door, the way I manipulated the wind, it's nothing. Everything that the monks do is a fraction of what we should be able to do, yet nobody properly investigates such things. Reports of the Second Country's king being able to hold the sun in his hands, or the mystical abilities of people within the Third Country, suggest that what the monks do can be understood beyond the simple explanation of faith. And yet everybody seems content to accept the idea that faith offers power. I believe that one day we might be able to understand what happens when I use the wind to open the door. And I think that refinement of the mathematical arts is the way to do it." For the first time, passion had crept into Leyana's normally measured voice. Given her normally taciturn demeanour, it was oddly moving.

"What should I do?" Lexa asked, feeling excitement stir within her. To unravel the mysteries of the world? If she could learn that at the Academy, it would be time well spent indeed.

Leyana offered her a triumphant smile. "I'll write you a list of books that you'll need to read. You will be able to find them all in the library." She pulled a scrap of paper and a nub of charcoal from a drawer in her desk. When she was done, she handed the paper to Lexa, rubbing her fingers together to remove the charcoal. "Once you've read them, come back to me. You may not want to speak too much of what I've told you here to your fellow students."

Lexa stood, greedy to begin. Yet she hesitated. "Why do you trust me with this? Surely at least some of what you have told me is not something the monks would want known."

Leyana regarded her for a moment, her face utterly inscrutable. "Some of us must be loved in spite of the things we do, and some of us must love people despite of the things they do. You will always be one of the latter," she said. She sounded resigned, as though she spoke from an old sadness that had long since ceased to sharply cut her. She almost looked old.

SEVEN

Lexa devoured the books Leyana assigned her. Three days after Leyana had pulled her aside, she was already halfway through the list. She practically lived in one of the library's chairs, curling her legs around herself for so long that she often discovered them numb when she went to stand.

She was on the final chapter of a book about a method to calculate certain angles and apply them to construction. Suddenly, the light was blocked by someone standing in front of her. Jaxen.

"Is something wrong?" she asked. A slight drowsiness settled over her at being pulled from the concentration of reading.

"I was going to ask you the same question," he said mildly.

"I'm reading." She held up the book to prove her point.

"I can see that."

"So now you know," she said, when he made no move to leave. She tried to continue reading as though he wasn't there, but she was too aware of his presence. "Is there anything I can do for you?" she asked, looking back up to him.

"Oh, I'm sure there are several things I could dream up."

Her heartbeat quickened slightly at his inference, but she managed to control her face to display no outward reaction. "Well, when you have something more substantial in mind, let me know."

"I cannot help but feel your mind has been elsewhere in my lessons," he said.

He was, of course, correct. She had been preoccupied with thoughts of the new things she was reading. Especially considering that she had all but given up on seduction as a skill she would possess. She figured it was a better use of her time to digest the information she was consuming at such a voracious pace. "Does that hurt your feelings?" she asked.

He laughed. "And once you were so shy."

She hoisted the book in a 'what-can-I-say' gesture, causing him to laugh more.

"Come on, tell me what's been occupying that lovely head of yours," he cajoled.

She sighed. He was not going to be deterred, it seemed. "Leyana suggested I do some extra reading. It's interesting."

"Extra reading? Leyana? She all but hates every one of her students." Jaxen fixed her with a sceptical expression.

Lexa shrugged. "I would hardly say she likes me," she said, causing him to laugh again.

"She tried to teach me maths once, you know. It did not go well," he admitted.

"You know no maths at all?" Lexa was shocked.

"A little. I can count, and I know how to add and take away." He did not seem to be particularly upset or uncomfortable with the gap in his knowledge. "I only learned to read and write properly when I came here."

"What?"

"There was little need for a child working in a pleasure house to know how to read. I only learned bits and pieces. I like reading." He nodded serenely at his last comment.

Lexa shook her head, wondering what other surprises lay in his past. She sighed and shut the book. She knew that she wasn't going to get any reading done as long as Jaxen was there. In any case, she understood the idea behind the final chapter. "I need to get a different book," she told him, picking up her satchel and slinging it over her shoulder.

He followed her lead, walking with that irritating grace. "You know you're quite alluring when you're focusing on something," he told her.

"I know you're trying to put me off," she said, checking the carving on the bookshelf at which they had arrived. The system by which the books were arranged was a curious one, but she was finally starting to understand it.

"Why would I do that?" He feigned shock and hurt.

"Because you enjoy it," she said, moving on to a different shelf.

"Well, yes," he admitted. "But you do also look very alluring. Especially when you're concentrating, and especially when your hair is pulled back like this." He pulled gently on the plait that hung down her back. She wheeled around and scowled at him. "Do you think that I'm your personal project, because I'm all but failing your class?" she snapped. A passing monk glared at her. "What is it with the teachers here making me their personal projects?" she hissed, her voice lowered in deference to the monk's glare.

"Leyana's making you a personal project?" His eyes sharpened and he grabbed the book in her hand, pulling it easily out of her grasp. He read the title and looked back up to her, his eyes narrowed. "Is she getting you to help her with her research?"

She snatched the book back, having found its space. The title of the book was carved into the shelf with the most precise hand. She wondered, briefly, despite the conversation with Jaxen, how the shelf was altered when a new book was acquired. She suspected the monks' powers let them change the inscriptions in the wood.

Ignoring his question, she searched for the next book on Leyana's list.

"Lexana." Jaxen grabbed her arm and pulled her to face him. His tone was suddenly no longer playful but almost a growl. She was within her rights to slap him for having the impudence to grab her like that. She even raised her free hand, but he easily caught her wrist.

She glared at him for several seconds. Something about the set of his lips and the beautiful grey of his eyes made her skin feel as though it was on fire. She took a step toward him and his hand tightened around her arm. The pain from the strength of his grip throbbed through her.

The hardness in his gaze shifted and he pulled her forward. She was now against him, her chest against his, the jutting point of her hip nestled into the curve of his waist. Her eyes fell to his lips and she wondered what it would be like to kiss him. She leaned toward him. He moved toward her in reply. His lips were so close to hers that she could practically taste him. Then the sound of furtive laughter broke them apart. She stepped away from him instinctively, his hand let go of her arm. She turned to see the source of what had disturbed them.

Then Jaxen grabbed her shoulder and pulled her backwards, against the shelf, and against him. She found her back pressed against his chest, his arm encircling her waist. His chin came to practically rest on her shoulder, his cheek brushed against hers. Through the fabric of their clothes she could feel the heat of his body and the pounding of his heartbeat. The proximity to him made her feel dizzy. Together, they looked out from the shadow of the bookshelves into the main aisle. Serenah was leading Kirrith by the hand through the maze of bookshelves. She turned back to say something and Kirrith took the opportunity to tug Serenah close and give her a lingering kiss. Serenah brought her free hand to curve around Kirrith's neck, pulling her even closer. Her back arched into Kirrith's body.

"Well, well, well," Jaxen whispered in Lexa's ear. She was still nestled against him, and the intimacy of how they stood, and the low murmur of his voice that only she could hear, sent a shiver across her skin.

They remained perfectly still as Serenah and Kirrith finally broke apart and moved on, too intent on one another to realise that they had been observed. Only then did Jaxen release her. Lexa moved away from him with reluctance. She turned to see Jaxen grinning.

"Perhaps I should get Kirrith to teach one of my classes," he said.

"You're outrageous," she said.

"Hardly. I saw the way she was looking at Serenah from that first day. It seems she got what she wanted." He looked impressed.

Lexa watched the sharp planes of his face as he smiled. She could not stop thinking about his lips practically on hers, or the way his hands had felt around her arms. If Serenah and Kirrith had not interrupted them, she wondered what would have happened. A part of her was almost glad that they had been interrupted, while another part raged at it. "I should go," she stammered.

Jaxen raised an eyebrow, but it was impossible to know what he was thinking or feeling. Before he could say anything else, she all but ran from him.

Lexa used the walk back to her room to try and understand her reaction to Jaxen. She could admit he was attractive, or rather, that she was attracted to him. But she had not considered that he made her uncomfortable for any reason other than his impropriety. She could count on one hand the number of times she'd kissed someone. She had never found any of the girls she knew to be particularly interesting, and while the boys who attended the parties and soirees of the Capital were there partly for the amusement and entertainment of the girls, she had never been particularly comfortable being with one of them, either. She had never been certain what information about any liaison might be recounted to a waiting ear. Of course, that reluctance had not been assisted by her reclusive tendencies. Not to say that she wasn't curious. But caution had always prevailed over desire.

Something about Jaxen's frank appreciation of her appearance had led her to believe that it had been a jest rather than him genuinely expressing an interest in her. Then again, men had urges, too.

She told herself to stop being foolish as she rounded the corridor to her room. It almost certainly wouldn't happen again, so she should probably put it out of her head.

She knew, immediately upon opening the door, that something was wrong. Everything was where she had left it, but there was a foreign scent hanging in the air, a fragrance that settled on the middle of her tongue in a strange way, a note out of place to what she was accustomed to in the room. Cautiously, she stepped inside, scrutinising the small space. Absolutely nothing seemed out of place, but Lexa could not help but shake the certainty that while she had been in the library, someone had been searching through her things.

She let her satchel fall to the floor and went over to her trunk, inspecting it for any sign that someone had touched it. She stared at her neatly ordered belongings. Everything looked to be exactly where she had left it. With a frown, she picked up her stack of correspondence. The last letter that she had looked at – a letter from her mother telling her that she and her first *elui* were to be gifted a wing of the Farwan country home and an entire floor of their city residence – still sat on top.

The second letter, too, was what she expected to see – a message from Emi suggesting that she organise a party upon Lexa's return. She had written back all but begging that they make it a small event.

Lexa flicked through all the letters, not seeing anything out of the ordinary. With a sigh she replaced her correspondence, wondering if perhaps she was imagining things to distract herself from what had nearly transpired between her and Jaxen. Nevertheless, she persisted in her examination, wanting to assuage any doubts or concerns. She picked up the sheaf of paper that she had carefully stowed so that it remained flat and crease-free, but there was nothing on the smooth, blank surface of the pages that suggested someone had rifled through them. If she had been expecting an incriminating finger mark, she was disappointed.

All of her clothes appeared to be untouched as indeed were the rest of her meagre possessions. She hadn't brought much to the Academy. There was one formal outfit that she had worn a few times when meeting with her mother's business associates, but that was now folded at the bottom of her trunk. There was no need for such things on a mountaintop. Lexa liked it here for that reason. There was no unnecessary frivolity, no pointless socialising, and there was no intrigue. Except for the fact that she was certain – despite the lack of any evidence – that someone had been sneaking through her room. Almost certainly the same someone who had been trying to discover the secrets of the monks. Just as she wavered, on the verge of dismissing herself as paranoid, the barest scent of that unfamiliar perfume caressed her nose once more. She knew beyond doubt that someone had been in here, even if she had no proof that she could take to Laskana.

Serenah's knock on the door made her jump. She turned to see the satisfied smile on her friend's face. "Are you busy?" Serenah asked.

Lexa sighed and shook her head. "I could have sworn that someone came in here and was looking through my things, but perhaps I was wrong." The presence of someone else dispelled the certainty that had grounded itself within her.

Serenah's smile disappeared and a worried frown took its place. "What?" She stepped further into the room, looking around as though she could see whoever it was who might have been in there.

"It seems silly now, but I thought I smelled perfume in here that isn't mine. But nothing seems to have been moved." Lexa threw her hands up in a small gesture of frustration.

"That doesn't mean that nobody's been snooping," Serenah said. She sat down on the bed in what had become her customary spot. "The art of spying is making sure you've not been caught."

Lexa looked at her in surprise. She hadn't thought her friend the type for intrigue. Then again, her grandfather had tried to orchestrate a coup in her name. She probably had listened to conversations such as this for far longer than Lexa, even if she herself had not participated in them.

Lexa sat beside Serenah. "So..." she began, wondering what exactly she should say of what she and Jaxen had witnessed in the library.

"Why is your nose suddenly buried in books?" Serenah asked, interrupting her delicate construction of the sentence.

"Leyana suggested I read them. They're fascinating." It wasn't a lie, it just wasn't the whole truth. Leyana's warning that she not reveal why she was learning the new formulae and ideas had settled over her. It was what had prevented her from telling Jaxen earlier, too. If someone had been in her room, then she felt the need to pull secrecy around her like a blanket, even when it came to those she trusted.

Serenah yawned. The movement scrunched her face. "I can't understand why you find numbers and sums so fascinating, but if you're enjoying it, that's good for you."

"It does mean that I'm spending a lot of time reading in the library," Lexa said cautiously. "You know, it might not be quite as private as you think."

Serenah looked at her, amusement scrawled across her face. "Is this your delicate way of telling me that you saw me and Kirrith?"

Lexa looked down at the weave of the blanket, unsure what she should say. Serenah laughed at the obvious discomfort. "You really are a treasure, Lexa."

Lexa glanced at Serenah. She did not seem upset at having been discovered.

"Yes, Kirra and I have been finding ways to fill our free time," Serenah said with a lazy smile.

"What about Kellen?" Lexa asked, remembering her friend's distress of only two day-cycles previously.

Now it was Serenah's turn to look down at the blanket's weave. "It still hurts," she admitted. "But if she's done with me, there's nothing I can do to change that. Kirra's here, and she wants me."

Lexa pursed her lips in thought. "But do you care for Kirrith?"

Serenah shrugged. "I could."

"Does she care for you?"

Serenah shrugged again.

"Have you considered that you might hurt her?" Lexa asked gently. She couldn't help but feel that Serenah was using Kirrith to help her forget her feelings for the girl in the Capital who had broken her heart.

"Or she might hurt me," Serenah said. Defiance was carved into her tone.

Lexa let the matter drop. It wasn't really her business. "Forget-me-not?" she asked. After the incident in the library with Jaxen, and the concern of feeling someone might have been going through her things, distance from her raging emotions was a welcome prospect.

Serenah nodded, a pensive look on her face.

Lexa went back to her trunk and pulled out the little box in which she kept her pipe and the leaves. As she brought it back to the bed, she stared at it.

"Is something wrong?"

Lexa ran a thumb over the box's latch. It required a firm press to ensure that the latch slotted home, otherwise it did not properly fasten. Yet it was clearly free now. "I don't know," she said slowly, opening the box.

At first glance, everything seemed fine. The pipe was in the little holder that kept it from rattling about in the box, and the leaves were contained in the little cloth bag. But Lexa was a creature of ritual, and especially when it came to forget-me-not, she would take everything out in a specific order, and replace them in a specific way. The bag of leaves was at a slight angle to where it normally sat. It was almost imperceptible, but Lexa knew she always put everything back in the exact same place. The latch alone could have been an unusual error for her to make, but with the items inside the box not where they should be, it was conclusive evidence that someone had opened the box. It was proof, but not proof that she could tell anybody other than Serenah. It was too insubstantial, and her habit of smoking forget-me-not was something she wanted as few people as possible to know.

"Someone has been here. The latch is open, and the bag of leaves is not where I put it." Lexa realised how much she sounded like someone pushed to the point of paranoia, but now she was utterly certain that she was correct.

Serenah looked at the box. "Is there anything that you can do about it?"

Lexa bit her lip. "I don't think so. If anybody's looking for secrets to help bring down my family, I'm afraid they'd be sorely disappointed. Mother is particularly strict about not revealing anything other than the most banal of trivialities in letters lest they be intercepted. And anyway, there's also much that she doesn't share with me, even in person."

Serenah snorted in amusement. "I've only ever seen your mother on the other side of a room, but she sounds especially frightening."

"You have no idea." Lexa shook her head. She stared down at the open box for a moment longer, then prepared the forget-me-not. She desperately wanted a reprieve from the fear and confusion that threatened to overwhelm her.

She gave Serenah the first inhale. The other girl leaned back so that her head was touching the wall, a dreamy expression crossing her face. "Do you really think that I might hurt Kirra?"

Lexa brought the pipe to her lips, the familiarity of the action soothing her agitation. "I don't know. I have very little practice with love," she admitted, her thoughts flicking to her impending marriage.

Serenah took the pipe and looked at her in surprise. "Why not?"

Lexa tilted her head as she considered. "I suppose nobody's really interested me."

"Never?"

Lexa's thoughts treacherously flashed back to Jaxen's lips all but against hers, his hands on her, the feel of him pulling her back against him as they covertly observed Serenah and Kirrith pass them. The forget-me-not was already pulling her away from her emotions, allowing her to observe them as though from a distance, yet she felt a flash of heat somewhere around her sternum at the memory. "Not really," she said.

"You've never wanted to have fun with someone?" Serenah pressed.

The way she had shivered when Jaxen murmured in her ear came flooding back as though she were once more pressed up against him. "Once or twice," she admitted. "But it's always seemed more trouble than it's worth."

Serenah's laugh was slow and warm. "Oh, it's always worth it. Especially when there's trouble."

Much later, when her friend had left and the haze of the forget-me-not had worn away, Serenah's words still rang in her ear. It was almost as though another Lexa took hold of her then, opening the door and stealing into the corridor. Night had long since fallen. The light spheres that illuminated the corridors cast just enough light to see by. No curfew existed in the Enclave, but Lexa did not want to come across anybody. The fact that someone had been in her room left her cautious.

She made her way to the corridor that led to Leyana's room and sneaked along it, trying to discern which door was Jaxen's. Before she could begin investigating properly, one of the doors swung open. Lexa flattened herself against the wall, hoping that the shadows would be sufficient to conceal her. Karra stepped out, turning as if a thought had occurred to her, to speak with Jaxen, who was just behind her and naked from the waist up.

EIGHT

Humiliation burned through Lexa as she watched Karra walk away. Fortunately, the other girl did not walk toward her but in the opposite direction. She chided herself for being so foolish as to believe that Jaxen could want her, that she could simply go to his room and he would accept her advances. Whatever had transpired between them in the library that day had been nothing more than a trick of the moment. He could have his pick of any of the girls who came to the Academy. Of course he would want someone like Karra with fun purple streaks in her hair. She had even seen them laughing together only a few days earlier.

"Lexa?" Jaxen called out to her softly, his voice easily carrying across the stone corridor. She did not move, frozen in this final shame of being discovered when all she wanted to do was slip away and nurse her wounded pride.

"What are you doing there, plastered against the wall? You look like you're trying to become a painting." He sounded as lighthearted as ever, even though he had to have known she had seen Karra leaving his room.

She stayed where she was, deliberating the merits of running away.

"Did you want to come in?" he asked, sounding slightly confused.

His question gave her the fire she needed to speak. "No!" Her furious whisper echoed across the space between them.

"Would you like to just stand there?" Laugher was in his

voice now.

"Maybe," she snapped.

"Is this about Karra?"

She responded with a particularly vulgar profanity.

"I never thought I'd hear such a phrase from your mouth," he said. He sounded even more amused than before, if it were possible.

"You deserve it," she told him, outraged to find tears forming in her eyes.

"Can we please not discuss such things in the corridor where any passer-by can hear?"

She did not reply, focusing instead on trying to not cry.

"Nothing transpired between Karra and myself, if you must know."

She took a half-step forward, despite herself. "What?"

He stepped back, gesturing to the interior of his room, then folded his arms across his chest. He made clear that he would say no more until she moved the conversation out of the corridor. After one more moment of deliberation, she crossed the corridor and walked into his room. She had to all but brush up against him still standing in the doorway to get by. As she passed him, she was very aware of his bare chest. Her gaze flicked across his skin, noting the lean frame, the hair tracking down his chest, and the small scar over his ribs.

His room had a large window that looked down the side of the mountain. In the darkness, Lexa could see distant flashes of lightning from the never-ceasing lightning storm. Curtains of deep blue hung on either side of the window, drawn back to offer the view of the dark night beyond. Unusually, there were no lightning-filled spheres in the room. With only the gentle light of the fire rather than the agitated flickering of the lightning, there was a serenity that was distinctly unusual and welcome.

A large leather armchair, the only chair in the room, was arranged so that whoever was sitting in it had a view out the window. A book was balanced on its arm. Rugs covered the floor in patterns and colours that were almost dizzying to regard. Lexa's gaze roved across to the bed, which was neatly made. She turned back to Jaxen, who stood with arms folded against the closed door. He looked at her with an even gaze that gave no inclination of his thoughts.

"If you must know, Karra did come here with the hope of seducing me, but I turned her down," he said.

"What?" It was all Lexa could say to this piece of news.

"Yes. Did you not notice how fast she left, or the expression on her face? I'd hope that someone I'd just been with looked far more happy," he said, wry humour easing itself into the end of his sentence.

"Why are you so naked then?" she asked. She averted her gaze so that she was looking a little to his right, at the painting on the wall. She blushed deeply when she realised that it depicted several lovers in various stages of congress.

He glanced to see what had embarrassed her and laughed. "I'm so naked because I was getting ready to sleep. I don't wear nightclothes to bed," he said, his voice dropping to become suggestive. It made her very conscious of the fact that they were alone in his room, with nobody to walk in on them.

"Oh," was all she managed.

He walked toward her, his expression becoming more focused, more intent. "Time for a question of my own, I think," he said. "What were you doing in the corridor outside my room?"

She stepped backward. Her leg hit the armchair and she was forced to stop. Jaxen advanced on her until he stood directly in front of her. Her breath came in irregular gasps at his proximity.

"Well?" He reached out his left hand and lightly traced a finger along her arm. It was the most delicate of touches, yet she felt it so acutely.

"I was coming to see you," she said finally. She swallowed and looked him in the eye. Perhaps that was a mistake. It was as though he was staring right into her soul.

"Were you?" His other hand was suddenly at the curve of her waist, settling there and lightly pressing in before he slipped it around to the small of her back and pulled her closer. She did not resist.

"Yes." She tried to keep her voice firm, but there was a definite quaver in it.

"What for?" He lowered his head so that his lips brushed against her neck, sending fire throughout her entire body. She whimpered softly.

"What for?" He repeated the question, the hand in her back pressing her more tightly into him. His knee came between her legs, parting them as he pushed her back against the chair. She opened her lips to respond and that was when he kissed her, his tongue slipping into her parted mouth. She moaned or sighed – she wasn't sure which – at the taste of him. Then he pulled back, a smile that was almost cruel on his face. "You have to say it, Lexana," he told her.

With the most tentative of movements, she raised her own arms now, running an uncertain hand across his chest. She had never seen a man display so much skin in front of her. It was transfixing. Her other arm slipped around his shoulders to the nape of his neck, tracing the prickles where his hair was cut short. Unlike most men, he wore his hair cropped relatively close to his head. Another way in which he differentiated himself from every man she had ever known.

"I want you." Her voice was almost a croak, made hoarse by the desire that coursed through her.

"Why didn't you say so?" he asked, pulling her back to him and kissing her once more.

Jaxen woke her from slumber. She didn't know for how long she had dozed, but it was still dark outside. The curtains remained drawn back, allowing glimpses of a lightning storm to enter the room at irregular intervals.

Jaxen's lips were on her shoulder, urging her to wakefulness.

"Again?" she mumbled.

He laughed softly against her skin. "Who would have thought you'd be so wild," he said.

She watched the way his features moved as he spoke, the quirk of his lips, the unwavering way his eyes remained on her. His face was partly shadowed, making it even more difficult than normal to read his expression.

For a moment she basked in the memories of the hours before, the crash and tangle of their bodies, her single cry of pain and then her cries of pleasure, the way he had moaned her name. She stirred, finally pulling herself to sit, bringing the blanket with her to cover her chest, even though such modesty was certainly unnecessary now.

Jaxen put his hand under her chin and pulled her to kiss him. She sighed against his mouth, aching with enjoyment.

She slipped her free hand to the back of his neck, drawing him even closer to her. He pulled back with a moan of regret. "You should go."

She was about to protest, but she understood why he was telling her to leave. Being caught sneaking out of Jaxen's room would not be good at all. She was not sure if there was a specific rule that prohibited students from sleeping with the teachers of the Academy, but it would almost certainly be frowned upon. Besides, if someone was looking for information that could be used against her and her family, this would be a very good start.

Resignation at the need for secrecy made her lethargic as she slid from his bed and dressed in her scattered clothes.

He accompanied her to the door, making no effort to maintain any distance between them. He was shirtless again, having only pulled on trousers, she suspected, in case someone was

passing by his door. Being seen farewelling a student while totally naked was far more difficult to explain away than being shirtless.

"Are you all right?" he asked, one hand cupping her chin
tenderly.

"Of course." She smiled at him, curving into his body, feeling an echo of the overwhelming desire that had raged through
her earlier.

He kissed her again, tenderly rather than passionately. "I'll
see you soon." It sounded like a promise more than a mere
statement of truth.

She slipped back to her room, mercifully unseen by anyone.
Judging by the darkness outside the windows, it was very late.

Once inside her room, she quickly changed into her nightclothes and slipped under the covers of her bed. Despite the om-
nipresent pleasant warmth of the Enclave, she still shivered at
the cool of the sheets. It was very different to being in a bed next
to the heat of someone else.

She had expected herself to fall asleep quickly, but her mind
refused to allow her to slip into slumber. Instead, thoughts of
what had just transpired invaded her mind. A part of her was
amazed that she had been so bold. Another part – the part that
was the product of a lifetime spent being warned to be careful –
was considering the risks of what she had just done. To enjoy
life's physical pleasures was completely acceptable in the Fourth
Country, but it did not mean that slipping into the bed of the
wrong person was not without consequences. Half the reason
people came to the Academy was not to learn a new set of skills
but for the prestige of being able to say that they had gone there.
Such prestige would almost certainly be destroyed if it were to be
discovered that she had bedded one of the teachers. Especially
the man who went about parading himself in such a shameful
manner. The thought crept into her mind that she had been fool-

ish, allowing lust for Jaxen to eradicate her common sense. That thought was accompanied by a sense of shame and of the first cold pangs of worry. Someone had been through her room that very day. She had to be careful.

Jaxen found her in the library the next day. A conspiratorial gleam in his eye made her smile despite her best efforts. "Head in books again?" he asked, coming to sit in the chair next to hers.

She nodded, marking her page and putting the book down. Previous experience had taught her that it was impossible to read if Jaxen wanted to speak with her.

"Have you unlocked the secrets of the world?" he asked.

"Well, if I stopped being interrupted, perhaps I would have," she replied.

He laughed at that. Then he reached out a hand in wordless request to see what she was reading. She handed the book to him, surprised to feel him pressing something into her hand as he accepted it.

"You should take that," he said furtively.

She glanced down at the large, thick leaves he had handed to her. "What?"

"Madras leaves," he said quietly.

She reflexively closed her hand around them, glancing around to ensure that nobody was nearby. Madras leaves were taken by women who wished to ensure that they did not have a child. She had no idea from where Jaxen had gotten them, but once more, she was struck by the foolishness of what she had done the previous evening. The possibility that she might fall pregnant had not even occurred to her.

"The easiest way to take it is like you would tea," he advised her. She realised that she had not given him any acknowledgment that she understood.

"How do you know this?" she asked, careful to keep her

voice low.

"I lived in a pleasure house."

"Oh, of course." She should not have forgotten a fact like that, especially given the previous evening. He had been so skilled at finding what she liked, the places on her body where the most delicate of touches made her gasp with delight. Somehow, it had never occurred to her to attribute that skill to years spent servicing the desires of anybody who had enough money to buy him. She wondered how he could possibly enjoy such things now. Yet he had seemed to enjoy himself the previous evening. And if the way he was looking at her now was any indication, he wanted to revisit what had transpired between them.

"Jaxen, I can't do that again," she blurted. The need to ensure there was no misunderstanding was overwhelming, overriding her self control and, apparently, her tact.

He raised his eyebrows but said nothing.

"It's not you," she continued awkwardly. "In fact you were..." she trailed off, realising she was about to start blushing again. She looked down at her fist curled around the madras leaves.

"I understand." His voice was soft.

She flicked her eyes back to him, wondering what he was thinking. He did not look overly upset. Perhaps more thoughtful than normal, but that was all.

"I should go," she said, and took her book back before she left.

Even the sight of him had made her heart beat more quickly. She tried to stop thinking about the way he had kissed her body, and what the feel of his lips on her skin had done to her. But such thoughts would not be denied. She desperately wished things could have been different.

For the next three days, Lexa's thoughts were rarely far

from the night she had spent with Jaxen. Only the distance that forget-me-not offered gave her respite from the mix of longing and regret that encircled her. Serenah asked if something was wrong, and she spoke the truth when she told her friend that it was nothing. Technically, nothing was wrong. She had made sure of that by telling Jaxen she could not return to his bed.

On the fourth day, the mail came. Lexa collected a small bundle of letters, giving her own to the gnarled woman who made the trek up the mountainside once a day-cycle to bring supplies and letters to the Enclave. Flicking through the bundle of correspondence, she recognised Emi's handwriting and happily opened the envelope to see what her friend had written. She missed her friend's counsel and keen wit, especially after what had happened between her and Jaxen.

Lexa, I have held off writing until things became more certain with your family, but to all of us here in the Capital, your family's fate seems to have been confirmed. Your mother, brothers, and her closest elui have disappeared. I can only assume that Tanita has some safe house prepared for such a time as this. I do not know what will happen to you at the Academy, but it is my utmost hope that you remain safe. I have heard that the monks take in people who find their family losers in a power struggle.

It is with great sadness that I must tell you that I must disavow you and the Farwan family. You know that this is not the action I want to take, but you also know that I must protect my own family.

My heart aches for you, Lexa.

Emi

Lexa re-read the note several times, trying to understand. Then she scrabbled through the rest of her mail, opening the bound leather envelopes with panic that was spiralling out of her grasp. The date at the top of Emi's letter was two-day cycles ago. Such was the amount of time that it normally took for physical letters to travel across the Fourth Country, if they weren't being sent by specifically hired messengers. This meant that she was scrabbling through the past, trying to understand something of which it seemed everybody else was well aware. Finally, she found the coded message from her mother. Dateless to ensure it gave as little information as possible, it told her in the most simple of words that a successful attack had been mounted against the Farwan family. Tanita and those she could manage to take with her had fled with barely their lives intact. That which Lexa had assumed was impossible because of the extent of her family's wealth and cleverness had happened: the Farwan family had fallen.

NINE

She returned to her room, fear and numbness spreading through her like poison. The falling of a family was a momentous thing, but it was also so commonplace that it was a possibility with which everyone within the Fourth Country lived. Yet Lexa had never truly considered such a thing might happen to her. The Farwan name was too synonymous with power, wealth, and prestige. Yet she had indisputable proof that the unthinkable had happened.

She re-read the letters, searching for any pieces of information that she might have missed. The only truths that she uncovered were the ones telling her that she faced ruin.

Serenah knocked on the door and opened it without waiting for a response. Her face was set in a solemness that Lexa had not thought possible for someone who smiled so frequently.

"Are you all right?" she asked without any preamble. She closed the door behind her and stood with her back against it.

Lexa felt tears burn at her friend's concern. She said nothing, not trusting herself to say anything without beginning to sob. Serenah came to sit next to her, uncertainly patting her shoulder. "I don't know everything. I was with Veleth and Kirra. Veleth's mother wrote to her and mentioned what had happened and I came straight here."

Lexa breathed deeply, pushing the feeling of sickness that had lodged in her throat down so that the nausea was bearable. "I'm fine. Thank you for coming to check on me." She put her hand on top of Serenah's. If there was anyone at the Academy who knew what she was going through, it would be Serenah.

"Do you know who was behind it?" Serenah asked, her blue eyes wide with curiosity and concern.

Lexa picked up her mother's letter once more and scanned it. "There's some reference to the Kalabath family, but Emi didn't mention it. I'm not sure mother knew exactly who was behind the takeover when she sent word to me."

"Kalabath family. Aren't they on friendly terms with Kaitlen and Karra's families?" Serenah asked.

"Mawani help me. Kaitlen. She'll be thrilled to hear the news." Lexa felt sick all over again at the prospect of seeing the nasty girl's face. Perhaps Kaitlen's family had even helped the Kalabaths to take everything from the Farwan family. It wouldn't surprise her to learn that it was Kaitlen who had gone through her room. The more she considered it, the more she thought it likely.

Serenah pulled a face which indicated she agreed Kaitlen would be most gleeful at Lexa's misfortune. "Is there anything I can do?"

Lexa drew her knees up to her chest. "I don't think so, not right now at least. I think I'm still trying to understand what's happened."

"Do you feel like coming to lessons?"

Lexa shook her head.

"I'll stay with you then," Serenah said resolutely.

Lexa shook her head again. "You should go. I'll be fine, I promise. I just need some time to think."

Despite the reassurance, Serenah still hesitated.

"Honestly, go. I think I need a little time alone, anyway."

"There's nothing I can say to make this better, but I promise it gets easier," she said.

Lexa squeezed Serenah's hand. "I never thought we'd be friends, you know," she confessed.

Serenah laughed. "Neither did I," she admitted. "I'll come and check on you after lessons."

Left alone, Lexa tried to imagine what life would be like without the protection and assurance of her family's position and wealth. It was a daunting prospect. The idea of being alone, of being nobody, was overwhelming. In the small confines of her room, Lexa felt like she was being suffocated. She gathered her letters and walked to the library. The few monks that were there paid her no heed. She wondered if they knew the misfortune that had befallen her. How many of them were themselves victims of a fall from grace and power? An even more unpleasant prospect: perhaps one of their brethren had assisted the Kalabath family to take over her family's lands. She had never thought much about the morality of the monks hiring themselves out to whoever could pay their exorbitant fees, but now it seemed uncaring, to be a mercenary like that. She sat in one of the chairs in front of the fireplace. Something about the crackle of the flames as they de-voured the logs, amid the expanse of the library was soothing.

With that newfound calm, Lexa re-read the letters, trying to find anything else within their contents that might be of use. A plan of sorts had begun to take shape in her mind when Jaxen found her.

He sat in the adjacent chair, regarding her with a sombre grey gaze. "Are you all right?"

She shrugged, unsure how she was supposed to respond to the question. It was especially odd given that they had main-tained a careful distance from one another over the previous days – or rather, she had maintained a careful distance from him.

"Do you know what you'll do?" He kept his voice quiet, gentle. She appreciated his consideration but at the same time hated the way she had suddenly become fragile, to be approached with caution and care.

"I suppose I'll just curl up here and die," she said, her anger giving her sarcasm a particularly unpleasant edge.

He did not give her the satisfaction of any anger. "Sorry," he said after a moment, his contrition only eked out.

"I've become an untouchable," Lexa said, not in reply to any particular question that he had asked. She gestured toward Emi's letter on her lap.

He did not ask permission, but simply took Emi's letter and read it for himself. "She wrote to tell you that she could not be friends with you anymore? That's horrible," he said, returning the letter to her.

"Even sending me a message was a risk," Lexa murmured, leaning forward and holding her friend's note out to the fire so that the edge of the page started to burn. She did not want anybody else to know her friend had taken the risk of contacting her one final time. Once she was certain that the words were on fire, she threw the page onto the blaze, watching as it curled in upon itself and became ash.

"Honestly?" Jaxen sounded faintly disgusted.

"Yes. She knows I'd do the same thing if it were her," Lexa said.

"Would you really though?"

She did not even need to think about her response. "Yes."

He shook his head. "It is a ruthless land that we inhabit," he said. She did not disagree.

"Will you stay?" His tone now was more businesslike, less like that of one speaking to a frightened child or wounded animal.

Lexa shook her head. "I have to go and help my family."

Jaxen's expression was sceptical.

"Mother, my brothers, and some of her *elui* escaped. Perhaps my father among them," Lexa explained.

"Do you know to where?"

She shook her head. "But I know where to go to find out."

"And what happens when you find them?" There was definitely challenge in his voice now. She couldn't blame him. From his perspective, even if her family were still alive and she managed to find them, they would have very little money, be hunted by the Kalabaths, shunned by everyone.

"My mother will have a plan," she said, certain of that, if nothing else.

Jaxen raised his eyebrows. "Are you sure?"

"The Kalabath family – even if they have the help of that sneak Kaitlen's family, won't manage to co-ordinate the trade routes. Even if they had the necessary information, they wouldn't be good enough to do it." Lexa lifted her chin in pride and defiance.

At the mention of Kaitlen, the first true expression of surprise crossed Jaxen's face. "Information?" was all he asked, though.

"They won't have the names of traders who have pledged allegiance to our family," Lexa replied. Traders and merchants within the Fourth Country kept their allegiances a very closely guarded secret. That way they were secure in the knowledge that nobody would dare attack a merchant who might be in the service of a powerful foe, or worse, a friend. Some allegiances were obvious, and it was to the well-known allies of the Farwan family that Lexa had gone on her way to the Academy, but most were secreted away. Only Tanita knew the true network of traders and merchants in the service of the Farwan family, and indeed the nature of their bond to her family's businesses. It was another reason that the Farwan family had assumed itself free from any external threat. Even if someone wanted their trade routes and trade networks, they would almost certainly never get the information to secure them.

Jaxen regarded her. "So you're going to go and find your mother and enact whatever plan she has?"

She nodded.

"You're going to cross the Fourth Country alone, move

through regions where families are fighting one another for control, with very little coin, and what, your wits?" He didn't speak in a pointed manner, he continued to look at her with a measured gaze. It was the most effective way to make her feel like a foolish child.

Despite the very valid point he made, she nodded again. "What should I do instead? Ask the monks to take me in? Then I'll have to live with myself, knowing that my mother is out there somewhere and I did nothing to help her."

"Your mother has almost certainly done some bad things in her time, Lexa," Jaxen said. "You might be forgiven for allowing her to face whatever fate may have in store for her."

"I love my mother despite the things that she has done. Most do bad things, Jaxen. We love them anyway," Lexa replied.

He sighed, perhaps agreeing with her. "For someone who's quite terrible at my class, I find you inordinately compelling, Lexana."

"Lexa." She corrected him without thinking about it.

He raised his eyebrows again in question.

"You should call me Lexa," she said.

"See? You've done it again. The thing I least expect." He shook his head. Amid the turmoil that the news of her family's fate had caused, his bemusement was a lighthearted moment. She liked that he had given that to her.

"You're honestly going to go?" Worry returned to his face.

She nodded, then took a final look at her mother's message before burning it, too. "I have to. The supply cart should be here for the rest of the day, I'll ask the driver to take me down this afternoon."

He sank back into his chair with a sigh. "Is this goodbye, then?"

She looked down at her lap, refusing to meet his eyes. Only then did she realise that whatever awkwardness had arisen between them since the night she went to his room had departed.

The uncertainty and hesitance felt so trivial now when Lexa faced the loss of everything.

"I suppose it is," she said.

"It has been a singular pleasure to meet you, Lexa," Jaxen said.

She looked at him. She could not quite accept that she would never see him again. But it had seemed impossible that anyone would ever dare to mount an attack on her family, too. "I..." She found herself unable to say what she wanted. "Goodbye, Jaxen," she said instead.

He nodded once and rose, leaving her alone by the fire.

Lexa returned to her room and began sorting through her things. Jaxen had made a good point. It would be unavoidable that she would traverse parts of the land beset by fighting, or the immediate aftermath of fighting. Taking trunks would not be practical, so she had to decide what among her possessions was the most important. Her hand hovered over the box in which she kept her forget-me-not. The box had been a gift from her father when she was ten years old. She could still remember the way he had procured it seemingly from nowhere. "Girls have secrets that they need to store somewhere," he had said, a conspiratorial gleam in his eye.

For all she knew, her father might be dead. That thought nearly made her sit and give in to tears, but she steeled herself. The only way to know if her father were still alive was finding her mother. With great reluctance she put the box aside. She wrote a note for Serenah and placed it on top. If there was ever a chance for Lexa to come back to get it, her friend would keep it safe for her.

A knock on the door forced her to pause.

"Yes?" she called, expecting it to be Serenah. Instead, Leyana stepped into her room.

"It seems Jaxen was correct," the woman said, casting a dispassionate eye over Lexa's things spread across her bed. Lexa said nothing. The prospect of telling Leyana that she was leaving was somehow harder than telling Jaxen and Serenah.

"You know you could have a place here," Leyana said eventually. "I've heard about how quickly you've read those books. It's quite exceptional. If you wanted, you could learn to control the elements like the monks, if you stayed here. You could learn so much."

Lexa closed her eyes briefly. It seemed everybody was trying to make her stay here. A large part of her wanted to stay in the Enclave, wanted to learn under Leyana's tutelage, and unlock the mysteries of their world. "I wish I could," she said.

Leyana nodded before Lexa could continue. "I thought it worthwhile to try at least," she said. "If you choose to return, for whatever reason, there is a place for you here."

There was no warmth in her tone, yet Lexa felt tears spring to her eyes nevertheless. She knew Leyana well enough to understand that the offer was a touchingly genuine one. "Thank you," she whispered.

"Good luck," Leyana said. Then she was left and Lexa was left alone once more.

She stared at the closed door, wondering if she knew exactly what she had just given up. She told herself to stop being foolish. Even had nothing happened to her family, she would not have been able to come here and live the life that Leyana offered. Lexa the student of mathematics was a person who could never have existed.

Lexa shook her head. There was nothing to be gained from such thoughts. They were going to slow her, or distract her from what she needed to do. Her hands moved almost of their own accord, selecting various items and putting them into the bag.

Then she exchanged the light clothes she had worn inside the Enclave for clothes more fit for travel. Instead of slippers, she put on boots. In the place of light trousers were sturdy pants. She retained the shirt but put a jerkin over it, and then her cloak over that. She plaited her hair quickly.

She didn't feel ready, and couldn't shake the feeling that she had forgotten something, but she was running out of time if she wanted to make sure that she rode down the mountain with the supply cart today.

Lexa went to the kitchen where the mail woman normally took a meal and rested before heading back down. Classes would still be taking place – Laskana's now. Lexa was grateful for that. It meant she did not have to see anyone; not Serenah's pity, nor Kaitlen's triumph. She hoped that Kaitlen was caught for the spying that Lexa was certain she had done. She hoped that Kaitlen's family lost their wealth as quickly as they had won it.

She was relieved to find the mail woman still there, chatting with a monk. The lack of ceremony with which the monk laughed and exchanged titbits of gossip seemed completely incongruous with the solemn monks she had seen. Perhaps there was something about the students that made the monks reticent to engage in any conversation with or near them. Another mystery she would never solve.

The chatter lessened when she walked in. "Should you not be in classes?" the monk asked.

Lexa shook her head. "I need to leave." She turned to the mail woman. "I was wondering if you might take me down the mountain."

Beady eyes regarded her from within a deeply lined face. The old woman pursed her lips in contemplation, emphasising different lines surrounding her mouth. For a heart-stopping second, Lexa thought she was going to be refused and that she would have to walk down, but then the woman nodded. "You're lucky you caught me," she said in a voice that rasped and wheezed. "I'll be leaving shortly."

Lexa was almost breathless with relief. "Thank you."

The monk gathered a few things and wrapped them in a cloth. Lexa's intrusion had put an end to their conversation. She would have felt bad were she not so completely overwhelmed by relief.

"Here." The monk shoved the bundle of food into Lexa's hands. Lexa thought she saw pity in the woman's gaze. Apparently everybody knew who she was and what had happened to her family.

"Thank you," she said, clutching it tightly. The small act of kindness made her feel tiny, but she was grateful for the effort, nevertheless.

The old woman sighed and heaved herself to her feet. Everything about her spoke of a hard life. Her clothes were sturdy, practical, and looked as though they had seen a long life of use. By contrast, Lexa felt her own clothes laughably flimsy. But they were the best that she had.

"Come on, let's go." The woman neither asked Lexa's name nor offered her own. Lexa did not attempt to redress either of those unknowns, fearing that she might do something to change the woman's mind about taking her down the mountain. She probably knew who Lexa was, anyway.

As they made their way through the Enclave, Lexa half expected someone to stop her, to prohibit her from leaving, but no such thing occurred. Instead, she walked out of the doors that it seemed like a lifetime ago she had entered for the first time. The carriage was waiting, a battered affair with no windows. It looked sturdy enough. The woman jerked her head in silent direction for Lexa to enter. She opened the door. The carriage's interior stared back at her, completely empty but for small and uncomfortable-looking benches along either side, and a few wooden crates neatly tied into place.

Lexa considered asking if she could sit alongside the driver, but thought better of it when she remembered that they would have to pass through the lightning storm. She had no desire to sit outside as they passed through it. She climbed in and the driver closed the door behind her. A few cracks of light shone through the door, saving her from being in complete darkness. She was left forced to listen to the disembodied sounds from outside. Lexa heard the driver as she walked around the carriage, and the creak that accompanied the swaying of the carriage as she heaved herself up to her seat. Then, Lexa heard another noise, one that sent frissons of fear through her: running footsteps coming toward the carriage. Her breath caught in her chest. Someone was coming to stop her. She believed it would be easy to simply walk out of the Enclave. She should have known better.

TEN

The door was flung open. Light flooded into the carriage, blinding Lexa. She felt the boards sway as someone scrambled aboard. The sudden brightness after the near-total dark of the carriage blinded her. All she could see was a menacing silhouette advancing on her. She raised her arm in the most feeble of gestures to try to ward off whoever was coming to take her.

"What are you doing?" Jaxen's voice surprised her. She lowered her arm, confused.

The door closed and Jaxen sat beside her, feeling his way in the dark. His hand brushed her leg and she flinched at the unexpected touch.

The carriage lurched as it began to move. "What are you doing?" Lexa echoed Jaxen's question.

"Coming with you." He sounded disconcertingly comfortable.

"What?"

"I'm coming with you," he repeated.

For a moment she said nothing. The creak and rattle of the carriage filled the space. "Why?" she asked finally.

"Because you have no idea how to survive. You'd be captured, or robbed, or killed within a few minutes of being on your own."

"But why are you coming with me?"

In the near-darkness, his hand found hers. "Because I couldn't let you do this on your own."

"Why?"

He sighed. "I told you. For someone who would all but have failed my class, you're very compelling."

She had no answer to that, so she remained quiet, listening to the sound of the carriage making its way down the mountain and feeling the warmth of his hand in hers.

"What of your class? Your life in the Enclave?" Some time had passed. She couldn't tell if they had gone through the lightning storm or not.

They were still holding hands. He shrugged, the gesture pulling her hand along with his. "I think my time there is over. Perhaps I'll try to get to the Second Country. They don't require their men to veil. Or the Third Country. I've heard that men and women are treated completely equally there." He sounded wistful. She had never given much thought to the idea that men might want greater freedom. Their service to women had been something she'd assumed was a constant for as long as she could remember.

"How would you get there?"

"I'm sure I could persuade a merchant or trader to take me across the border." Something about the way he spoke made it sound as though he'd considered it before.

"But what would you do once you were there?" She couldn't help but ask. The idea of leaving the Fourth Country was an impossibility to her. Even though it was a place of violence and political intrigue, the place that had allowed the fall of her family, the Fourth Country was her home. Outside its borders were lands where men went unveiled, were considered the equals of women, where Mawani was not worshipped; a thousand other differences would remind her every single day that she was a stranger.

He shrugged again. Perhaps it was an accident, but the movement pushed him a little more closely up against her. "I'm sure I could find something to ensure I don't starve. Maybe I'll charm some rich woman." Despite the carefree way in which he spoke, she couldn't help but feel he was being more serious than he was trying to suggest.

She let the silence between them return, not sure what she should say to the man who had just left everything behind to help her.

The journey down the mountain took the afternoon. First, Lexa's backside felt like it was on fire from the hard seat. Then, her backside all but went numb. Finally, she arrived at the belief that if she had to stay cooped up in the dark, rattling, uncomfortable box for much longer, she would lose her mind. She shared the food that the kitchen attendant had given her with Jaxen. It made the time pass more bearably, but she was still beyond grateful to Mawani when the carriage came to a halt.

When they finally stopped and the driver opened the door, it was dark outside. They were in the small settlement at the mountain's foot. It was controlled by a minor family who had enjoyed a secure hold over their lands thanks to the preference of the Enclave's monks to not have war on their doorstep. Few wanted to alienate the monks who would almost certainly guarantee them victory if hired. Lexa resented the family on whose land she now walked for that security.

She stepped out of the carriage first, wincing as tingling rushed through her backside and down her legs. For a moment she walked about stiffly, assuming that she looked ridiculous. Jaxen followed her, looking far less uncomfortable. The old woman looked past Lexa at him with a pointed gaze. Lexa turned to see what the woman found so offputting. She was so accustomed to seeing Jaxen unveiled that she hadn't thought anything of it. But if he were caught in such an improper state, he would be punished. Unpleasantly. She unfastened her cloak and handed it to him.

Because he was nearly a head taller than her, the cloak only reached the back of his thighs. But it had a hood, which Jaxen drew up, offering some modesty.

"If you'll be wanting lodgings, the roadhouse is there." The old woman addressed Lexa, averting her gaze from Jaxen. Lexa wondered if the woman had seen Jaxen in the Enclave before, or if he had carefully avoided the kitchens on delivery days.

"Thank you for allowing us to ride down with you," Lexa said formally, pretending that Jaxen, or his state of undress, were not present.

The woman gave a grunt and turned her back on them, going around to the front of her carriage.

Lexa led Jaxen to the roadhouse. She had stayed there the evening before her arrival at the Academy. Rather than only a few day-cycles, it seemed like years had passed since she had stayed there. The woman behind the roadhouse counter glared suspiciously at Lexa and Jaxen as they entered. "I'd like a room," Lexa said, trying to sound confident, as though there were nothing unusual about two people, one of them an improperly dressed man, requesting a room to share. Men and women rarely shared where they slept, even when travelling, unless they were very poor. Women were not expected to share their quarters – let alone their beds – with those who served them.

"One?" The woman raised an eyebrow.

Lexa glanced at Jaxen, but his face was hidden by the shadow of the cloak's hood. It shouldn't matter that she couldn't see his face. No woman took any direction from a man. "Yes," she said firmly.

The woman made a show of finding a key and passing it over to Lexa. "Payment is due in the morning," she said gruffly.

Lexa clutched the small bag of her belongings close and ascended the stairs. She felt the woman's gaze on her as she climbed, Jaxen following an appropriate three steps behind. Only when she had unlocked the room and put her bag down did she realise how odd it would have looked that she carried her own bag when she had a man to do such menial things. When she had last been at this inn, she had not even considered carrying her own things. The *elui* who had driven her had done that for her.

As soon as the door was closed, Jaxen removed the cloak. Only then did she realise he wasn't carrying anything, not even a coin purse tied to his belt.

"Didn't you bring anything with you?" she asked.

He shook his head. There was no self-consciousness in the motion.

"Don't you need some of your things?"

"They were nice to have, but I don't need them. More of my life has been lived not having things than having them."

She could imagine. Pleasure houses were not known for the kind treatment of those indentured to their service. But if she been in his position, the moment she had been freed, she would have wanted to surround herself with things that were hers and never let them be taken away.

"You'll need clothes, though," she pointed out.

"Yes, I suppose I'll need to veil too, won't I?" he said thoughtfully. He didn't sound particularly bothered by the prospect. But he had spoken too longingly of the Third and Second Country to make her believe that he didn't resent the necessity of giving up the freedom he had enjoyed at the Enclave. "And we'll need to get a new cloak for you," he added. His afterthought surprised her away from the question of how he felt about being veiled like any other man.

"This is an excellent cloak," she protested, gesturing to the garment he had cast aside.

"Exactly."

She looked at it. The inside lining was soft fur, the outside was made from beautiful leather. It was an item whose luxury and expense she had taken for granted for as long as she had owned it. Jaxen was right. It would draw far too much attention. Especially given that they were almost certainly not going to travel in the style to which Lexa was accustomed.

"Ask the woman downstairs to find us some clothes," Jaxen

told her. "You did bring money, didn't you?"

She bristled at his inference that she had thought of nothing. "Mawani above, I knew I forgot something important," she said sarcastically. It felt good to let out some of the tension that had wound itself into her very bones.

He laughed, stepping close to her and putting a hand on her arm. Even with the worry and fear of what had happened to her family and the danger she risked in trying to find them, she amazed herself by blushing at his touch. "I'm sorry. I don't like to assume such things," he said. His reconciliatory tone was like a soothing balm on a stinging wound.

She tilted her head to meet his gaze. "Sorry for snapping at you," she said, bashful at her outburst.

He gave her arm a little squeeze. "It's all right."

She went downstairs to ask the innkeeper if she could assist them in acquiring clothes. The woman glared, but said, "I'll have them sent up. But make certain your man's decent." Her tone was far more insubordinate than it should have been. Lexa normally would have taken issue with it, her mother's maxim to never allow any display of weakness when dealing with strangers drilled into her from a young age. But that guideline did not take into account how much latitude she should give others when accompanied by a man not veiled in the proper manner, inviting shame for all who saw him. So Lexa pursed her lips in irritation, but pretended she had not heard the woman's rude tone, and returned to the room.

Jaxen was sitting in the solitary chair, looking quite comfortable. The sparseness of the room struck her anew. Unlike the many light spheres that illuminated every part of the Enclave, a solitary sphere was placed in this room. Regret for what she had left behind speared through Lexa, hot and serrated. She did not particularly care that she had given up luxury and comfort, although she would certainly miss them. It was Leyana's offer of knowledge that she truly regretted turning her back on. Jaxen appeared to have no such qualms about what he had left behind. He looked as peaceful in the ugly chair as he did anywhere in the Enclave.

"So where are we going?"

"We need to go to the Capital."

"Your mother is hiding there?" He looked impressed by the audacity it would take for someone to hide within the Capital.

"I doubt it. However, she has information hidden there that will tell me where I can find her. It's in one of our warehouses."

"Wait, so your mother didn't even tell you where she would go if your family fell?" Jaxen sat up straighter in surprise.

"She always taught me never to spread information that didn't have to be known by others," Lexa replied. "It is a lesson that I was not particularly good at putting into practice." She gave a wry smile and sat on the bed. "Thank you for coming with me," she said hesitantly.

"You're welcome," he said with a solemnity that was undercut by the way his eyes scrunched up in amusement. "You know, I've been unable to stop thinking about what happened between us." It was unclear if he was telling her or confessing to her.

"Is that why you followed me here?"

"No." His answer was just one word, yet there was so much meaning imbued into the single syllable that she felt herself trembling as she met his gaze.

It only occurred to her then that they were alone in the room. The lack of any social restriction left Lexa exhilarated and frightened in equal measure. With a deliberateness to her movements, she stood. For a moment, she remained still, with Jaxen's eyes on her. Then she crossed the space between them as his gaze never left her. Yet he did not move. It was clear he would do nothing until she acted first.

Her breath became shallow. Her skin began to feel hot under his gaze. She wanted so badly to feel his hands on her skin again.

She could remember vividly what it felt like, that it almost felt as though he was touching her now. The smile had vanished from his face, replaced by something more serious, more intent. Her arm was poised to pull him to her when a knock on the door interrupted.

She wasn't sure if she was relieved or upset. She opened the door, coming face to face with a pile of clothes thrust toward her. "When you've decided what you want, come down and let me know. I'll tell you how much it is, then you can pay me," the innkeeper told her. Before Lexa could take objection to the manner of the woman's address, the door was pulled shut in her face.

Lexa laid down the mixture of men's and women's clothes on the bed, irritated as much by the woman's demeanour as the interruption. Jaxen left his chair and began to sort through the garments, efficiently dividing them into piles. "You should take some, too," he told her.

"But I brought clothes with me," Lexa pointed out. His instruction rankled her.

"These are better. Less obvious," he replied without looking up. Suddenly he was abrupt, focused. It was as though the tenderness and passion that had flared between them only moments before had never been there. The sorting done, he began to pick up various clothes, holding some up for inspection, measuring a few against himself. From these, he began to create another two piles.

After she had done nothing but watch him for a while, he pushed the pile of women's clothes toward her. "Here."

Reluctantly, she unenthusiastically sorted through the dull-coloured fabrics while covertly watching his efficient movements, fascinated. This was so different to the relaxed or amused Jaxen she knew.

"If you're watching me, you'll never be done," Jaxen said, startling her. He hadn't even taken his gaze from the hooded top he was holding aloft.

Lexa blushed and turned her attention more properly to the chore, choosing two tops that would likely fit her, and one pair of trousers that was so drab in colour and appearance she could not believe she had ever seen anything more underwhelming in her entire life.

"Is there a jerkin there?" Jaxen asked, startling her. She hadn't even realised he had finished making his selection.

She pointed to the offending item. And offending was indeed the correct word. The jerkin she wore was made from beautiful material, cut so that it hugged her sides. It was comfortable, warm, flattering, and a world away from the beige monstrosity that she had cast aside after barely a second of examination.

"Take it," Jaxen ordered.

Lexa delicately picked it up. Her jerkin was cut to the waist. This was tailored – although that was a generous term – to be formfitting until the waist, then flared out to more freely fall down to mid-thigh. Perhaps with proper material and the technique of an actual seamstress, it might look quite arresting, but the item that Lexa held was an abomination. "Oh, no," Lexa said without even pausing for thought. It was even worse the second time.

"What you're wearing is—" Jaxen paused as his eyes roved over her body, an appreciative look returning to his face, "— extremely flattering. It emphasises every lovely part of you."

Lexa felt the tension between them return with a snap. The jerkin fit snugly along the curve of her waist, the top running along the side of her breasts, drawing the eye to their shape. Now more than ever, she was particularly aware of this.

"As much as I enjoy the way you look in it, it's too nice. It will draw too much attention," Jaxen said. "That other garment will make people want to avert their gaze from you as quickly as possible. Nobody would ever think you have anything worth stealing, let alone that you were someone worth capturing."

Lexa could see his point. With a sigh, she threw the jerkin

onto the small pile of clothes that she had picked for herself. Jax-en sorted through them with a dispassionate efficiency, seem-ingly satisfied with her choices. Once more, the heat that had made her flush to her very core had gone as suddenly as it had appeared.

"All right, that will do for now," he said.

In any other circumstance, Lexa would have bridled at his tone. Never in her life had she allowed a man to speak to her in such a manner, nor had a man ever told what to do in the way Jaxen had. Yet she could recognise the wisdom in everything that Jaxen had said. Indeed, only when he had mentioned the terrible things which might befall her if she set out across the Fourth Country by herself had she realised what peril she was courting in trying to find her family. He was already proving to know far more than her about how to travel without drawing attention to herself. If she wanted to find her family, perhaps she would need to cede some authority to him, despite her discomfort with the prospect.

She took the remaining clothes back down and paid the woman what she thought was an overpriced number of lighter, valuable coins known as feathers, for those they had kept, espe-cially given their subpar quality. But she fought her instinct to haggle over the price, and simply handed over the money. She had no wish to draw any further attention to herself, certainly not mark herself out as someone who was accustomed to trading goods.

As Lexa left, the innkeeper looked at her in disapproving confusion, all but wondering aloud why Lexa was performing such mundane tasks herself when she had a man who could and should have been doing them. Lexa resisted the urge to snap, not wanting to make herself any more memorable to the woman than she and Jaxen already were. But when she returned to the room she shared with Jaxen with a heavier coin purse, weighed down by larger coins of far lesser value, she hesitantly brought up the subject of his unusual independence, and how that might draw unwanted attention to them such as would be elicited by a man with such freedom and authority.

"Jaxen, I think if we want to be inconspicuous, from now on, you'll need to do many of the menial tasks."

Jaxen, sitting in the chair, looked at her for a moment. The blankness of his expression made it impossible to know what his true thoughts were. Finally, he nodded. "Now that I have a veil, I should be doing most of the work. You're quite correct."

It had been a while since she had truly felt awkward around him, but now she did. "I'm sorry," she stammered. In the back of her mind, she was aware that it was ridiculous to apologise. It was the place of men to serve women. Jaxen was an anomaly, and now that he was away from the Enclave, that exception no longer applied to him. Yet here he was, helping her, even though he did not have to. For that, she felt awkward that he would appear to be in her service.

"In fact, I think it would be easier if you say that I'm your *elui*," Jaxen said.

"First *elui*," Lexa added, grateful that he had agreed so readily. "It would be easier then to explain why you share my room."

Something flared in his gaze, but it was gone too quickly for her to understand what it was. "You want to share a bed with me, then?" He smirked, but there was something unpleasantly sardonic about the smile. Normally such a comment would leave her flushing and unable to suppress thoughts of his hands on her body.

"I think it would be better if we're not separated," Lexa said uncomfortably.

"Do you know the name of Mawani's husband?" Jaxen asked. He sounded almost meditative.

Lexa shook her head. In no text or teaching that she had ever encountered was Mawani's husband given a name. She had always merely presumed that it was a fact which had been lost to time and collective forgetting.

Jaxen leaned back in his chair, regarding her from lowered lids. "I thought it was forgotten, but I came across an older book of stories in the Enclave. It was nearly four hundred years old. His name is referenced there."

"Really?" Even though Lexa knew Jaxen was leading to some point she might not like, she was intrigued. "Why would that be not mentioned in more recent writing?"

One side of his mouth was tugged upward in a sort of smile. "Perhaps it suited the purpose of whoever was writing later versions of the story to exclude it."

"Why? What was his name?" Lexa asked.

Jaxen's smile broadened. "Elui."

ELEVEN

Their decision to share a single room required them to share the bed. The faint mockery in Jaxen's expression had remained as he prepared to sleep. He had stripped to the waist, his eyes barely leaving hers, and a blush had worked its way along Lexa's cheeks as she remembered him telling her that he normally slept naked. There was a cursory invitation in his eyes as he lay on the bed, but Lexa averted her gaze and placed herself practically on the edge of the mattress.

Sleep claimed her and brought with it nightmares of faceless figures in the Farwan house in the Capital. They pursued her brothers, her mother's *elui*, and laughed as her family fell under their swords.

She woke to predawn light, sweat coating the back of her neck. For a moment, she stared at the rough timber beams of the ceiling, trying to understand how she was somewhere so quiet after the tumult of her dreams. She became aware of the fact that she was alone not only in the bed, but the room, too. A few minutes passed, then she got out of the bed and dressed. Wondering where Jaxen was, she paced the small room before settling on the task of ensuring all of their newly purchased clothes were in her bag.

Jaxen returned as she was halfway through. The door opened so quietly that had she been asleep, she would not have heard it. Two plates of food were balanced on one arm. When he saw she was awake, a look of mild surprise flitted across his face before his calm expression asserted itself. "You're awake."

She nodded. "Where did you go?"

He hefted the plates in reply. He held one out to her in offer.

Lexa's memory of the food at the inn was that it was very acceptable fare. She took the plate, realising with some chagrin that this might be the last decent meal she would have in a while. If they wanted to remain unnoticed, the comfortable accommodation to which she was accustomed would likely not be what they sought.

The bread was warm and the curried fruit heaped atop it danced upon the tongue in a pleasing fashion. She chewed slowly, savouring the comfort it offered.

"You did not sleep well." His eyes were green-grey as they looked her over in some kind of appraisal.

"No."

"Nightmares?"

She took another mouthful of her breakfast before she answered. "Yes."

When she looked up, she saw compassion in his eyes. His voice was firm, but there was a gentle edge to it. "During the day we may direct our minds away from thoughts we would rather not consider, but such things will be heard, and if they are denied in wakefulness, they will slip into our dreams."

"Are you saying I should try to think about what happened to my family?" Her voice had more of a bite than she intended.

He did not seem at all upset by her tone. "No. All I meant to say is that nightmares are what we would rather not see happen to the best of us – and the worst of us."

Her appetite abruptly fled. Knowing it was foolish, but unable to stomach eating any more, she put the plate down. "I don't want to think or dream about what might have happened to my family. I just want to find my mother." She worked hard to keep herself from snapping at him.

He shrugged. "Are you not eating any more?"

"No, I'm full." Now she did snap.

With another shrug, he took her plate and quickly ate the remainder of her food while she finished packing in contrite silence. She regretted her anger. It hadn't been directed at him, not really.

"Jaxen?"

"Mm?" He sounded wary. She couldn't blame him.

"I'm sorry. I should not have spoken to you like that. You were only trying to make me feel better."

He crossed the small room to stand next to her. She looked up into his eyes. The sun had not yet fully risen, and the shadows of the room echoed the grey of his eyes. "You've had a shock. You must be feeling a great many things."

"You don't have to help me." The words tumbled out before she could order them.

"I know." That gentle amusement she knew so well entered his voice.

"No, I mean that I would understand if you wanted to go back to the Enclave, or to head your own way from here." She bit her lip and looked down.

"Lexana." A gentle hand under her chin lifted her gaze back to his face. "If you wish to find your mother, you will need my help."

"I'm sure I could manage by myself," she protested.

His laugh was kind, but it stung nevertheless.

"I could," she insisted.

"All right, now how would you get to the Capital?" he asked.

"I'd go with the mail carriage," she replied smugly.

"We should certainly take the mail carriage as far as the next town, but then we must find a cart of our own. People are bound to be looking for you and we don't want to be easily tracked." Now his voice was brusque.

"Won't that take longer? The mail carriages are the fastest way across the Fourth Country if you don't have your own, good-quality cart," she pointed out.

"Not necessarily. Mail carriages have to stop at every town they pass to collect and drop off their supplies."

"Yes, but they're direct."

He gave her ego no respite. "And they're also the obvious way to travel. You might get to the Capital quickly, but you might also never get there. If I were looking for you, the first place I'd look is a mail carriage."

"So why travel with the mail at all?"

"Because this is a small village. Where and how we leave will be marked by almost everybody. Better to start with the obvious manner of transport and then find another way at a bigger town."

"What if people are waiting for me in the next town?" She folded her arms across her chest.

"We deal with that problem if it arises." He ended the debate by pulling a veil across his face, picking up her bag, and striding to the door.

They were fortunate -- the mail carriage was leaving that day. Jaxen's warning about her being hunted hung in her mind as she paid the innkeeper, found the mail carriage, and bought berths on it for passage to the adjacent town. Two other travellers boarded the carriage. Locals, by the look of them, although she could not help but wonder if they were disguised assailants seeking her. Then again, the grandmotherly-looking woman likely could not move fast enough to apprehend her, if it did turn out she'd been hired to find Lexa.

Bags of letters and parcels were heaved into the mail wagon, squashed between the passengers' knees. The large carriage in which they were travelling was similar in design to the cart in which they had descended the mountain the previous day. However, crude windows had been cut in the side to allow passengers some light, rather than the force them to sit in darkness as she and Jaxen had been forced to do the previous day. Unlike the carriages in which Lexa was accustomed to riding, there was no glass filling the gaps in the rough wooden sides. Curtains made from thick material hung on either side and would be firmly fastened across the gaps in the instance of rain. To add to the barren furnishings, the seats were unforgiving on the backside with no cushioning of any kind to offer any succour. Lexa took her cloak and folded it underneath her to try and prevent the painful experience of the previous day. She would certainly miss the garment when they sold it – Jaxen had told her they would divest themselves of it at a larger town, where the transaction of such a finely crafted item would draw less attention. Jaxen sat next to her, pressed against her in deference to the cramped space in the carriage.

A man clutching a small child clambered into the carriage, panting slightly. He sat himself down and adjusted his grasp on the child. It let out a squall, and Lexa prepared herself for an extraordinarily long ride, but the child's father rocked it and it settled in his arms without so much as a further peep.

With a rattle that promised a day of discomfort, the carriage set off. The grandmother took out some crocheting and began to deftly loop the thread into an intricate pattern. Lexa wished she had something with her to pass the time, but she had been forced to leave almost all of her possessions in the Enclave. The other passenger, a middle-aged woman whose stomach gently strained against her belt, almost immediately began to doze, the sound of her snores a counterpoint to the rattle of the carriage wheels.

So much time with nothing to do meant that her thoughts wandered to the dreams that had stalked her the previous evening. She shuddered, not wanting to think about the awful figures which had so cruelly laughed as they murdered her family. She breathed deeply as the fear that had lain beside her when she woke up crept through her once more. Jaxen's words about nightmares drifted back to her. "Jaxen." She kept her voice soft, not wanting the other passengers to hear.

"Yes?"

"Do you have nightmares?"

His silence lasted for so long that she worried she'd asked something she shouldn't have and had upset him. But then he spoke. "Yes."

"Often?"

"Not as often anymore."

"What is in your nightmares?"

"Memories," he said simply.

"What do you do when they come?"

"I read, I exercise, I find someone to share my bed so that they can chase away the nightmares. Whatever needs to be done, really." His tone was still pleasant, but it was clear he was no longer willing to speak on this.

Silence lapped at the space between them. Lexa worried she had pried too far, but then Jaxen spoke again.

"How are you feeling?"

She considered his question. A part of her wished he hadn't asked, as it required her to examine the fear and anxiousness that had been sitting inside her since she had received Emi's letter. "You know, I never thought about what happens when a family is overthrown."

"Really?" The way he raised his eyebrows led her to believe her confession had amused him.

"I realise it's silly. But I've lived my entire life with this sort of thing. It's never seemed … wrong."

He snorted. "Of course it didn't. It never affected you."

"That's not fair," she retorted, hurt by the accusation. "We've lost friends to takeovers."

"You're very fortunate if the only thing you've lost is people close to you."

"What do you mean?"

He shook his head, his expression hidden by his veil. "I've seen people who have lost their very selves. Friends, possessions," he shrugged, "losing them is nothing compared to being stripped of your will to live, or will to fight."

She did not press him, certain he would not answer her properly. She wondered what he had endured during his years in the pleasure house. If he was talking about himself, then he had certainly made an excellent recovery. Yet for all his veiled comments, he had given her something to consider. Certainly, she had never considered the ruthlessness that pervaded life in the Fourth Country. The rise and fall of families had been the backdrop against which her life had been staged. The suddenness of her family's fall was shocking, and she still struggled to comprehend that it really had transpired. But her mother's letter gave her certainty that Tanita still lived, as did her brothers, and perhaps her father, too. She was fortunate. Many families were killed by those who came for their position. She had Jaxen helping her – many of the survivors were alone in the world. She had the determination to find her mother – the more she considered Jaxen's words, the more she understood that many would crumble in the face of their loss.

Despite her certainty that the carriage's discomfort would keep her awake, she dozed against Jaxen's shoulder. The noises of the carriage filtered through her dreams, and when he shook her awake to tell her they had arrived, she was relieved to have escaped the previous evening's nightmares.

They walked alongside one another rather than Jaxen remaining the customary few steps behind her. He carried the bag containing their combined possessions. Uncertainly, for she had never followed the guidance of a man before, Lexa followed Jaxen's murmured directions to an inn.

Darkness was falling, leaving them no time to arrange any transport for the following day, or to sell Lexa's cloak, so they went to the adjoining tavern for dinner. Lexa's hunger surprised her, even though she had left her breakfast unfinished and barely nibbled at the food Jaxen had procured for their lunch. Since she had received the news of what had befallen her family, her appetite had fled. Yet now, with a primal insistence, her body demanded to be fed.

As they worked through a platter of cheeses and vegetables, Lexa leaned back into the wooden seat and listened to the noise of the tavern around her.

People were beginning to stream in, their working day complete. Good-natured gossip and chatter filled the space.

Lexa had only been in this kind of establishment a handful of times, usually on matters of business, either with her mother or as her mother's emissary. Yet even when she had stopped in this kind of inn, she had never really sat among people as they came in to catch up on the trivialities on their daily lives. It was a curious experience. Then three women came in and their conversation chilled her.

"I 'eard the Farwans' land 'as been totally taken," a woman said to her companions

"Yes, the Kalabaths declared victory."

"No warning," the third woman added. Her accent turned the 'w's to 'v's. It suggested she came from somewhere near the Farwan territory itself. She, like her companions, didn't sound particularly bothered by the brutality of what they discussed.

"Of course there was warning," the first woman said scornfully. "The Kalabaths've been 'iring mercenaries for a long time now."

"Still, to move on the Farwans."

"They 'ad it comin'." Scorn dripped in every syllable of the woman's voice. "Anyone of 'em 'as it coming. They's dripping in blood."

Jaxen's hand on her arm kept Lexa from yelling at the woman who spoke with such callous delight about the violence that had been unleashed upon her family.

The cloth of his veil brushed her ear as he spoke to her in an urgent undertone. "Everybody gossips. Whenever a family falls, it is the subject of intense speculation, and often delight. The only thing you will achieve by yelling at this woman is that you will draw attention to yourself."

Lexa pulled away and glared at him, wishing she could yell at him. "The entire world seems to know," she hissed, not caring if she attracted attention.

His eyes seemed to glitter in the dancing illumination of the room's three light spheres. "People gossip. They delight in the misfortune of others. Especially when those others are rich and powerful. It is the way of the world. If all they are doing is talking, then you are lucky."

Her jaw was clenched so hard that it felt as though she was going to grind her teeth into nothingness.

"All we need to do is wait for the Kalabaths to be taken over by someone else." The comment floated over, spoken by the woman whose accent.

"See?" Jaxen's voice was soft. "This isn't personal, Lexa. Everybody waits for those who have power to be toppled."

Tears gathered in her eyes, blurring her vision. Her throat hurt from the effort of keeping those tears at bay. "They knew before me," she said, her voice so low it was almost lost to the din of the tavern. "They're catching up on the latest gossip."

Perhaps compassion overtook his expression – she could see only his eyes through the gap in the veil – but certainly, the hand he placed on her arm was gentle. "And you never gossiped like this?"

The fact that he was correct made her feel even worse, and she looked down so that Jaxen wouldn't see her crying.

She had to hurriedly hide her tears as the server – likely an *elui* of the owner – delivered two bowls of soup. She averted her face as he placed them down and left, hating herself for showing such weakness so publicly. Her mother would never have cried like this. Indeed, she didn't think it was in Tanita Farwan's nature to cry at all.

The soup was hot and good, although she barely tasted it, her appetite receding as grief and rage replaced it. However, Jaxen's insistence that she eat had her thoughtlessly spooning up mouthfuls of the food as she tried to not listen to the three women who were now gossiping about an absent fourth friend.

Jaxen's curse drew her attention to the spill of soup on his veil.

"Mawani-cursed thing, it's impossible to eat in one of these," he growled.

"We'll wash it," she reassured him.

Even with the veil, she saw the anger slip into the delicate lines around his eyes. He did not reply, merely mopping up the excess liquid as best he could.

She made no further attempt to placate him, too preoccupied with her own sentiments to be able to offer him any true comfort.

Only when they returned to their room and Jaxen had removed his veil did his normal serenity return. She sat on the bed and listlessly tugged off her boots. He came to sit beside her and waited until she turned to acknowledge him before speaking.

"I'm sorry about those women in the tavern. You're likely to hear more of that kind of talk. You need to ignore it as best you can, though."

The truth of his words had struck her in the tavern, but she had ignored it, too overcome with emotion. "I didn't expect any of this," she confessed.

"We rarely expect what happens to us. I never anticipated that someone from the Enclave would buy out my service, yet it came to pass."

"We'll never be able to get to the Capital, let alone find my mother." The worry that had lain with her all day now found voice in the face of Jaxen's kindness.

"Certainly we will face many risks in getting to the Capital," he agreed. "In the tavern, those women were also talking of a takeover in the Gemesh lands." He named territory held by a minor family.

"But the closest crossing of the river Sorrow is at their heart. Any other bridge will triple the time it takes us to get to the Capital," Lexa said, fighting alarm.

"Yes, I agree. We'll just have to go through them." His face was thoughtful.

"But mercenaries often remain in the lands which are taken over, and they offer no quarter to anyone," she pointed out. "If they find out who I am, they'd..." She trailed off as she considered the extent of the danger they were going to encounter. None of these things had occurred to her when she decided to leave the Enclave and set out across the Fourth Country.

We'll have to be careful to avoid drawing any attention to ourselves. I think we'll have to walk for at least a little while."

"Will that keep us safe?" She asked, her voice small.

"I can't promise that we won't be apprehended, or worse," he told her.

The world had never seemed so unfriendly. Tears once more invaded her eyes. She did not want the truth, she wanted reassurance. "You said that lying is about telling people what they want to believe. Lie to me," she begged.

He put his arms around her in an embrace that was devoid of the heat and passion that so often sat between them. It was an embrace of comfort, and she leaned into his chest as he promised her something he could not know to be true. "Everything will be all right."

AFTER THE FALL

TWELVE

Lexa's breath came in fits and starts. She was acutely aware of every part of her body, as well as the feel of Jaxen pressed up hard against her in the darkness. The darkness of the room heightened her other senses. His breath sounded in her ear, rough and harsh. Her forehead rested against his chest. His arms were wrapped around her, his heady scent inescapable. In different circumstances, she might have mistaken his arms folded about her for tenderness.

Around them, the souls who had been irreparably broken by the horrors of the bitter battle for the town lay haphazardly across the space. The acrid scent of forget-me-not hovered over the room, rising from the mugs and bowls discarded on the floor. Everyone there except for Jaxen and Lexa was completely lost in the drug's embrace. Screams from outside permeated the forgetting den's walls. There were far fewer than when the wailing had first started. Lexa buried her head further into Jaxen's chest, desperately hoping that the raiders butchering the remaining citizens of the town which was otherwise so anonymous it was only remembered for being on the bridge that crossed the river Sorrow, would pass them by. His grip tightened around her at the sound of footsteps in the room. Heavy. Menacing. She squeezed her eyes shut, not wanting the intruder to see the absence of forget-me-not's tell-tale violet hue in her eyes. The footsteps came closer. It sounded like two or three people, but Lexa kept her head buried in Jaxen's chest and dared not peek out to see she was correct. Each step was like a blow driving fear through her. A part of her wished that she were as distant from the world as everybody around her. Then she wouldn't need to battle this sick feeling.

"Just a bunch of forgetters." A voice that sounded disconcertingly normal came from only a few paces from Jaxen and Lexa.

"Mm." The noise was punctuated by another footstep, this time coming toward Lexa and Jaxen. "Look at those two, dreaming together." It was a man speaking. That almost caused Lexa to look up in surprise. She pressed her head even harder into Jaxen. Surely she would leave a bruise.

Footsteps came even closer. Lexa was sure that she and Jaxen were being inspected. Not knowing was agony. Any moment she expected to feel the sharp pinch of a blade being driven into her. She wondered if it would hurt immediately, or if there would be a few seconds between when the blade entered and when pain began.

"Pathetic," came a third voice. Boredom was interlaced with disdain.

"Do we have the owner of this ... fine establishment?" a woman close to Lexa and Jaxen asked.

Sarcastic chuckles came from her companions.

"She's no longer with us," the man said.

"Burn it." The woman gave the order with a casual indifference that Lexa found the most shocking part of the entire exchange.

The footsteps receded.

Lexa chanced moving her head so that she could look up at Jaxen's face. "What do we do?" she whispered.

He did not let go of her, keeping her tightly pressed against him. She was grateful for it. The contact was immeasurably comforting.

"Wait," he breathed.

She strained to hear what was going on outside. Jaxen must have heard something she hadn't, because suddenly he stiffened, released her and urged her to her feet. She stood, picking up the bag that had been underneath them and clutching it close.

"Come on," he whispered. He grabbed her hand and pulled her through the room. She could hear an ominous rustling noise coming from one of the forgetting den's other rooms. Jaxen pulled her the opposite way to that sound, his hard like a vice around hers. They made their way into the kitchen. Jaxen released her hand so he could listen at the door to outside, then cracked it open cautiously. He peered through the small gap, then threw it wide open, beckoning for Lexa to follow him as he left the building. She did as he bade without question. He had repeatedly proved that he was the more competent of the two of them over the two day-cycles for which they had been travelling. The little lane that ran behind the forgetting den was deserted. It was disgusting, filled with a multitude of refuse, but Lexa only let that bother her for a second before she followed Jaxen along it, trying to place her boots on the clearest parts of the ground.

She glanced behind her and saw smoke trickling from the forgetting den. "Jaxen, they've set fire to the building."

He didn't even look back. "Keep going," he instructed.

"But there are people still inside," she protested, panting from the effort of speaking as they ran. Running was not something Lexa had done often through the course of her life.

"Keep going," he repeated.

"But Jaxen," she gasped.

"No!" He did not even pause, but his voice rang along the laneway with enough force to compel her to drop the issue.

They reached the end of the lane. She almost collided with Jaxen, who had stopped to peer around the corner. She risked another glance back. Smoke was beginning to pour more profusely into the sky. Jaxen, still surveying the scene, reached his hand behind him to find hers, giving it an absent-minded squeeze of reassurance. The bridge they needed to cross was only a short distance away from them now. It looked deserted, but then again, the town had looked devoid of any threat when they had entered it, too.

Jaxen remained where he was for some time, observing the area. The crackle of flames echoed down the lane as the forgetting den burned.

"Okay, let's go," he said suddenly, stepping out from the cover of the lane, still holding her hand.

As she followed, she looked around, expecting assailants to emerge. Evidently she was not walking quickly enough, for Jaxen pulled her into a trot as they stepped onto the road leading to the bridge.

"What if they came from across the river?" Lexa asked.

Jaxen shook his head. "That's Lix territory. Those raiders were fighters from the Yendel forces. I'd bet they felt they might be able to get a little more for themselves."

Lexa should have remembered that the land across the river Sorrow – an apt name for the river – belonged to the Lix family and was peaceful. But the information had been chased from her mind by the horror of the morning. Their shoes tapped on the timbers as they broke into a run as they reached the bridge. She glanced behind her into the ruins of the town. The view as she retreated was even worse than entering it had been, now that she knew what horrors lurked within it. Buildings lay in ruins. A few corpses were sprawled across the street, some looking days old. A broken signpost hung in the still. And now smoke billowed above the forgetting den. The people inside were almost certainly dead. Perhaps that was a mercy for them. They were the survivors of the initial invasion by the Yendel family. Most people who survived such attacks sought escape from the loss of their loved ones, their homes, or simply the misery and desolation which surrounded them. Forget-me-not provided it to them. Yet the brewed forget-me-not would only offer a painful, drawn-out demise. Flames may be a quicker mercy than drug-addled loneliness.

Their pace increased into an outright sprint as they neared the halfway point of the bridge. She fought the urge to look back again to check whether someone had seen them. That would only slow her down if they had in fact been spotted. She clutched her bag and focused on putting one leg in front of the other, and the feel of Jaxen's hand in hers. The far bank was in sight. Lexa's chest burned as she fought to breathe in enough air. She wanted more than anything to stop and heave in huge breaths, but Jaxen pulled her on. Finally they made it across onto the neatly packed road, lined by trees that had not been hacked at or used to hang people. Anyone who was caught engaging in such behaviour in undisputed territory that was guaranteed a quick and painful retribution. Besides, there was almost always some other dispute to which they could lend their sword in exchange for the promise of coin and violence.

Jaxen let go of her hand and they both stood, gasping for breath. Lexa looked back across the wide river to the town on the opposite bank. It appeared so still, so devoid of life or hope. The cloud of smoke from the forgetting den was even bigger now and had turned from white to grey-black.

"That..." Lexa stopped, struggling to find the words for what she had seen. "They killed those people in the forgetting den."

"Yes."

She could feel Jaxen regarding her as she looked back at the ruined town.

"They were all defenceless. And they just burned them."

"Yes."

"That's inhuman," she declared, her gorge rising.

"What you saw there wasn't nearly as bad as the areas near the borders. Those areas are lawless at the best of times. But when one of the families tries to take from the other, it's everybody for themselves," Jaxen said. The dispassionate way in which he said it horrified her, perhaps as much as the fact that such awfulness existed in the world.

"Is that ... is what happened over there ... is that what will have happened to the people in the Farwan lands?" she asked. The thought sent horror rippling through her bones. Her initial grief had long since receded, pushed aside by the day-cycles of rough travel. It was as far as she could imagine from the life she had previously led.

"Maybe. What happened back there was unusually brutal. But it's what happens when the people play games of power with one another. The lives of everybody else are ruined. Become that." Jaxen gestured wearily back toward the town they had just escaped. He began to walk along the road.

After a moment, Lexa followed him. "But why destroy the buildings?"

"To make the people surrender their allegiance," Jaxen replied, not bothering to look at her. "We should be able to make Fabriel by night," he added.

With that, he pulled up the hood of his shirt and secured the flap across his face, hiding his features. It had come loose when they had scrambled into the forgetting den. It was the most simple of veils, but they had long since discarded any clothes or trappings which might make them seem to be of any wealth. Like that, only his eyes were visible, the grey almost lost amid the shadow.

Lexa fought back a shudder at the brutality that it must take to burn down half a town. "So why burn the forgetting den?"

All she could see of his reaction was the rise and fall of his shoulders in a shrug. "The raiders who fight for coin are a people unto themselves. The men who join don't veil, and the women who lead the packs are ruthless. I've never tried to understand them. Only avoid them where possible and do what they want when I can't." His voice was now muffled by the cloth and Lexa had to pay attention to hear what he was saying.

"Have you encountered them often?"

"They have a lot of coin. Sometimes they would come into the pleasure house." He elaborated no further. Lexa did not wish to push into that part of his past. He had spoken fleetingly of his time in the pleasure house, but when Lexa sought more information, he gently deflected the conversation away. She had learned that it was best to let him share what he wanted.

Lexa's stomach began to growl after they had walked for an hour. She made a comment about it and Jaxen called a halt. They walked a little way off the road and sat down on the grass. Even though it was near the middle of the day, the first bite of winter kept the moisture there. Lexa pulled out the sorry excuse for lunch – a few fruits and vegetables, a hunk of bread that probably should have been thrown away the day before, and a hard nub of cheese, while Jaxen unfastened his veil. It was the last of their food, but hopefully they would be able to buy more when they reached Fabriel, the town only a day-cycle's journey from the Capital. Lexa divided the food between them in silence. As she passed it to Jaxen, their hands touched. A thrill ran along her skin at the contact and she glanced into his face. His eyes were intense, locked with hers, and she fought with the contradictory emotions that had settled within her over the time they had been travelling. She wondered if he felt it, too, that dormant passion between them.

His hand lingered on hers, and she remembered the way he had held her close to him as they hid in the forgetting den. Because it was a place nobody would go unless they were already broken, it had been a perfect hiding place from the raiders they'd suddenly heard as they walked through the town had they assumed to be deserted of anyone who still clung to hope and life. She wanted to be held like that by him again. But the way he had ruthlessly left those people behind without an apparent second thought would not leave her mind. That ruthlessness had kept them alive as they went through towns filled with people that would have captured or killed her without a second thought had they known she was Lexa Farwan.

Those two sides of Jaxen – the one who would place their survival and reaching their destination above everything else, and the one who spoke with seductive warmth and intimacy – were at war in her perception of him.

"Are you all right?" It was the second Jaxen who spoke now, his hand on hers, his thumb moving in the tiniest motion of comfort and reassurance.

She dropped her gaze but left her hand in his. "I still can't believe how violent everything that happened to the Gemesh lands was. We'd heard stories of what takeovers are like, but I never expected it to be like that," she confessed, saying nothing of her struggle with the fact that he had so easily left so many to be burned. She knew he would tell her it was had to be done so they could survive. Today was the most imminent danger they had faced, though, having to cross through the former Gemesh lands to cross the Sorrow. It was a calculated risk. The towns should have been free from any lingering raiders seeking to take a little more for themselves from the land they had taken for someone else. Without Jaxen's callousness, she likely would not have made it out of the town.

"No story can properly convey the way a dead person looks, or smells, or feels. Nor can it properly explain what it feels like to watch someone's home burn down with every piece of furniture, every memory, inside it." He let go of her hand and took a bite of the food. "Were you afraid back there?" he asked when she said nothing in reply.

"I prayed for Mawani to watch over us," she confessed.

He let out an amused breath that stopped just shy of being a snort. "Do you really believe that the goddess looks over the lives of individual people? I thought you didn't find comfort in prayer."

She shifted uncomfortably at the suggestion of his ridicule. "I don't really, but it seemed the right thing to do."

"Do you believe the stories then, that Mawani does actually look over women?"

"And men," she added.

He shook his head, the motion definite. "Not if you believe the stories. They claim Mawani charges women with that task because she failed."

Lexa narrowed her eyes in thought. "I've never heard a story told like that."

"That's because the common stories are twisted to suit the purpose of the storytellers. There's an earlier version of *Fabiane's Wishes* in the Enclave's library called *Fabiane's Shame*," he said. "Think about the fact that almost nobody remembers where the name *elui* came from."

Before Lexa could reply, he dusted crumbs from his hands and asked, "Are you finished? We should be off."

She put the last of the meagre lunch in her mouth. He refastened his face covering and led the way back to the road.

Jaxen was the most interesting, unusual man she had ever encountered. He taught at the Academy, walked around uncovered, and had experienced things she that if she was lucky, she would never undergo. Without his assistance there was no way she could have survived her journey to find her family. That realisation was humbling. Her gratitude for his protection and help further complicated her feelings for him. As she watched him walking ahead of her, her mind shot back to the night in the Enclave she had spent arched in passion underneath his fingertips, and the various moments in the past day-cycles when they had almost returned to that night. Yet each time she had been on the verge of giving in to her desire for him she had found an excuse to dispel the moment. But she knew she wanted him. Desperately.

As Jaxen had predicted, they reached Fabriel just as night was falling. It was a larger town than the ruined one at the bridge, built on top of an underground spring that had given it a reputation as a destination for relaxation. It felt almost surreal to see the bustle and life here, given the devastation of the ruined town, not even a full day's walk away.

Jaxen found the inn he wanted, holding the door open for Lexa so that she could go in and order a room for them. They had sold her cloak on the third day of their travel. It had fetched a handful of the more valuable smaller coins, feathers, rather than the larger and heavier, less valuable stones or pebbles. She had never realised what wealth she had thoughtlessly draped around her shoulders. The feathers she had received for her coat had kept her coin purse light. That too had been some cause for concern. A smaller coin purse suggested wealth. A heavier coinpurse spoke of unwanted, cumbersome large coins and as such, less wealth. Jaxen had taught Lexa how to create the illusion of a purse filled with the larger coins of smaller denomination, and managed with near militancy what coins they spent and when. It was a small detail, but it added to the facade that made them completely unremarkable. It was interesting to think in terms of finding the least efficient way to spend coin rather than the most. Not that the calculations were difficult for Lexa, but they were not the ones her mind had been trained to make.

The woman behind the counter passed an eye over Jaxen and Lexa and seemed to find nothing particularly objectionable about them. Lexa had become practised in giving Jaxen commands whenever someone was nearby. She had never given a second thought to commanding a man before. Yet Jaxen was his own man, and it felt somehow wrong to perpetuate even the semblance that he was in some way yoked to her, especially given how much she had relied on him to survive.

Once in the room, Jaxen immediately took off his veil. Lexa sat on the floor, and began to tremble. He was immediately beside her, saying nothing, but putting his arm around her shoulders. She leaned into him and inhaled his scent. His arms around her, her nose buried in his chest, made her think of that morning in the den, and her shakes became even more pronounced.

Jaxen pulled her closer and she cried softly into his chest. Only now that they were definitely safe could she properly express the terror she had felt.

"You've done so well." Jaxen soothed her, running a hand through her hair.

"I'm sorry," she sobbed. "Thank you for everything." That was all she managed to say before her tears began to flow even harder, making further speech impossible.

He held her until the emotion had passed and she was exhausted. Then he scooped her up and put her on the bed, tugged off her boots and covered her with a blanket. The day and the day-cycles behind it were crashing down on her, and it was all she could do to stay awake. "You should eat," she whispered.

"I'm all right." Jaxen lay down next to her, his body curling against her. His warmth was so comforting that she couldn't help but fall asleep, feeling safe and protected.

THIRTEEN

Lexa awoke feeling ravenous. Jaxen was still beside her, although he had rolled onto his back during the night. Daylight crept around the edges of the shutters. Lexa sat up and looked down on his face. Relaxed in sleep, he appeared much younger, closer to her age than she would have thought. A smile curved his lips and she knew that he had woken.

"Are you hungry?"

He nodded without opening his eyes.

"I'll get them to bring us something," she said. The exhaustion and despair that had clung to her the previous evening felt swept away. The sense of lightness was unlikely to last for very long, but she was nevertheless glad for the reprieve that the night of sleep had given.

She slipped on her boots and went downstairs. The woman looked at her strangely – fetching breakfast was a task for *elui* to perform – but Lexa ignored her and returned with two bowls of porridge.

Jaxen opened the door when she knocked awkwardly with a foot. He was fully returned to wakefulness. The truth of his age that she had seen in his sleep had been erased, replaced by the air of quiet confidence and serene amusement which loaned him an extra few years. She handed him a bowl and he took it with a word of thanks.

"I think we should try to get a cart," he said once he had taken a bite.

Lexa personally disliked porridge but ate it anyway, too hungry to truly care what she was eating. "Is it safe?" she asked with her mouth still full. They had alternated between buying and selling carts and walking. Especially when traversing the doomed Gemesh lands, caution needed to be balanced against speed. The last few days they had spent walking to avoid drawing attention to themselves in a land where most people had lost everything. Lexa was sick of it. Even after a full night of rest, her feet ached. Nevertheless, she worried that Jaxen had proposed they take a cart out of concern that she was struggling to cope on foot. She did not want him to make concessions for her, or to think of her as weak.

"We are on Lix land now, and they are a powerful family. Order is well maintained within their borders. We'd look more out of place on foot than on a cart."

"The Farwan family was powerful, yet we fell," Lexa pointed out.

He stared at her for a moment. "You're right. Even so."

She watched him covertly as they ate. She remembered the feel of him curled against her as she had fallen asleep, the warmth of his body on hers. The intimacy of the way their bodies had fitted together left her with a sense of longing to be pressed against him like that once more. Whatever hardness he may have displayed in the service of keeping them alive, he had never been cruel or unkind to her. She shook her head. All this time spent with him had meant she was losing focus on finding her family. The worry that had initially hung over her, invading her every thought, had receded until it was a faint constant in the background. The nightmares she had experienced on the first night had come intermittently. On more than one occasion, she had awoken with tears on her cheeks. But in the past few days, her sense of urgency had receded and been replaced with a monotonous sense of purpose.

Distracted, she spilled a spoonful of porridge onto her shirt.

She cursed as the surprisingly hot food not only landed on her shirt but somehow managed to get on her skin as well. Jaxen laughed kindly.

"Well, it doesn't make much difference. I reek," Lexa said once she had recovered from her initial embarrassment.

"Did you want a wash, my lady?" he asked mockingly, the charming, playful Jaxen she had first met suddenly appearing.

"I really don't think that's an option," she said regretfully.

"Nonsense. We're in a town known for its springs. Come with me." He put his empty bowl aside and stood, replacing his face covering. Lexa hastily finished the final dregs of her meal and followed him. He led the way downstairs and quietly, respectfully, asked the woman if she had a free wash room. She gave him directions and he led Lexa along a short corridor.

"See?" he said, opening a door with the number 3 painted on it. Steam filled the small room, which was dominated by a sunken pool. It looked decidedly inviting.

Lexa's clothes stuck to her skin as the steam enveloped her. "Did you know about this?"

Jaxen laughed as he closed the door behind them. He took off his shirt. "I had an idea. Fabriel is known for the hot springs. Most inns here have wash houses."

Once more, Lexa felt stupid for forgetting something like that. She watched as Jaxen tugged off his boots and unbuttoned his trousers.

"Are you going to clean yourself fully dressed?" he asked, looking in her at amusement.

A blush made its way along her cheeks as she hesitantly took off her clothes, leaving them in a pile by the door.

Jaxen, naked, put their clothes through a hatch in the wall. "They'll be cleaned and dried by the time we're done," he said, certain of the inn's efficiency. "Now, are you going to get in or just stand there in that very enticing state of undress?"

Lexa had stripped to her loincloth, her hands self-consciously covering her bare breasts as she watched Jaxen. Aware of his eyes on her, she hastily made her way to the pool. It was sunk into the floor - like those at the Enclave – and the water in it looked inviting. The water was delightfully warm as it swirled around her calves.

"You can remove everything, you know."

"I really do believe you enjoy making me uncomfortable," Lexa said, keeping her back to Jaxen as she removed the final item of clothing.

"Oh, I honestly do," he admitted with a laugh.

She quickly immersed herself up to the neck, trying to maintain some modesty. She distracted herself from the thoughts of their nudity by mentally calculating the volume of water that would be needed to fill the pool.

Jaxen came into the water beside her a moment later, at apparent ease with his state of undress. He sighed in contentment as the water enveloped him. "This is much better than hiding in a forgetting den."

"Yes," she agreed. The nightmare of the previous day began to feel less and less proximate amid the steam and hot water. The heat of the water melted through her skin, wearing away at the fear and grief which was knotted inside her. She dipped her head under the water, running her fingers through the grimy strands, using her nails to separate the hair out from her scalp. It felt as though she were able to remove the awful memories of the arduous days of journeying. Once it felt as though the grit was finally out of her hair, she rested her head against the edge and closed her eyes, enjoying the heat and peace of the room.

"Are you enjoying yourself?" Jaxen's voice floated across to her.

"It's so nice," she replied dreamily.

He chuckled. The sound echoed around the room. Then he lapsed into silence, and they remained together in the water for a time.

"I should actually clean myself," Lexa said eventually. She took a bar of soap from the pool's edge and began to scrub herself. Her hand was arrested by one of Jaxen's on her shoulder. His other hand plucked the soap from her and began to run it across her back.

"What are you doing?" she asked softly, enjoying the sensation of being pampered.

His voice, when he replied, was the low, seductive tone that left shivers on her skin. "One of the many tasks of an *elui* is to clean his wife." The soap moved down to her lower back in deft strokes.

"But you aren't my *elui*," she said, her voice barely above a whisper. Jaxen brought the soap up to her shoulders, skimming it along the top of her right arm and then down along the underside.

"Maybe. But it can be fun to pretend," he murmured, moving the soap to her left arm. His body didn't quite touch hers, but she could feel how close he was to her and was keenly aware that the only thing between them was water.

"Is it, though? Fun, that is," she asked, her breath shortening as desire uncoiled itself within her.

"It depends on the circumstances." His lips were at her neck, gently kissing the skin above the water. He slipped his hand around her waist to drag the soap along her stomach.

"Does it?" She half turned to better face him. The motion caused his lips to graze across her jaw line. He had apparently let go of the soap, because the hand that had been holding it was now gripping her side, almost tight enough to be painful. Lexa's arm came to his shoulder, pulling him close so that their lips were just shy of touching. She could almost taste him on her, feel him on her, when the knock on the door interrupted the inevitable.

She pulled away from him. "Yes?"

"Your clothes are ready," a voice called from the other side of the door.

Her ardour dulled by the interruption, Lexa moved farther way from Jaxen, fear of the passion that had nearly carried her away replacing the arousal. "Thank you," she called back. "How long have we been here?"

"Longer than you'd expect," Jaxen said, looking entirely unruffled.

Not trusting herself to say anything further, Lexa finished bathing and got out. As she crossed to take a towel from a hook, she could feel Jaxen's gaze on her naked body, but she pretended to ignore it. When Jaxen came out, she averted her gaze.

Their clothes had been expertly washed and dried. Putting them on after nearly a day-cycle of wearing them nonstop was delightful. The fabric was no match for the beautiful soft clothes to which Lexa was normally accustomed, but when she first put on the clean shirt, it could have been an equal to the finest cloth in all of the Fourth Country as far as she was concerned. She sighed with pleasure at being free from the grime of the road.

The woman who had a cart to sell was not the shrewd trader Lexa had expected. Humming dreamily to herself, the old woman introduced herself as Alani, invited them into her house and all but forced them to have tea with her while they discussed the sale.

"So this is your first *elui*?" she asked Lexa.

Lexa nodded, resisting the impulse to glance at Jaxen for encouragement. "The marriage ceremony was held only a few day-cycles ago."

"And will you seek more *elui*?"

Lexa shifted in her seat. "I hadn't thought about it yet."

"Mmm. If you do, you must make sure that they are compatible with you."

Lexa looked at her in surprise. "Compatible?"

"Yes, my dear. It can't be helped that you haven't done it with your first, but if you make sure the ones you choose next are born on compatible days to you, then you will give yourself much happiness."

Lexa fought not to raise an eyebrow. "I'm not sure I follow, Alani."

"Birth days, Lexana. What do they teach you these days?" the woman exclaimed, blue eyes turned pale with age widening in emphasis.

"Oh, of course," Lexa said. The attribution of temperament to the day on which a person was born had been in vogue years back. Neither Lexa nor any of the people she knew in the Capital paid particular heed to it, but many older people still clung to the idea that one's day of birth gave an indication of what a person was like. They also considered certain days ideal for certain activities and planned their calendars accordingly, much to the irritation of those who did not feel the need to contort their schedule to satisfy pseudo-religious nonsense.

"You know it's very interesting that you came to me on the Day of Sight," Alani said enthusiastically. "The ideal day for making decisions, such as when to sell an old cart I've had lying in my yard for over a year now."

Lexa nodded weakly, somewhat overwhelmed by the fact that she was apparently trying to conduct business with a superstitious crackpot.

"I always feel better on the Day of Sight, you know. A day for a fresh start. Rarely do I find myself cheerful on the Day of Sorrows," Alani continued, her voice taking on an almost song-like quality. Each day in a day-cycle was named to chart the story of Mawani and her human lover. The Day of Sorrows was named for the time when she found herself left behind, following his death.

Lexa let the woman chatter while she covertly shot a look of alarm at Jaxen. Because his face was covered, she was unable to see his reaction. For the first time in her life, she envied men the ability to hide their reactions behind a veil while she struggled to keep a straight face.

"When were you born, Lexana?" Alani asked her.

She surprised herself by offering the answer immediately. "The Day of Ageing."

Alani nodded sagely. "You see things the way they were, my dear. I myself was born on the Day of Joy. It's why I've such a cheerful disposition. My life is linked to the happiness of Mawani and her love." She turned to Jaxen. "And you?"

He noticeably stiffened at the question. "I don't know on what day I was born," he said shortly.

"Ah, you're given the Day of Sorrows then, along with all who don't know," she said. "I'm sorry," she added, seeming to really mean it.

He inclined his head in an ambiguous gesture.

Lexa cleared her throat, regaining Alani's attention. "If we could return to the issue of the cart – we were hoping to leave today, if possible."

"Ah, yes, of course." Alani returned her attention to Lexa, the superstition given to meaningless trivialities left behind, or at least, remaining unspoken as they turned to business.

Once they were on the road outside Fabriel, Lexa brought up what had happened at Alani's. "Can you believe that she believed in that nonsense?"

Jaxen was driving, holding the reins with a relaxation that suggested he had driven many carts. Lexa wondered if that had been part of his duties when he was in the pleasure house, or something he had learned to do before he had entered into service at the pleasure house. "Are you certain that it's nonsense?"

"Yes. Don't you?"

He stayed silent.

"Don't you?" she pressed.

He tilted his cloth-covered head. "I'm always cautious to completely dismiss something," he said.

"But to say that someone's life and the type of person they are can be determined by the day they were born is nonsense," Lexa argued.

"Who's to say what's superstitious and what's not? The monks of the Enclave perform the most incredible feats, controlling the very world around us, and they claim that this comes from their faith. The Sun King of the Second Country is said to be able to quite literally bring the sun into his hands. People from the Third Country tell stories of figures who can perform feats no normal person can. And we know where the First Country is, or rather, where it should be -- beyond the Keth mountain ranges. Yet anybody who tries to cross them either never comes back or reports the mountains are impassable. The only way to get to the First Country is a precise sea channel that few captains go through. It may as well be unknown.

"These are all things some might call superstitious, but some might say is beyond the understanding of many, perhaps most. What's the difference?"

He had a very good point, although the initial conversation was now of less interest to her than this reflective, philosophical side that he had revealed.

"Well?" he prompted when she didn't answer.

"Maybe," she admitted. "But I still think it's silly to say that you can know anything about someone because of the day on which they were born. When did you think of all that?"

Jaxen shrugged. It was interesting to see how much more physically expressive he was when veiled. Of course, it was necessary given she couldn't see his face. She was surprised by how quickly he had adopted the more physical responses in conversation, given that he had gone unveiled for many years.

"I told you, I read a lot at the Enclave. And I would often

speak with Leyana. Understanding how the world works is a passion of hers, as I suspect you know."

Lexa shifted in her seat, remembering with some measure of discomfort that on the mountain, she had avoided telling Jaxen that Leyana had asked her to help with her research. After the many day-cycles she had spent with him, that unwillingness to tell him of what she and Leyana had spoken seemed so silly. With a rush of heat, she also remembered the way they had come so close to kissing when he had interrogated her about with what Leyana had tasked her to research. That in turn made her think of what had nearly transpired between them that morning in the bathing house, and the heat intensified. With the time to reflect now as they moved along the road, free from danger, she wondered what would have happened had they not been interrupted. She indulged herself in imagining what would have transpired in the steam-filled room, his hands over her, his lips on hers, her gasps, his moans.

A rattle brought her back to the present, and she turned to see Jaxen regarding her. Looking into his eyes, she found herself almost drowning in her want for him, and she wondered if he saw it on her face. Unlike him, she did not have a veil that hid what she was thinking.

"What were you thinking?" he asked.

She dropped her gaze and saw, out of the corner of her eye, him turn back to the road.

"Nothing important," she said, her body still practically thrumming with desire.

"You looked like you were in a completely different place," he said. Even the low tone of his voice sent a wave of longing across her. She wondered why, in the time that they had travelled together, she had not acted on that desire. He had more than proved that she could trust him, and she no longer had to consider the implications of what giving in to that desire would have on the reputation of her family.

"I suppose I was," she said.

FOURTEEN

Thanks to the cart, they reached the Capital in only three days. Their journey was expedited by the fact that the lands near the Capital were always secure. The Lord Protector did not appreciate unrest near her lands, and while she technically had no authority to actually put a cease to any ongoing warfare or conflicts between families, she controlled the land through which almost all of the Fourth Country's trade had to flow in order to get anywhere of consequence. Of course, it was possible in theory that someone may attempt to wrest the Capital from the family of the Lord Protector's family – Veleth's family – but given the defensibility of the Capital and its surrounding land, it was all but impossible to mount any form of successful attack. Lexa could attest to that herself. She and her mother had often looked over maps of the Capital in the intellectual exercise of deducing how they might take the land for the Farwan family. Little tactical advantage had made itself known to them no matter how many times they tried to find one. Lexa had always assumed it was for their own amusement, but she wondered now if her mother had harboured a desire to claim the most integral part of the Fourth Country and the glory and power that accompanied it. Witnessing the destruction that the Yendel family had caused in claiming the Gemesh land, Lexa had been forced to wonder if there was no limit to greed.

Lexa had spent an agonising three nights next to Jaxen. The onset of winter had made the nights unpleasantly cold, and they now slept pressed together. Despite the chill, Jaxen still slept in only a loincloth, and while Lexa studiously avoiding overtly staring at him, it was almost a physical pain to be so aware of his skin so close to hers. Yet his flirtatious mannerisms had never gone beyond a wicked look or comment, and that had made her reluctant to be the first to change things between them. Despite the fact that women customarily initiated physical contact, she did not think Jaxen the type to let things happen to him. So she waited for him to give her some signal that he wanted her.

They sold the cart and its beasts at a trader's store on the edge of the Capital. Many such traders located themselves near the fringes of the Capital to take advantage of those in need of acquiring or divesting themselves of, some item or service to successfully conduct their business in the Capital. Some of those stalls were even part of the Farwan network – used to be, Lexa had to remind herself. Although they sold the carriage for a third of its value, they were happy to pay the price for the anonymity. Their entrance into the city proper was noted with extreme indifference by the troopwomen they passed. As they worked their way closer to the centre of the trading hub, the sprawling wooden buildings and dirt roads of the outskirts gave way to sturdier, sanctioned buildings made of stone and timber lining, and paved streets.

Jaxen guided her through the undercity, a place where she had never gone before. The crowded buildings, the assault of various stenches, and the air of latent menace left her confused and intimidated. Fortunately, the apparent intimacy of Jaxen's knowledge had them off the street relatively quickly. He'd even found a guesthouse of superior quality to those around it, although the neighbouring buildings set a low bar.

"Wait here," he said, once they had been shown to their room.

Lexa dubiously looked around at the surrounds. The meagre

blanket that covered the bed was a grey colour that suggested it had not been washed in some time. Rather than light spheres, a little fire burned in the hearth, giving the room a dingy light that emphasised its simplicity. She thought with longing of the Inn at Fabriel. At the time, it had seemed so simple, but in hindsight it was a luxury.

"Where are you going?"

"I'll be back soon," he said.

"But where are you going?"

"Don't worry, I'll be back soon," he promised again. Then he left, offering no further word or explanation.

While she waited for him to return, she unpacked the bag that had faithfully accompanied them from the mountain. She examined the contents to ensure that the clothes and few items were still in acceptable condition. Jaxen had made her sell or discard many possessions to keep the bag light. Almost nothing in it she had originally owned. All her actual possessions had been lost in the takeover, or left at the Enclave.

The small map of dubious accuracy that she had bought two days earlier, she kept out with a nub of chalk. From memory, she drew a rough sketch of the city on the back of the map so she could consider how they would get to her mother's warehouse. The lines which formed the city where she had spent so much of her life slowly formed a picture that she recognised. She had never realised how little of the Capital she had ever seen. Her life had been so restricted to the residential areas of the wealthy that she had never ventured into much of the city, nor considered the people who comprised the majority of its inhabitants.

Her mind returned to the town in which she and Jaxen had hidden from the raiders. That desolation had been wrought in the name of the Yendel family. She knew the eldest daughter, a sweet-faced girl named Denna. Lexa was certain that Denna would not know what her mother's decision to take those lands meant for the people who had lived there – who the family's hired fighters had trampled across without a thought. Perhaps if she had, she might have begged her mother to reconsider. Or she might not have cared. Lexa certainly had never given any thought to the people who might have been in the way of an invading force employed by the Farwan family. An echo of the town's smell – rotting meat, burnt wood – drifted into her senses. Even though Jaxen claimed that the land through which they had walked had been treated with unusual severity – perhaps the Gemesh family put up a significant fight to keep their territory – she could not help but wonder if the people on her family's conquered lands would have to rebuild from similar desolation And those other families, many of them here in the Capital, would all know what had befallen the Farwan house, and none of them would particularly care about Lexa, her family, or the people on her family's lands. But it wasn't as though she had been any different. She still remembered the way she had felt upon learning of the demise of a family. The only emotion that she had ever experienced was a detached regret, or perhaps a vague sense of sorrow. It was the way of the world, she had reasoned. The strong endured and the weak or careless slipped into ignominious demise. After a few days, those who had fallen were all but forgotten, by her, by everyone.

Her hand paused on the map she had drawn. Her family's house had been built by her great-great-great-grandmother. Now, it would have been plundered by the greedy hands of the Kalabaths. The prospect of boots tramping through her house, her room, with an appraising eye that reduced all sentiment or memory to a heap of coin seemed an injustice of the highest order. It was not a prospect she had allowed herself to consider much, but now that she was alone, she could not help but think of such possibilities. Almost certainly, the sentimental tokens she had kept in her room would have been relegated to some rubbish fire. The abacus she had been given when she was four meant nothing to anyone other than her. The portrait of her, Emi, and Kellen had not been painted by someone of any noteworthiness. Equally, the little tapestry her youngest brother, Ket, had made for her only the previous winter was so clumsy that it would be thrown aside without a second thought.

Lexa wanted to cry. She wanted the anger and sadness over the invasion of her home and the almost certain destruction of her family to come out in a flood of hot, bitter tears. Yet her eyes stayed dry.

As he had promised he would, Jaxen returned shortly. She waited for him to tell her where he had gone, but he said nothing, sinking into the room's dilapidated chair and uncovering his face with obvious relish.

"Where did you go?" she asked.

"To get this." He slipped a hand into his pocket and withdrew a bundle of cloth.

Lexa looked at him in surprise. "Some fabric?"

He threw her an amused look before unwrapping a knife with a wicked-looking long blade.

Lexa gasped, shocked at the menace exuded by the gleaming metal. "We won't need that," she said, almost as a reflex.

Jaxen folded the cloth back over the knife. "We might."

"So you went to buy a knife? Why didn't you have one when we were going through the country where law and safety barely existed?" She heard the shrill edge to her voice and forced herself to take a breath.

"The safest way to go through areas like that is without being a threat. Besides, if we'd been stopped by people who meant business, one knife wouldn't have helped us." Jaxen was completely calm, completely restrained. "In a city like this, however, it's often useful to have something very sharp and very pointy about you."

She shrugged in angry acknowledgment, wondering how he spoke of such things with such confidence. Jaxen came to her. The knife had disappeared without her seeing where he had put it, or how. "What's wrong?" he asked, putting a hand on her arm.

She knocked his hand away. "My family was toppled and I have to find my mother, father, and brothers. I'm in the Capital in this questionable establishment while some ugly, undeserving person sleeps in my bedroom. Do I really need to continue?" Here at last was some of the release she had craved. Anger felt better than sorrow.

She turned away from him, finding the serene expression on his face irksome. His hands were almost immediately at her shoulders, his thumbs seeming to find the tight spots in her back. Under the skilled pressure of his hands, the muscles that had knotted themselves into hard, tight places of tension and pain, melted. She let out the softest of moans. The anger she had intended to hold had gone.

"You know, for someone so very pampered, you've impressed me," he told her, his right thumb working at a particularly entrenched point of tension.

She tipped her head back, all but arching her back into his fingers. "Mm?"

"Yes. Most would never have survived the trek." The warmth in his voice was intoxicating.

"I had you," she replied.

"True," he acknowledged.

"Why did you come with me?" she asked. Perhaps this time she would get a real answer.

Now the thumb of his left hand dug in, drawing from her a gasp of pleasure and pain laced together. "Do you really not know?"

"I honestly don't," she told him, delighting in how what he was doing felt.

"Lexa." He caressed her name. The sensuality of the sound made her shiver. "I'm a cynical man. I've seen a great many beautiful people do ugly things. It leaves a certain fatigue on your soul. And you arrived at the Enclave, shocked by my immodesty in a way that was so honest. You made me want more, to be better because of the freshness with which you see the world.

"You were so immediately willing to go and find what remains of your family. And it wasn't even that you didn't care about the peril someone in your position might encounter. You didn't even consider how dangerous the world might be for someone like you. You come from a world in which any threat is calculated against risk and reward, yet none of those things meant anything when you decided you had to find your family. It was quite enough for me to want to help you. The thought of you dead left me feeling as though the world would be a little less bright without you." His right hand moved lower as he spoke, coaxing the tension out of the bottom of her shoulder blade. The fingers of his hand curved around her side to rest against the underside of her breast.

"You make it sound so devoid of any nobility of sentiment," she murmured.

"Quite the opposite. You touched me when I thought I could not be touched," he told her. "Does that seem so impossible?"

She hesitated, weighing his words. The truth was that she wanted to believe him. "But you gave up your freedom in the Enclave." She did not like how plaintive her voice sounded.

"It was not freedom," he countered, his voice gentle. "But even so. Do you know how rare you are? We live in a world where friends betray one another as a matter of habit. The bonds of family might be stronger than those of friendship, but not by much. Yet you never even considered not trying to find your family. You and I both know you could have chosen a safe, comfortable life in the Enclave." Then he surprised her. "And you, Lexa, why do you look at me in the way you do?" he asked.

Her breath caught. "What do you mean?"

"You look at me as though you want me not just for my body or what I could do for you, but for my mind. For me. I'm not sure anyone has ever looked at me like that."

"I do?" Inelegant though it was, it was all she could manage.

"Yes. It makes me feel as though taking everything I can possibly get from everyone foolish enough to give might not be the only way to live." His hands stilled. Without the movement, the intimacy of his touch became very noticeable. Almost painfully so.

"I don't know what to say," she admitted.

His hands squeezed softly as he laughed. "You don't need to say anything."

It was then that she turned, moving quickly enough that he didn't have time to reposition his hands. She looked into the grey of his eyes, dark with some emotion that she fervently hoped included desire.

He remained utterly still, his hands on her shoulder and waist, as she tentatively bridged the distance between them. When their lips met, the hand on her shoulder slipped down to mirror the one on her waist. His moan against her mouth was almost inaudible, but it was more than enough to ignite the lust for him that she had kept constrained for so long. Fire bloomed in her chest and her arms came around him, greedily pulling him to her so that she could feel him against her. After the days of resistance, of longing for this exact moment, she could hardly believe that now they stood locked in this embrace that made her forget where she ended and he began.

After what could have been an age, or a few heartbeats, he pulled away from her. She was drunk off that one kiss, swaying slightly. His hands, still around her waist, steadied her. He did not ask if she was sure. He did not say anything. Eyes so dark that they were nearly black, he brought his lips to hers once more. If anything, this kiss was more urgent, even more filled with the desire of the past days that had gone unanswered. Lexa did not think that she would ever be kissed like that again, and that knowledge made the kiss all the more wonderful. When they pulled apart for the second time, both of them were panting, staring at each other with surprise at the force of their need. Then, by some unspoken agreement, they began to tear at each other's clothes.

When he pushed her onto the bed, her earlier concern over its cleanliness barely passed through her mind. All she could think of was the consuming need for Jaxen. He invaded her senses, his scent filling her nose, his skin on hers, the sound of his ragged breathing all she could hear. The way he felt against her was what she imagined it would feel like to walk through the lightning storm surrounding the Enclave. For as long as she lived, she could not imagine anything would ever feel like this again.

They lay together as their blood cooled, him on his back staring at the ceiling, she curled into his side, using the space on his chest just in from his shoulder as a pillow.

"I didn't know a man could take a woman from above like that," she said, reaching out her hand to gently run her fingers along the strip of hair down the centre of his chest.

He laughed and pulled her closer, turning his head so that his nose nuzzled her hair. "You would be amazed at all the things that can be done. Were you taught that a woman should always be astride a man?"

She nodded, causing him to laugh again.

"How you were misinformed," he murmured seductively. Then his voice took on a more reflective quality. "It's strange how we are taught that women have desire, will take charge of a man for her pleasure. Very rarely is the desire men feel even acknowledged. But we are creatures of passion, too, Lexa, and we are not simply to be taken in service of a woman's need."

"Was it that bad, in the pleasure house?" she asked, assuming this was what prompted his comment and the bitter tone in his voice.

His exhalation was long and controlled. "There were times when it wasn't so bad. Some of the people who came in were looking for comfort or contact. Some were foreigners, away from home. Some people came wanting me to take charge, like I did with you just now. But there were others who thought that because they'd paid for my body, they could do whatever they wanted with it, provided they left no marks – we all had to be beautiful, you see. They, even when they were underneath me instead of above me, they were—" He stopped, unable or unwilling to find the words to complete his sentence.

"I don't make you feel like that, do I?" she asked. Sadness that he had endured such things filled her, its taste bitter in her mouth.

He laughed. "No, Never."

FIFTEEN

The river district was more reputable than the area in which Lexa and Jaxen had stayed for the night, but not much more. Whenever Lexa's mother had gone to inspect the warehouses owned by the Farwan family, she had been accompanied by several guards, some of them even her *elui* who had been given special dispensation to train to fight without their veils. When she had been much younger, Lexa had snuck into the training yard and watched them, fascinated to see the focused expressions on their sweat-drenched faces as they moved. They would likely have been the first to fall in the takeover of the Farwan family, defending their wife and mistress.

Lexa had often been obliged to accompany her mother on the inspections, a task that increased in frequency as she got older. It was a duty she had done most begrudgingly. Aside from the menace that each corner promised, she found the rows of warehouses lining the river eerie in and of themselves. Why she could not say exactly, but whenever possible, she found an excuse to avoid the chore.

The job was as much performance as actually ensuring the quality of goods. Many of the warehouses used by the Farwan family were never visited or inspected by anyone with even the most tenuous of public connections to Lexa or her family. Secrecy was key when it came to trade in the Fourth Country.

Yet despite Lexa's deep-rooted dislike of the river district, here she was, walking along the rows of warehouses. Much as with the allegiance of traders, the exact ownership of warehouses was often murky. Some were obvious, and indeed, if anyone would have invested enough coin and time in the effort, they likely would have deduced which warehouse belonged to whom. Even so, those more crafty, like Lexa's mother, were paranoid enough to ensure that no one linked to the family went near one or two particular warehouses owned or rented by the family – some under the false names, or a variety of other ways to place distance between themselves and the properties. It appeared that paranoia had been well founded, for as she walked, Lexa was confident that the warehouse whose number was seared into her mind at her mother's behest – Tanita would not even write it down – was not known as being in her family's ownership by anyone other than Tanita and herself.

Jaxen walked beside her as she glanced up at the large yellow numbers painted above the doorways of the stark, dirty-white buildings. After the afternoon and evening they had spent together, she was keenly aware of where his body was in relation to hers. Despite the worry for her family and the as the yet-uncompleted task of finding them, she could not suppress a certain elation, incited by what now existed between her and Jaxen. She glanced at him, attempting to be subtle, but he noticed and gave her what she was certain was a smile behind his veil. That made her stomach feel as though it were flipping over. The giddiness was tempered by the knowledge that he carried the knife he procured the previous day in his pocket. If Jaxen thought there was a need for a weapon, the danger was real.

Down the narrow alleyways squeezed in between the warehouses, Lexa could glimpse the green-grey of the river Joy that ran through the Capital. The Joy was so wide that many barges could easily traverse it at the one time. This was what made the Capital the great trading hub of the Fourth Country. The barges would easily and discreetly load or unload their contents into the warehouses, and the goods flowed across the Fourth Country. Wagons loaded with wares rattled past, the drivers intent on delivering their cargo on time so as to avoid their payment being docked for tardiness. Lexa felt a shock of familiarity when she saw the Farwan family motto stamped on the crates of a passing wagon. The letters proclaiming "quality is the secret to success" seemed a disturbing jibe, especially when she realised whoever was trading those goods must have seized them from Farwan holdings and was profiting off the blood of her family.

"Are you certain you know what we're looking for?" Jaxen asked, pulling her attention away from thoughts about the remnants of her family's legacy. His voice was muffled by the veil. Having initially found his unveiled state at the Academy confronting, Lexa now found it even stranger to see him covered. From the recesses of his hood, his eyes shone, their grey colour curiously bright in the shadow.

"I'm certain," she said. She pushed aside the shock of seeing the Farwan crates and glanced up at the number on the warehouse they were passing. She really hated the buildings. Constructed from white clay bricks to ensure that fire would at the very least be contained, the buildings were tall but bereft of any sense of grace. The Lord Protector's family had built them two generations earlier and sold half of them at an exorbitant price to whoever could afford them. The other half, she had leased out, and her family continued to do so. It was a brilliant way to make even more money for the family.

"How do you plan to get inside?" Jaxen asked. There was no malice or challenge in his voice, merely calm curiosity.

Lexa waved at him to tell him to be quiet as they reached the warehouse she was searching for. It looked identical to any of the surrounding warehouses, nondescript in every way. She walked up to the doors, which were the height of at least two people. Through them, carts could come into the warehouse itself and load or unload their wares. Lexa's mother had experimented with ways to mount cargo on tracks to easily slide them along the length of the warehouses so that loading cargo could be expedited. Lexa had suggested this process could be expedited by altering the design of the tracks. She had even produced several sketches of her proposed changes. Tanita had promised her that she could experiment with the design once she returned from the Academy. Realising that took a small slice out of Lexa's heart as she wondered if that promise could ever be fulfilled.

One guard stood at the worker's entrance in the narrow space between the enormous structures. Lexa steeled herself, then strode up to the guard. It was cold in the shadow of the huge buildings. The woman looked bored. Lexa could hardly blame her. Standing for hours at a stretch to deter anyone from trying to rob or investigate the warehouses was dull work. Perhaps it would have been a kindness to double the guard for the sake of companionship. But two guards inferred that there was something inside worth stealing. One guard was what almost every warehouse had as a matter of routine, even if its contents were of the highest value.

"Morning," Lexa said, her voice conversational and light. The guard looked at her with suspicious eyes, saying nothing in return. She didn't even glance at Jaxen. After all, he was only a man.

"Been here long?" Lexa asked, unconcerned by the silence. Guards were not known to be chatty.

"Long enough," the woman answered in a clipped commoner's accent.

"Must be dull," Lexa said.

"Could be worse."

Lexa was surprised by the woman's unwillingness to engage in even the slightest conversation. The script she had prepared in her head had seemed so flawless. Uncertainly, she slipped a hand into her pocket and jangled the coins there. It was not a subtle action, but she hoped the guard would not be put off by such overtness. Snooping on the contents of the river district's warehouses was far from uncommon. Provided nothing was stolen or destroyed, it was an accepted part of both the area and the game of trade.

The guard narrowed her eyes. "You might want to be careful about that noise," she said. "Some might think you've got quite a few feathers in your pocket."

Lexa relaxed. It seemed this woman was amenable to the idea of being bribed after all. Greed was written into the sharpness of her eyes, and she was looking fixedly at Lexa and the coin she offered. The woman paid no attention to Jaxen as he slid to stand behind her.. Lexa looked at him in confusion. His eyes behind his veil were intense and unreadable.

"I'm sorry," he said, to Lexa or the guard, it was not clear. Then he pulled the guard against him with a hand over her mouth and sliced the knife across her throat. Bright red blood sprayed out from the right of the neck almost spattering Lexa, while darker blood poured down the left side of her neck. For a moment, the guard struggled fiercely. Lexa could hear her wheezing scream against his hand, air whistling around the line he had scored across her windpipe. But with obscene speed, the guard went limp, dark blood flooding from her throat. Lexa was paralysed with horror, transfixed by the guard's staring eyes – the fact that her eyes remained open somehow made everything worse. Finally Jaxen let the body fall to the ground with a careless thud, as though the person whose life he had taken hadn't been a friend or daughter or lover to someone.

"Come on," he said, bending down to rifle through the woman's pockets. Due to his veil, it was impossible to see if remorse or indifference had settled on his features. He did not seem particularly bothered that one sleeve was soaked with blood, nor did he seem to notice the spatter of blood on his veil.

"You killed her," Lexa said somewhat stupidly. It was all she could manage.

"Yes." Jaxen was so matter of fact.

"She did nothing. I would have bribed her and she would have let us in."

"No." The absolute certainty in his voice was almost as shocking as his terrible deed. "At best, she would have called for help to remove us. She was going to take the coin and either call for help or try to get rid of us herself." This certainty was so unnerving. For the first time, Lexa noticed the menacing baton at the guard's hip. A well placed hit with that could be just as lethal as a sword's bite. But Jaxen's claim seemed so preposterous that she couldn't accept it.

"She'd done nothing."

Jaxen retrieved a small chain of keys and straightened up. "I promise, Lexa, she was never going to accept a bribe." He spared no time to soothe her and began trying keys in the lock.

"How can you be so sure?" she asked. She did not add "sure enough to kill her", but she certainly thought it. The idea that the hands that had caressed her the previous day were the same that had ended someone's life with cold indifference seemed impossible.

"I just am," Jaxen told her, apparently feeling no need to elaborate. The lock gave a click and the door swung open. "Come on."

Lexa stayed where she was, staring at Jaxen with mute horror. Who was this cold, brutal person who stood in the doorway, waiting for her with obvious impatience?

"Lexa." In the one word there was enough meaning to convey his frustration. "You can come in and find your family or stay out here, be discovered by a passer-by, and never get to your family."

That galvanised her. But she had to step over the body to get inside. She had to look down at the corpse to avoid stepping in the puddle of blood settling around the body. The sight was gruesome. Lexa had once heard that the dead looked asleep, but there was no way she could make that mistake here.

Jaxen pulled the door closed behind her. The sound of it shutting echoed around the huge space. Aside from wan light through a few small windows high up on the walls, it was very dark, and very cold, too. Jaxen was looking around. Blood on his veil glistened in the low light. "You have blood on you," she said.

He undid his veil and let the hood fall back to expose his face and hair. "I'll sort that out later," he said. He did not look like a vicious, remorseless killer. He looked the same as always. "Do you know where to look?" he asked.

She swallowed and with an effort, nodded. Her face felt like stone or wood. He grabbed her by the arm. His blood-stained sleeve brushed against her wrist. "Lexa, I'm sorry. I did what I thought was necessary." His earnestness ignited a war within Lexa. She wanted so badly to believe he hadn't done something wrong, but she could not stop herself seeing him pull the knife across the guard's throat.

"I'll be fine, Jaxen, I just need time," she said. She hoped that was true.

He released her and stepped back to give her a little more space, a little more of the lead. Even though she knew he was doing it to make her feel comfortable, as though he hadn't just murdered someone, she appreciated the courtesy. She looked along the rows of crates. "Sixth row from the side entrance, fourth crate closest to the docks," she said softly, her voice carried away from her by the vastness of the space. In her periphery, she saw him nod, and they set off, their steps dull, echoing thuds.

The crates were made from fresh timber roughly sawn into boards which were then made into boxes. They were obviously part of the Farwan enterprises which were kept away from public knowledge. The wood was bare; the familiar sight of the stencilled family motto was not present. Lexa put her hand on one of them and pulled it back quickly, worried that she might get a splinter. She could smell the mouldy scent of the green timber mixed with something else, something familiar, although she couldn't quite place what it was. She stepped carefully through the rows of crates, her mind niggling as it tried to place that other smell. Briefly, she wondered if she was focusing on this little mystery to distract herself from what had transpired outside. Yet the scent was so familiar that she could feel it in the back of her mouth, as though all she had to do was part her lips and allow the name of that scent to come forth.

Jaxen kept a respectful distance behind her. She wondered how she would know him now. Lover? Murderer? She did not look back at him but kept her eyes resolutely forward, counting the rows as they passed. It soon felt as though they were lost amid the neatly stacked boxes. Here, no rail system was in place to allow the crates to be easily slipped along to a waiting cart. It was as though Tanita had gone to great lengths to create the appearance that goods of poor value were housed within the building. Lexa wondered what her mother had been doing with this warehouse.

They reached the sixth row and turned left, toward the riverbank. She could hear nothing from outside. Someone might have found the body and raised an alarm, but she couldn't hear enough to know if that had in fact happened. They should have dragged the body inside, but the prospect of touching the woman's still-warm corpse left her feeling ill. What left her even more unsettled was the fact that she had thought of a 'they' rather than ascribing the crime to Jaxen. He was, after all, here to help her. She banished these considerations from her mind. They would do her no good now, only stop her from finding her family. Soon, they reached the crate Tanita had instructed Lexa to find. Jaxen stood beside her as she surveyed it. She could feel the heat from his body near hers. In the cold of the warehouse, it should have been a comfort, but it felt almost too hot.

"So now what?" Jaxen asked. His voice sounded hollow in

the vastness of the warehouse.

There was nothing about the crate that was even remotely unusual. Although, had there been, it would have been unforgivably careless. Tanita was not that kind of woman. Lexa crouched beside it. The smell of dampness rushed to invade her nose. The packed dirt floor was dry, but the bottom of the crate was slightly wet. Crates were often damp if they came straight off river barges. It often led to cargo being spoiled. The familiar scent, the one that Lexa couldn't quite identify, was stronger, too. She knew that it shouldn't be her preoccupation, but it was maddening.

"Lexa?" Scepticism brushed the upward inflection of his question.

"One moment," she said absentmindedly. She rubbed her hand along the crate's lowermost panel, wary of splinters that may lodge themselves into her skin.

"Do you actually know what you're looking for?"

"She only told me once," Lexa murmured, some impulse keeping her voice low. "She said that I should – ah." Her hand found impressions in the wood. Her fingers traced lightly over the letters pressed into the slat. With her other hand, she took the chalk from her pocket and rubbed it over the wood. The scrape of the chalk against the wood cut through the eerie stillness of the warehouse like a ripple in water. She wished for a light sphere, even a simple open flame, to better see what she was doing. Fortunately, it only took a moment. The address was pressed into the wood like a brand or stamp. "I wonder," Lexa whispered to herself, pivoting to the adjacent crate. Again, on the bottom slat, she found an indentation. With a swift motion, she swept the chalk across the indentation. It was not as thorough as her pass on the first crate, but she saw enough to know that it was the same address.

"Clever," she whispered, still speaking to herself.

"Lexa?" The confusion in Jaxen's voice brought her out of her reverie.

"The instruction was pointless, just designed to confuse in case I was caught and forced to give up the information," Lexa said, standing.

"Your mother thought you might be captured and, what, tortured for information?" Jaxen was standing in a particularly deep shadow, but she didn't need to see his face. She could hear the faint disgust in his voice clearly enough.

"It was a precaution, perhaps just giving a little extra ambiguity. The address is on all of the crates. That's where they are, in the business address of whoever manufactures the crates," she explained. She felt the slight sense of dismay that her mother had been obscure with her out of a belief that she might be taken, but it was more like she was observing the emotion rather than experiencing it.

"I do not understand your world," Jaxen told her.

She shrugged. "It's actually brilliant. Who would hide somewhere so obvious?"

"I don't understand how you aren't angry she didn't just tell you where to go in the first place, rather than have you run around finding clues like this," Jaxen said.

She stared at him blankly for a moment. He was right. She should have been at least a little frustrated by the circuitous nature of her mother's clues, especially given how easily Tanita could have told her where to go. A suspicion worked its way into the corner of her mind. She sniffed again. She definitely knew the smell that softly pervaded the warehouse. She surveyed the lid of the nearest crate. Like the rest, it was secured by tightly tied cord. She began to unpick the knot. The coarse fibres of the rope burned her fingers, but she paid it no heed, too intent on her task to let pain distract her.

"What are you doing?" Jaxen asked.

"Help me," she said, finally undoing the knot and putting her fingers into the gap between the lid and the side of the crate. Underneath the delicate skin of her fingers, the wood felt gritty and swollen with moisture, but it was almost soothing after the burn of the rope. With Jaxen's help, the lid easily lifted.

She lifted one of the wax-covered cloth bundles neatly stacked in the crate and unwrapped it.

"Mawani," she whispered. Without the scent of damp wood between her and the package, the smell was unmistakable despite the fact that the substance was not being burned or brewed. Really, she should have immediately recognised it. But she would never have associated a warehouse – especially a warehouse owned by her mother – with forget-me-not.

SIXTEEN

"I don't understand," Lexa said, for perhaps the fifth time, as she paced the room.

As he had done the previous four times she had uttered the statement, Jaxen said nothing. He merely sat in a chair and regarded her with a contemplative expression.

"Are you going to say anything?" Lexa demanded.

They were in another anonymous Inn. The sound of raucous laughter seeped in from the bar downstairs. Such merriment made everything feel even more unreal.

"What is there to say? I think it's reasonably obvious what we saw," Jaxen said, as calm as ever.

She stopped her pacing to throw a glare at him, then resumed her incessant trek around the room. She didn't want to be still. Jaxen's serenity was setting her on edge.

"She must have been leasing out the warehouse to someone else," Lexa concluded. It was the only explanation that made sense.

Jaxen's look conveyed his thoughts on the likelihood of that being true. "Even if that were true, and mind, I've never met your mother, she surely had to know what was in those crates, given they've the address on where to find her."

"Perhaps I got it wrong. Perhaps that isn't the address after all," Lexa said, a sense of desperation swirling inside her.

"Lexa." Something in his tone caused her to pause her pacing and actually look at him. She'd been unable to do that since he had killed the guard. Even when he had gently told her to turn her shirt inside out because it was speckled with blood – she didn't even remember blood jumping across the distance between her and the guard – she had not looked at Jaxen.

"What?" Her arms came to curl around her stomach as though she could hold herself together.

"You and I both know that your mother gave you those instructions never actually considering that you'd find out what was in those crates."

"But mother thinks of everything," Lexa protested, her voice sounding child-like to her ears.

Jaxen said nothing. He did not have to.

"Do you really think that my mother trades in forget-me-not?" Lexa asked. Her voice was so small it was almost inaudible. She hugged herself more tightly. The idea that her mother, Tanita Farwan, a woman whose fearsomeness preceded her entry into any room or situation, was trading in forget-me-not, a drug that was viewed with disdain and shame by even those who used it, left her feeling distinctly unwell. She did not wait for Jaxen to answer her question.

"I wasn't supposed to take over a trade empire built on drugs," she whispered.

"Haven't you ever wanted to be someone other than your mother's daughter?"

"Well, yes," she confessed. "But I've always enjoyed doing the accounts and understanding the numbers behind what she did." She shrugged. "So I supposed there were far less pleasant things in the world to do."

"Less pleasant than supplying people with a drug to make them forget the way in which their lives have been ruined by a conflict caused by people like your family?" His challenge was soft, but it felt as though he'd physically struck her.

"That's not fair." His voice was soft. "You murdered someone today." She knew she should not throw an accusation of her own back at him, but she was too upset to stop herself.

He did not appear particularly upset. "I did. I never claimed to be a good person, or a kind person. If the gods exist then they are unlikely to smile on me. But this isn't about me, it's about you, and what you've discovered about your mother."

She looked at the man who had followed her across half of the Fourth Country. Without him, she knew that she would have been caught by raiders, or recognised as Lexana Farwan, or been harmed in a thousand other possible ways. He sat there completely composed: murderer, lover, mystery. Every time Lexa thought that she was beginning to understand him just a little, she realised how completely she did not.

"You're upset about what happened in the alleyway." Jaxen did not ask a question but stated a fact. He looked completely comfortable where he sat regarding her. She wondered what, if anything, made Jaxen angry. Perhaps that was what had unsettled her the most about his decision to kill the guard – the complete calm with which he had done it.

"How could I not be?" Her voice was calm – despite the hysteria thoughts of the murder evoked.

He ran a hand through hair that had grown noticeably longer in the time they had been travelling. "I know it was upsetting. I'm sorry. Perhaps I should have warned you. Lexa, you must believe me that I will only ever do what I think is necessary to protect you." He leaned forward, earnestness making his eyes seem like bottomless grey lakes.

"Her blood was on me," Lexa protested, looking down at her abdomen where the blood had sprayed. She could still see the blood there, even though the stained garments had long-since been thrown into the fire, all evidence of the crime destroyed.

"I know, I'm sorry." He did seem genuinely contrite – although she would have bet it was about upsetting her rather than ending the guard's life.

Lexa looked directly into Jaxen's eyes and she was lost. The truth was that she wanted to forgive him. She didn't want to think of him as a callous murderer. Especially not after the shock of finding a warehouse owned by her mother full of forget-me-not. She crossed the distance between them and leaned down. His lips were so soft against hers, his mouth so warm. As she kissed him, it felt as though she could forget for the tiniest moment everything that had happened and fall into his kiss.

Their lips did not part as he pulled her onto his lap. She could not have said for how long they remained like that. When their lips finally parted, the sweet headiness that she had discovered kissing him induced, had settled over her. What she had seen him do did not seem to matter anymore. It was as though a different Jaxen had committed that unthinkable act, not the Jaxen whose lips had just been on hers, who kissed her so tenderly.

She tugged at his shirt. He gave a laugh and gently captured her hands. "What do we do next?" he asked.

"We need to go to Ketter," she said.

"The port city?"

She nodded.

"Why?"

"Because that was the address on the crates."

"So you'll go to find your mother?" Jaxen sounded surprised.

"Whatever she may have done, she's still my mother."

His hands enfolding hers tightened. "Lexa, forget-me-not might be fun for people who can afford it in enough amounts to smoke rather than brew, but for those who are desperate to escape some hardship or horror that haunts them, it ruins them, both for themselves and anybody who might know or love them." His voice had taken on an unusually serious note.

"I know, Jaxen. I was in that forgetting den, too," she said.

"No, Lexa. You have no idea. Where we were was clean and nice and there were only a few people there. If you were to go into a proper den, you would think that Mawani herself had turned away from such a place. Often you can't walk through the area without stepping on someone, because the floor is so crowded. And the stink is overpowering. Some people lie there for days, soiling themselves and lying in their own mess, knowing it but not caring.

"The people who care about those who walk into forgetting dens lose them for days at a time, wondering if they will ever come back, or if they will drift away on the dirty floor of some miserable den, lying in their own filth. That's what your mother is feeding." His eyes were completely flat, his face eerily similar to the way it had been when he had killed the guard.

"Jaxen." She found herself whispering his name, her ardour dulled by the image that he painted and his expression. She did not know what else she should say.

"My mother was addicted to forget-me-not, Lexa," he said. His voice contained no emotional flourish, only the quiet heaviness of the truth.

"Oh, Jaxen, I'm so sorry."

"I had brothers and a sister, and we would wait for days for her to come back. Mostly we would run out of food by the third day. We were always so hungry." His grip on her hands became almost painful, but she didn't want to interrupt, so she endured it. "One day, of course, she didn't come back. For over a day-cycle we waited for her to return. She did not. So I offered myself into service at a pleasure house. In exchange for what I provided, they gave me food and a warm room. I was able to slip food to my brothers and sister, but they stopped coming after a year."

"Do you know what happened to them?" She couldn't help but interject with a question.

He shook his head. She did not see remorse or sadness in his face, simply acceptance. "I did what I had to do, so that I survived. I couldn't have done anything to help them. Don't forget that's what forget-me-not does, Lexana Farwan. That's what your mother helps to do."

She silently stared at him as she tried to think of what she should say in response to this terrible story. Jaxen had given her a peek into a world that she had never even considered. He was watching her closely. A smirk formed in the corners of his mouth. "Yet you'll go and find your mother anyway," he said.

She nodded, battling the discomfort of knowing how Jaxen viewed her mother. "She might have done terrible things, but she's my mother, and I love her despite them," she told him.

"In the same way that you're still here and you still want me, even after what I did to that guard," he said. He shook his head, his incomprehension clear.

"I want to believe that when I do something terrible, something unforgivable, that someone will love me anyway," she said simply.

He crushed her against him and kissed her. There was no tenderness, only the raw force of his desire. His urgent hands and bestial growl that was ripped from his throat drove any semblance of rationality from her mind. Near-frantic with her answering desire, she pulled his clothes from him, tearing off buttons when they would not immediately yield to her shaking fingers.

She brought her lips free of him for long enough to begin to ask if they should move from the chair, but he answered the question for her, simply pulling her onto him with a single minded certainty. Their union was furious and intense. Afterward, Lexa remained draped across him, the aftershocks of frantic desire and pleasure shortening her breath. Jaxen's hands were splayed across her back, his cheek against hers.

Eventually, they had to move. As she gathered her scattered clothes, Lexa felt transported back to the first time in Jaxen's room, gathering clothes which had been strewn about the room amid their passion. So much had happened since then. She hardly felt like the same person who had left the Enclave.

"So what do we do?" Jaxen asked as he examined one of the

buttons she had torn off.

"We need to get to Ketter," she repeated her earlier answer.

He grimaced. "By foot? We'll be noticeable."

"We could take one of the mail carriages," Lexa suggested.

He shook his head. "You're too recognisable. The daughter of Tanita Farwan will still be sought by the Kalabaths and their allies. Especially if they want to try to find your mother."

Lexa bit her lip. He was right. The information on the network of Farwan traders was too valuable to let go. Especially given how many people travelled between the Capital and Ketter, someone was bound to recognise her if they went there in any normal manner. "I have an idea," she said.

Kellen Falren had been friends with Lexa for as long as she could remember. For this reason, she knew her friend's weekly schedule by heart. On the Day of Sight, Kellen would go to the temple of Mawani in the jewellers' district and pray by herself. It was an area Kellen and Lexa often used to explore together, delighting in discovering the various jewellers for whom the district was named, as well as the other artisans who made and sold their beautiful wares amid the tiny streets. Before she had gone to the Academy, Lexa had harboured dreams of being a woman known for her discovery and patronage of many craftspeople, as women of great standing had done before her. As she and Jaxen wandered through the streets that she had spent years discovering with Kellen, Lexa felt a sadness for the naivety that had been lost when she had learned of her family's fall.

Jaxen, as ever, walked beside her, his face covered by a more comprehensive veil that conformed more closely to the lines of his face. It was more appropriate to the area and would draw less attention than the simple flap on either side of a hood, which he usually wore. He had put it on without any protest, but Lexa could not even begin to imagine how resentful he felt of the custom which required men to veil themselves. She could not believe she had never given the practice of veiling men a second thought before meeting him.

The sun gave the crooked bare trees and yellow-plastered buildings of the district a warmth that Lexa had always associated with the area. The familiarity and atmosphere of welcome was so at odds with the terror and uncertainty she felt.

The temple was halfway up the hill to the Lord Protector's residential area, where the landowning families kept residences. Lexa avoided looking toward the area where her family's home stood. She concentrated on finding Kellen and securing her friend's assistance, determined not to be waylaid by memories and regret. Besides, it was not her house anymore. Members of the Kalabath family would reside within its walls, now.

At the entrance to the temple, Lexa hesitated. She had never been particularly devout. Going into the temple was something Kellen had almost always done alone. Perhaps Kellen's faith in the goddess, prompting her frequent observance of religious practices, had given her family more fortune than Lexa's, despite the fact that the Farwans had been more wealthy and more powerful. She looked up at the magnificent structure. From her vantage at the entranceway, she couldn't see the white rounded dome. The façade seemed to touch the very sky itself, the pink-toned stone which had been brought from the Third Country for the temple's construction, glowing in the morning light. The building itself looked infused with a certain divinity. Then she dismissed her silly superstition and entered the temple. Jaxen silently went into the garden around the side of the building. Men were not permitted into temples on the Day of Sight. He would await her exit along with the other elui. The elui who had accompanied Kellen would be waiting there, too.

Globes of flickering lightning lined the interior of the temple, casting pure white light amidst the mellowed gold beams of morning sun streaming in through the windows. It felt like peace and agitation quietly fought for dominance in the vast space. As was the case whenever she entered one of Mawani's houses, Lexa took a deep breath, feeling almost as though she was underwater. She easily recognised Kellen's kneeling form. Her friend was a creature of habit in this observance, and she had often come to meet Kellen once her friend had finished her worship.

Lexa measured her steps as she approached Kellen, ensuring that she did not seem too hasty. She did not want to draw attention to herself. Somewhere a woman was singing. The sound was beautiful in the high-ceilinged space. She knelt beside her friend. "Do not react," she said quietly.

Of course, Kellen started violently. She glanced at Lexa, then returned her gaze to the meditative pattern in front of her. It was said that following the design to its completion induced a trance that brought the individual closer to Mawani.

Lexa observed Kellen's face out of the corner of her eye. She thought that in the time since she had last seen her friend, some of the youthful roundness had slipped from it. It seemed that adulthood was being forced upon them, either through the fact that they could not be forever protected from the events of the world, or simply through time.

"Lexa, what are you doing here?" Kellen whispered.

Some hysterical impulse made Lexa want to reply that she was in the temple in search of enlightenment, but she restrained herself.

"I need your help."

"When I heard about what happened to your family, Lexa, it was terrible. And then when Emi wrote that awful letter to you ... How are you here, Lexa?" Kellen started to turn to face Lexa but stopped. Lexa could see her friend's agony for her. It was quite moving. She had feared Kellen, like Emi, would disavow their friendship and call for guards immediately upon seeing her.

"Someone has helped me. I wouldn't be here without him."

"A man? You've been helped by a man?" Kellen's shock almost seemed to outstrip her upset at what had befallen the Farwan family.

"Yes. I can't explain now, but I trust him. Believe me, I can trust him," Lexa whispered urgently.

Kellen looked as though she wanted to say something but instead she bit her lip, her disagreement clear, if not unvoiced..

"Kellen, I need to get to Ketter. I need – we need -- your help to get there," Lexa said.

Kellen gently pinched the tip of her nose in thought. It was such a familiar gesture that it nearly brought Lexa to tears. "I'm sorry that I must come and ask you for a favour like this," she added.

Kellen lowered her hand to rest on top of one of Lexa's. "There is no need to apologise for requesting my help. Unlike Emi, I will do everything I can to help you," she said vehemently.

"Don't be angry with Emi. She did what she had to. She's a first daughter; her obligations require her to put aside what she would like," Lexa said. Kellen was the second daughter of her family. Sometimes it meant that she spouted a certain idealism that Lexa knew was unsustainable in practice, but it was one of the reasons she loved her so dearly.

"You're too kind, Lexa. She could have offered you her help. She should have offered you her help," Kellen said. It was clear she had made up her mind not to forgive Emi, and Lexa knew better than to push her friend.

"Can you help?" Lexa asked. She felt unbearably callous for her insistence on asking her friend, but Jaxen had told her to remain focused. She could not afford to remain in the jewellers' district any longer than was necessary.

Kellen thought for a moment, her eyes losing their focus as she contemplated. Finally, she nodded. "Be on the corner of fishermen's street and the plague lane tomorrow morning at the hour of trade. I'll have come up with something by then."

"Thank you. I cannot tell you—"

"Lexa," Kellen interrupted her, risking a direct look. "Are you certain you can trust whoever this man is?" Concern made her amber eyes wide.

"I'm certain."

SEVENTEEN

Lexa left the temple first, the whisper of her clothes loud in the high-roofed temple. She did not look back at her friend, who remained staring at the meditation pattern.

Lexa stood on the steps for a moment, waiting for her eyes to adjust to the harsh light. Her eyes watered and she brushed away the false tears. The beginnings of cramps curled around her hips. She hoped they would not be severe – the bleeding days she had endured so far on her travels had been mercifully gentle.

She went around to the garden where *elui* waited for their women. It was filled with tall trees and ornately carved wooden benches. The men were either occupying themselves with some task, or quietly conversing among themselves. All were veiled in the traditional demure charcoal blue, grey, or dark green. The garb made them all look disconcertingly similar.

"Jaxen?" she called.

Heads turned in her direction. Across the distance, it was impossible to know which among them was him. Nobody moved.

She took a step into the garden. The climbing vines that crawled along the side of the temple were in bloom. Huge violet kerrel flowers were intermittently spaced along the plant. The twelve-petalled blooms were Lexa's favourite. Yet she took no delight in the sight of them. Concern over Jaxen preoccupied her.

"Jaxen?" she called again, the uncertainty in her voice causing a stir among the men.

When still nobody moved, the cold edges of panic began to

work their way up her legs. Had he left? Worse, the possibility that he had been apprehended occurred to her. Perhaps they had been tracked or recognised. Truly panicked and with ever-increasing pain blossoming in her abdomen, she looked around, her movements wild with agitation. She feared that at any second, someone was going to grab her. Her breathing began to shorten. Sweat made her armpits clammy. She had come so far only to be thwarted now.

"Lexa." Jaxen's voice was a panacea for her fear. A veiled man strolled toward her from the direction of the temple entrance.

"Jaxen?"

Yet she need not have asked. She recognised that rolling gait, and as he drew closer, those grey eyes behind his veil.

"Where did you go?" She kept her voice low, mindful of the *elui* in the garden behind her.

"To buy some things." He gestured to the small bag he carried. She hadn't noticed it.

"You should have told me," she said, the last vestiges of her panic turning into the beginnings of anger and frustration. The discomfort curling around her pelvis was becoming almost unbearable, and it meant that her voice was even more clipped than she intended.

"It was a decision made in the moment," he replied, something defensive in his voice.

"What if I'd come out earlier?"

"Perhaps we shouldn't discuss this here." His eyes drifted beyond hers and to the *elui*. She glanced around and saw studiously uninterested heads. Yet the conversation which had been taking place as she first came to the garden was absent.

She walked off, uncaring if Jaxen was following her. She wanted to lie down as soon as possible. The bones of her fear were still there, rattling around inside her, and she said nothing to him as she made her way into the narrow, fetid streets of the undercity. She remembered the way to the inn where they had spent the previous two evenings. If they stayed in the city any longer, they would need to move again so that they would be harder to trace. As the thought occurred to her, she realised how much she had learned from Jaxen. If he had gone off to buy something, he probably had a very good reason. Yet she couldn't help but be angry with him for the fear he had caused her.

Only when they were inside their squalid room did she speak with him. "What did you buy?"

From the small cloth bag, he procured what she recognised as madras leaves. "I thought better you take the precaution."

That left her completely speechless. She had not expected him to think of such matters. She herself had not considered it, although she should have.

"You should take it now," he urged when she said nothing.

She nodded, taking the leaves from him.

"I'll get hot water," he said, when still she remained silent.

As she brewed the tea, the cramps redoubled their efforts to seemingly tear her apart from the inside. She wondered if she should abstain from taking the tea if it was a bleeding day. Through the pain, she asked Jaxen. If he knew about madras leaves, he likely knew about this.

He looked at her as she clenched her jaw against the pain. "You can still become with child, although it would be unlikely."

"Wonderful. Lucky me," she muttered. She took a sip of the beverage, willing the hot water to slip all the way down her and soothe the needling pains in her abdomen.

"Would you like some sweet-tea?" Jaxen offered, evidently seeing the discomfort on her face.

She shook her head. "I have an allergy."

"Let me see what I can do." The gentle Jaxen was back, understanding and empathy sunken into the lines of his face as he left.

Cradling the wooden mug, she sat in the chair and curled

her legs up. Sometimes the pain was lessened if she sat like that. After a few moments, she concluded that, unfortunately, this was not one of those times.

Jaxen returned with a heated clay brick wrapped in a blanket. He placed it tenderly on her abdomen. She gasped as the heat nearly seared her, then relaxed as the warm tendrils melted away the extremes of the pain. "Where did you even find a brick?" she asked, taking another sip of the tea.

He removed his veil to reveal a smile. "You'd be surprised how resourceful I can be."

She smiled back around the pain. "I know how resourceful you can be."

He perched on the edge of the bed, still rumpled from the previous evening. "What did your friend say?"

She sipped before she replied. "I need to go back and speak to her tomorrow."

He frowned. "Why?"

"She needs to organise things."

"She doesn't know where we're staying, does she?" His tone was suddenly sharp.

Now it was her turn to frown. "No. Why?"

He regarded her for a moment. "I think we've seen enough to establish that ours is a land where the ruthless thrive."

"She was incredibly angry at Emi for renouncing me. I really don't think that what you're insinuating is correct."

"Anger is very easy to feign," he countered.

"I've known her for as long as I can remember," she protested. "She would never do something like that."

"Your friend Emi did that," he pointed out.

She sat up straighter, then winced as her abdomen viciously protested. "I trust her, Jaxen," she snapped.

He allowed his disagreement to sit in plain sight on his face, but said nothing.

Regret at allowing her anger to drive her reply swirled

around her. "I'm sorry, I didn't mean to sound as though I don't trust your judgment. I do." She took another sip of tea to disguise her discomfort at apologising to a man. He had insinuated she was wrong, after all – something which ordinarily was unpardonable for a man to do to a woman. "But you need to trust my judgment. Kellen isn't like Emi. She's unusually loyal."

"Like you," Jaxen noted. It was obvious that he still doubted Kellen's loyalty, but he said nothing more.

"Thank you for the madras leaves," Lexa said, seeking to change the subject. "And the brick," she added. The warmth had done its job, and the pain was now only a dull growl.

He smiled, obviously seeing through her attempt to distract him. Yet he indulged her. "It's the least I could do. The women in the pleasure house would use bricks. They were cheaper than sweet-tea. I would curry favour with them by fetching heated bricks for them when their bleeding days came."

"Is that what you're doing with me – trying to curry favour?" she teased.

He came to stand in front of her and bent down to graze her forehead with a tender kiss. "I think we're a bit past that, don't you?"

She freed a hand from encircling her mug and caught one of his. She brought his fingers to her lips and kissed them, an unexpected rush of tenderness for him filling her. "Yes," she agreed.

They waited for Kellen at the appointed place and time the next day, Jaxen standing discreetly away from her. The hour of trade was the busiest across the city, the point of midmorning when businesses had been open for several hours, and people were rushing to complete their chores so that the afternoon could quietly fall into the evening. Lexa felt conspicuous, standing on the corner of the busy streets while everybody rushed around her. Her head snapped around as the tramp of feet signalled hired swords marching through the street. It could only mean that one family was making a claim on another. Once, the sound would only have evoked a mild curiosity within her, as she distractedly wondered which family was being assailed. Now, she wondered if those people who had come to the Farwan house in the Capital sounded like that as they approached. She wondered if they were the same people – the swords could be hired for any cause. They would fight against a family who had paid them previously without a second thought.

Her eyes connected with Jaxen's and she knew he was wondering if those swords were for her – if Kellen had betrayed her. The briefest flicker of doubt in her friend's loyalty flared within her as the steps came toward her. She watched, apprehension bringing the burning taste of bile to the roof of her mouth, as the swords drew ever closer. The crowd scrambled to get out of the way as the armed mercenaries walked down the street. They were dressed in well-worn clothes and openly carrying a variety of weapons, and menace streamed off them like some toxic vapour. The woman who led them had a smirk on her face that intensified the bitterness of the taste in Lexa's mouth. She looked as though she was enjoying the reactions they were getting. Fear kept Lexa motionless as the mercenaries approached, but they moved past her, and she released the breath she hadn't even realised she had been holding.

Kellen hurried toward her in the wake of the mercenaries, and warm relief coursed through her. Kellen wore the 'drab' clothing she and Lexa had worn to blend in on their excursions. Looking with eyes that had been trained by Jaxen's finely tuned instinct for survival, Lexa almost laughed at the naivety she and her friend had possessed. The cloth of Kellen's clothes was so fine that even without the ornate embroidery or deep colours normally worn by the powerful, it was clear that she was a wealthy woman. Lexa's clothes, purchased with Jaxen's approval, were truly the type that made her blend in with the poorer members of the city: ill-fitting and made from inferior cloth.

As she approached, Kellen's pace slowed, and Lexa fell into step beside her. They walked along the street as they had countless times through their youth. It was almost possible to forget they had not slipped into the past where their cares were so much lighter, so much more trivial. Almost.

"Why do you need to get to Ketter?" Kellen asked.

"I think my mother might be there."

Kellen inhaled sharply. "Tanita is still alive?"

"She sent a message to me after the Kalabaths took over. In a code that only she and I know."

Kellen was silent for a moment. They passed a pharmacist. The shutters were flung wide open, and an *elui* sat behind the extravagant display of vials and remedies on display. Passers-by could quickly buy something from the display, while more serious customers could enter the store and consult with the woman who ran the store. This was the style of most stores in the lower parts of the city. The places where the families of power normally shopped all had glass windows which shut out the rest of the world, but here among the middle section of the city, those who walked along the streets called to the people inside the shops, creating a tapestry woven from myriad fragments of conversation, the strands spun across the street and the interior of the shops. It was chaotic and loud and Lexa loved it, had always loved it.

"I assumed you wanted to get to Ketter to seek passage to the First or Second Country," Kellen said after they had moved on.

"The First Country? Only a few people are even permitted passage there."

"There are rumours that they occasionally permit foreigners to settle on their shores." Kellen paused ever so briefly to examine a tailor's display. A veiled man sat behind the blouses and veils, hunched over a piece of sewing.

"I didn't know that," Lexa said. "Anyway, it doesn't matter. I need to get to Ketter to find mother."

From the corner of her eye, Lexa saw her friend bring a hand to the tip of her nose in thought. "All right, I should be able to help you to get there. I can get a carriage to Ketter tomorrow."

"Kel, I can't tell you how much I appreciate it." Lexa's rush of gratitude brought tears to her eyes. She knew the risks Kellen would be taking to help her.

"You're my oldest friend. I'll do anything I can to help you."

By unspoken consensus, they paused at another tailor and inspected the garments. The quality of the cloth there was less fine than the previous one, but perhaps the stitching was better.

"Would you like to try something on?" A woman, rather than a man, sat behind the display. She appraised the friends with a dealer's eyes.

"No, thank you," Kellen said with a polite smile. They moved on.

"Where should we meet the carriage?" Lexa asked once she was certain they were out of earshot of the tailor.

"We?" In her surprise, Kellen stopped walking.

"Yes, me and Jaxen," Lexa said defensively.

"This man who's helped you." Kellen's disapproval and suspicion were etched across the set of her mouth, shaping the downward inflection of her words.

"He left the Academy to help me, he's risked his life countless times as we've travelled across the country. You should believe me when I say he would never hurt me."

Kellen pinched the tip of her nose again before she spoke. "You won't be dissuaded from bringing him?"

"No."

Kellen's heavy exhalation was so slight it was almost lost to the hubbub of the street. "I'll leave through the Gate of Sighs. Can you be there tomorrow at the same time as today?"

"Will it be safe? It's one of the main gates of the city."

"If I go another way, it's likely to attract more attention. Besides, it's so busy that nobody is likely to notice if one carriage stops to collect two people."

Kellen had a point. Even she, despite her innocent loyalty, had a nuanced appreciation for the subterfuge that was required to remain in power within the Fourth Country.

They reached a divide in the road. One path led into the undercity, the other up to the high city. Kellen did not hesitate, did not embrace Lexa. They both knew that such an act might draw attention given the differences in their garb. Those with power did not hug those without it. With only the most imperceptible of lingering glances, Kellen took the road to the right and began the climb up the hill. Lexa remained a moment longer and allowed Jaxen, who had been following them, to catch up to her.

She felt his presence by her side. Warm, solid, reassuring.

"Your friend will help?"

She nodded.

"And you're certain she is to be trusted?"

She pursed her lips in irritation. "Yes."

"Worse things have happened than one friend betraying another, you know." His hand brushed against her waist as they began to walk. She was acutely aware of the contact, craving more.

"And stranger things have happened than friends remaining loyal to one another."

EIGHTEEN

"Are you certain that you can trust her?" Jaxen once again asked her from beneath his veil.

"I trust her as much as I trust you," she told him above the bustling noise of the city as they stood on the street near the Gate of Sighs, waiting for her friend.

"Perhaps you trust me too much," he replied. She glanced at him, trying to understand what exactly he meant by the comment, but the deep shadow the veil threw across his eyes made it impossible to properly see even them.

"What do you mean?"

He shook his head. "It was a poor attempt at humour."

Before Lexa could reply, a carriage pulled up and Kellen's head appeared out of an opened window.

"Lexa," she called.

Kellen's hair was pulled back from her forehead, exposing the clear arch of her brow. The rest of her hair cascaded around her face. A series of small plaits interspersed throughout the tumbling blonde locks lent them an extra volume that made her look like she was surrounded by a halo of light. Her friend looked magnificent, and among the rattle of carriages and wagons, the holler of conversation, argument, and negotiation, she was a welcome sight.

They boarded the carriage quickly with hurried glances to ensure that nobody was paying them any heed.

The first thing Lexa noticed was that Kellen was dressed

with the intricate care befitting a daughter of a high house. Lexa felt threadbare by comparison, dressed plainly in the fashion of a servant. Indeed, she wore the ugly long vest that Jaxen had insisted she purchase on that first night away from the mountain. She was uncomfortably aware of the unflattering shape it gave her. Seeing Kellen so beautifully adorned in a vibrant mauve blouse made her ache for those luxuries. Coarse wool and cottons had scratched at her skin for so many day-cycles that she had ceased to notice their irritation. Now that she was looking at the delicate, soft material that clothed Kellen, it was as though she could feel every rough fibre chafing at her anew.

Kellen leaned across the space between them and took Lexa's hands. Her wide brown eyes searched Lexa's face. It was the first time that they had properly looked at one another in so very long.

"It's so good to see you." Kellen smiled, her attention fully focused on Lexa. "I feared the worst when nothing was heard of you."

"Thanks to Jaxen, I've been fine." Lexa squeezed Kellen's hands. She smiled at her friend's concern, and the warmth of knowing Jaxen had always been there to look after her.

"Jaxen." Kellen's smile was wiped from her face and she withdrew her hands and sat straighter, looking at Jaxen who had unveiled himself as soon as they entered the carriage. Kellen's eyes widened with shock and she averted her gaze to look to the left of Jaxen rather than at his bare face. A faint blush tinged her cheeks.

Lexa glanced uncertainly at Jaxen, irritated that he would so brazenly unveil himself in front of Kellen without so much as a word of warning or request. "I'm sorry to shock you, Kellen." She rushed to ease the discomfort that Jaxen had caused her friend. "Jaxen does not normally veil himself."

"It is perfectly fine, just unexpected." The stiffness behind Kellen's words belied her assurance.

Out of the corner of her eye, Lexa saw the smirk on Jaxen's face.

"My apologies, my lady." Jaxen's voice was that smooth melodious sound that Lexa knew he used when he was trying to enthral someone. "I should have been more courteous to your sensibilities."

Despite the sweetness to his tone, there was a sardonic twist to his smile that meant Kellen could interpret his words as being insincere. Lexa bit her lip in consternation at Jaxen's apparent unwillingness to defer to the norms of their society, the norms by which Lexa and Kellen had lived their entire lives. Fortunately, Kellen seemed to decide not to take issue with Jaxen and gave him a slight incline of the head that indicated she had accepted his apology. With that, Kellen turned her attention wholly on Lexa and appeared to forget that Jaxen was even in the carriage.

Lexa winced at her friend's treatment of Jaxen. There was a time when she would have behaved similarly. Indeed, to specifically acknowledge or speak to men in the presence of women was uncommon. Their place was to be seen and not spoken to unless it was a woman's wish that they do otherwise. But Jaxen was no ordinary man. As Kellen assaulted her with questions about how they had crossed the country, she wondered how she could make this point about Jaxen to her friend.

However, he looked unoffended and leaned comfortably back against the carriage's wall. The plushness of the cushions and throws piled into the interior made the space comfortable. Despite the fact that it was two very long days' ride from the Capital to the port town, Ketter, the luxurious carriage was a far more pleasant way to journey than any of the modes of transport that Lexa and Jaxen had used.

As they exited the city, Lexa felt herself slip into a familiar rhythm of conversation with Kellen. She occasionally glanced at Jaxen, but he seemed content to be ignored, regarding through half-closed eyes the two girls as they chattered. The light sphere in the carriage made the grey of his eyes almost colourless. She wondered how she must appear to him. Despite the fact that her hair was pulled back into a simple plait – done in fact, by him that morning – rather than the intricate arrangement of Kellen's hair, despite the difference in garb, there was an undeniable similarity between them that she could not help but notice as she spoke with her friend. Friendship with Kellen was a part of her life as a member of a powerful family. While he had not spoken of it overtly, Jaxen had clearly conveyed a certain disdain for the world from which she came. It made her self-conscious to realise how much she must remind him of her origin as she spoke with Kellen about what had occurred in her absence; who had done what, what power moves were being played where. She had never realised how much of the conversation with her friends had been consumed by the machinations of those who surrounded them, as well as their own games and plays for greater authority and power. Considering it from Jaxen's perspective, it seemed facile and distasteful.

"You may not have heard, but we'll be travelling along disputed land," Kellen said after many hours had rolled beneath the wheels of the carriage. The carriage moved at a far quicker speed than the little one-beast carts that Lexa and Jaxen had used. Even here was a reminder of the benefits offered by wealth and power.

"The Aranjay land is in dispute?" Lexa was surprised by that. The Aranjay family – the family of Serenah's former lover – were even more powerful than the Farwan family had been due to their ownership of land on which the road between the Capital and Ketter had been built. To attack them was a bold move indeed, especially given that much of their land was so close to the Capital and the Lord Protector's territory.

Kellen nodded, her lips pursed in disapproval. "The Jelreth family."

Lexa muttered several colourful curses, earning an approving chuckle from Jaxen and raised eyebrows from Kellen. Kaitlen came from the Jelreth family. Lexa could not suppress a sense of unease at the fact that Kaitlen's family, alongside Karra's family – the Rewin family – were closely allied with the Kalabath family who had stolen her lands. It seemed that the Kalabaths' success in claiming the Farwan fortunes had emboldened their allies. It explained the presence of the mercenaries who had so terrified Lexa in the Capital the previous day.

"Kaitlen was at the Academy with me," Lexa explained once she had mustered her emotions. "She was spying on me," she added.

Kellen turned a cool gaze to Jaxen, who nodded a confirmation. "It doesn't surprise me," she said after a moment of consideration. "They always were conspicuous in how recently their family ascended to power." She sniffed in disapproval.

Now it was Lexa's turn to chuckle. She, Kellen, and Emi came from families who had held onto their power for generations. The knowledge of the wealth and power into which they were born gave them a certain air of superiority over those whose fortunes were more recently acquired. Tanita had never done much to dispel that attitude within Lexa. However, she had cautioned her daughter to not assume that their position was guaranteed. That warning seemed eerily prophetic now. For perhaps the first time since she had made the decision to leave the Enclave, Lexa felt a true sense of urgency compelling her to find her mother. Perhaps being reunited with Kellen made her remember just how ruthless the families of power could be in securing their positions. She had always assumed that her family would be safely hidden until she found them, but she wondered if someone had tracked them down before her, if she would walk into an office that had been long-since ransacked, its walls stained with the blood of her mother, brothers, and her mother's *elui*, Lexa's father among them.

"There." Kellen drew her from her morbid reverie and pointed out the window. They were travelling across plains, and a storm front on the horizon blocked the sun, making the day dismal and grey. The storm spoke of fighting under conditions altered by the monks from the Enclave – on both sides, in fact. As they neared the battle, growls of thunder invaded the carriage, louder and louder until they were nearly deafening. Lexa leaned across Jaxen and peered out at the distant figures of men and women fighting in the name of the Aranjay or Jelreth families. She wondered how desperate someone must be to receive money to risk their life for someone else's gain. Especially given the fact that the mercenaries who hired themselves out would often take land for one family, and then take it off them for someone else. It seemed an almost pointless existence.

Gusts of wind buffeted the carriage as it came closer to the fighting, even though the mercenaries were some distance from the road. Both forces knew better than to interrupt the flow of trade unless it was the only way to secure victory, and that victory was worth incurring the ire of the other families. Silence descended upon the carriage, the attention of its occupants on the battle as they slowed behind a line of wary carts, carriages, and those unfortunate people who were walking. Lexa fancied she could make out the figures of two monks, far behind the ranks of fighters, each wielding the formidable power to contort the weather to their whim.

Hawkers rode alongside the laden vehicles, selling forget-me-not with the promise that it would dull the fear of being so close to the fighting. As she leaned away from the glass of the window, Lexa saw Jaxen's eyes tightened with anger. There was a time when she would have gladly taken the forget-me-not, letting it coil itself around her and lift the quaking within her inspired by the sight of the sleeting rain and hail bombarding the opposing forces.

"Why would anyone risk their life for someone else?" she asked.

She felt Jaxen shrug beside her. "When men fight they are

not required to veil. Perhaps that alongside the promise of coin is enough incentive."

Lexa shivered as she remembered the way the male voice in the forgetting den had been so coarse with menace and glee.

"If you aren't veiled, Jaxen, does that mean you're a fighter?" Kellen asked with exaggerated politeness.

"Perhaps. My lady, I'm curious – how is it that you are able to suddenly announce a trip to Ketter?" Jaxen's question came abruptly, perhaps a response to her earlier interrogation of him.

Kellen pointedly averted her gaze from his naked face. "Being the second daughter has its advantages. I told them that I'd heard of a shipment of Katan plates coming in and wished to see if I could buy some as a wedding present for our friend, Emi."

Hearing the Katan name spoken in relation to the fine porcelain from which Serenah's family once had made their fortune made Lexa feel as though her life were turning in on itself.

"Emi is marrying?" Lexa asked in surprise.

Kellen nodded with obvious reluctance. She had avoided mentioning Emi during the gossip they had exchanged, and Lexa knew it was deliberate. "One of my brothers."

"Her first *elui*," Lexa murmured. Despite her own terror at the prospect of taking her first *elui*, it was a significant step in the life of any young woman to take her first slave-husband. That she might never celebrate this occasion with her friend left her on the precipice of tears. She had already missed the announcement of Emi's betrothal. What else had she missed in her friends' lives, she wondered, and what else would she miss if she failed to find her mother and restore the Farwan family fortune?

Jaxen gave a slightly derisive cough. "Do you not remember which brother is marrying your friend?" he asked Kellen, the taste of hostility in his tone as unexpected as it was unsettling.

Kellen looked Jaxen directly in the eye. "Lexa may trust you, but I cannot see the benefit to a man such as yourself helping someone in Lexa's position. What do you stand to gain from aiding my friend?"

Jaxen's opened his mouth to reply, his lips curved upward, almost as though he were delighted to have the opportunity to open overt hostilities with Kellen.

Lexa interrupted the exchange of mistrust between her friend and lover with the first thought that came into her head, a comment which she directed at Jaxen. "The monks, they're fighting against each other." "Yes?" He turned to look at Lexa, very obviously snubbing Kellen.

"But isn't that a problem?"

"How?"

"Well, they're fighting against each other."

"When both families are wealthy enough to be able to afford the monks, whoever ends up going views their task as friendly competition. The one rule is that they are not allowed to try to kill each other. However inventive they may be in conjuring sleet or lightning, or in one very inventive instance that I've read of, an extraordinarily hot summer's day, to encumber, maim and kill enemy fighters, they may not touch one another. Besides," he added, sitting back and insolently arranging himself to be slightly more comfortable, "they are able to protect themselves."

With that answer, silence rolled around the carriage, and Lexa dared not break it for fear of eliciting a judgmental comment from Jaxen, or a declaration of war from Kellen. The silence grew heavier with every hour, and she took to glancing between the two. Kellen serenely read a book, while Jaxen appeared to doze, his arms folded across his chest and head tipped back against the carriage wall. Lexa distracted herself by calculating the speed of the carriage. She had travelled the route between the Capital and Ketter many times in her life. She knew the distances between each of the waymarkers; the barley farms, the cattle fields, the timber milling yard. As the carriage passed by each landmark, Lexa noted the time it had taken and adjusted her mental average of their speed, comparing it to the wagons they passed, or the riders who passed them, determining their speed in turn. It was a soothing enough task that she soon forgot her fear of the storms both inside and outside the carriage.

That night they stopped, as all travellers between the Capital and Ketter did, at the town of Sunruse. The town had grown almost exclusively to house those travelling between the Capital and Ketter. As a daughter of wealth, Kellen stayed in nothing but the finest accommodation. The carriage pulled in to one of the rest houses that Lexa had stayed at on several occasions. It boasted excellent food, soft beds, and a wash house to which water was carried by the owner's own *eluis* rather than fed directly by the hot springs, as in Fabriel.

Kellen strode imperiously from the carriage, Lexa and Jaxen, who had put his veil back on, trailing in her wake as would be expected of servants. Lexa wondered if someone might recognise her, but nobody looked at servants, and her appearance was so different to the picture of wealth and power that Kellen portrayed that nobody would ever even consider the possibility that she might be Lexa Farwan.

Normally, word would be sent ahead of a traveller like Kellen, and rooms would be prepared in advance, scented with crushed wildberries and well warmed by a long-burning fire. However, Kellen's abrupt departure from the Capital that morning meant there had been no time for that. Of course, that had been deliberate, to make it more difficult to track her and the two people she was helping reach Ketter. Nevertheless, the owner of the *Dancing Sunset* snapped orders to her *elui* as soon as Kellen crossed her threshold.

"I'm sorry to not to have given you adequate warning." Kellen gifted the woman with one of her most endearing smiles. She had always been the most beautiful out of her, Emi and Lexa.

Under such charm, the woman melted, waving away Kellen's apologies, taking the little cloak that Kellen had settled about her shoulders for the short walk between the carriage and front door, and offering her a warm drink, or cold drink, or food. Lexa watched with longing as her friend was fussed over, while Lexa was relegated to impersonating a servant who was barely noticed. She remembered when she had been fussed over like that because of her family's name

"Perhaps some refreshment sent to my room," Kellen said. "Jaxen will go there and unpack my things. Before I could possibly eat anything, though, I'd like a wash. My woman will assist me in bathing."

Lexa risked a glance at Jaxen and saw a dull gleam of resentment in his eyes at being ordered around by Kellen, but he nevertheless did as she bade, fetching Kellen's bags.

"Come." Kellen all but snapped the order at Lexa as they followed the owner to the wash house.

Unlike the inn in Fabriel, there was no steam in the *Dancing Sunset*'s wash house. Sunruse was not constructed on top of a hot spring. However, the room was heated thanks to a large fire that had obviously been burning for many hours. Its heat had spread across the tiny blue tiles that completely covered the room. A light sphere was placed in each corner, the captive lightning storm in each globe flickering at its own pace and rhythm.

Kellen undressed with little bashfulness. Like any woman of power, she was accustomed to being assisted in the process of bathing. She allowed her garments to fall on the floor with a soft thud.

"Would you mind braiding my hair?" she asked Lexa casually.

Lexa obliged, her hands almost thoughtlessly separating her friend's golden locks into three parts, her fingers gently brushing against the curious texture of the tiny plaits interspersed throughout her friend's hair. Within a few breaths the braid was complete and secured with a piece of cord.

Kellen murmured a word of thanks and stepped into the elevated tub of steaming water in the middle of the room. Lexa took one of the buckets of water by the door and poured it into the tub. Kellen reclined, the enjoyment of the warm water against her skin obvious on her face. Then she sat up and looked at Lexa, a serious expression on her face. "I wanted to speak to you away from that man," she said softly, her words reverberating around the room.

"Who, Jaxen?" Lexa asked.

Kellen nodded.

"Why?" Lexa looked at her friend in bemusement.

Kellen splashed some of the water onto her upper arm and ran a thoughtful hand along the water's path. "You and he are lovers?" There was a measure of wariness in her tone that Lexa had never heard before.

"Yes," she admitted.

"That complicates things," Kellen said. "He was one of the teachers at the Academy, yes?"

Lexa nodded, absentmindedly handing Kellen soap.

"I've heard rumours about the Academy. People don't often speak of it, but it is said that the best way to find out someone's secrets is to go to the Academy with them." Kellen soaped herself with efficient circular motions, working the soap into a lather.

"That may be because they get to know one another," Lexa protested, thinking of Serenah's romance with Kirrith.

Kellen shook her head in an agitated motion. "It's more than that, Lexa. Mother didn't want Yaellen to go because of it." Yaellen was Kellen's older sister, heir to her family's fortune.

Lexa retrieved one of the folded yellow towels and returned to the tub. "This sounds paranoid, Kel," she said.

"No. Something at the Academy seems to be in the business of discovering secrets." Kellen leaned forward and took Lexa's hands in her own. Water dripped onto the blue tiles of the floor, but Kellen didn't seem to pay it any heed. Her gaze implored

Lexa to listen to her. "How much do you really know about this Jaxen?"

"I know enough to know that he's earned my trust," Lexa said, heat that might turn into anger filling her.

Kellen sighed. "Have you fallen in love with him, Lexa? You always were the most sentimental of us."

Lexa's face burned with embarrassment. Love for a man was rarely spoken of so openly. It was a shameful thing to fall in love with a man, to be beholden to him by that love. "It doesn't matter if I love him. It matters that I trust him," she retorted. She almost told Kellen that Jaxen had even killed someone to help her, but she could not see her friend taking that knowledge well.

Kellen relented and released Lexa's hands. She rose from the water and took the towel to dry herself. "Are you certain that you aren't confusing how you feel for him with certainty?"

"Yes," Lexa's irritation with this line of questioning was obvious, even in the single syllable. "Please, do not ask me of whether or not I trust Jaxen again."

"I did not mean to upset you, Lexa. I worry for you as your friend," she said. Despite the coolness of her voice, her eyes were warm and imploring.

Lexa let go of her anger. She had never been one for grudges. "I'm sorry for snapping. I know you only have my welfare at heart."

Kellen hugged Lexa. The comfort of her friend's embrace was enough to make Lexa easily forgive Kellen her suspicion. After all, she did not know Jaxen like Lexa did.

NINETEEN

Lexa and Jaxen slept apart that evening. It was the longest time they had spent separated in the many day-cycles since they had left the mountain. Lexa had not realised how accustomed she had grown to sharing a bed with Jaxen until she was in the dormitory for female servants on a mat by herself. There was a certain comfort to his presence by her side.

The next morning, before Lexa could confer with Jaxen, Kellen summoned her to assist with her hair. Normally, a male servant would help with such a task, but occasionally female servants would manage their employer's hair. Kellen stood in her room, dressed today in a vibrant green shirt and grey pants. Even with her hair down, she looked every bit the life that Lexa had lost. Once more, she felt a pang of grief whisper through her.

"I'm sorry you had to sleep in the dormitory," Kellen began as soon as Lexa entered the room.

Lexa waved the apology away. "I understand. It would have been very odd for you to have given me and Jaxen rooms."

At the mention of Jaxen's name, Kellen's lips pursed slightly, but she did not say anything.

"Have you eaten? I ordered extra in case," Kellen said, instead of making whatever comment about Jaxen that Lexa was certain had passed through her mind.

Lexa nodded. The bread and jam she and the other female servants had been given had been adequate, but it was a poor meal in comparison to the bowl of gently steaming porridge, or the plate of tiny poached eggs in sauce – one of Lexa's favourites. She hadn't consumed food like this since the Academy and her mouth watered at the prospect of once more eating food she had taken for granted for nearly her entire life. She did not need to be asked twice.

The creaminess of the leatip eggs – a bird so small that two could easily fit in her cupped hand – nearly left her breathless. After the barren meals that she had eaten over the previous day-cycles, it seemed outrageously decadent that anything so rich and subtle in its taste could exist. Lexa closed her eyes as she ate, savouring the flavours as they rolled down the back of her tongue. "Mawani only knows how much I've missed this," she confessed to Kellen once she had devoured the plate of eggs.

Kellen smiled at her friend, the warmth reaching her eyes. "I'm so sorry that you've had to go through all of this."

Lexa looked down at her scuffed shoes rather than her friend. A part of her was overwhelmed by shame at what had befallen her family and the fact that she required Kellen's help. Another part of her was sad for the life she had lost and feared she might never regain. "I should do your hair," she said eventually, stepping across the space between them.

Kellen sat and allowed Lexa to begin sorting through her blonde tresses, brushing out any snarls or knots

"Thank you for your help," Lexa said as she worked.

"Of course. You're my oldest friend. What else was I supposed to do?"

"You could have said no. It's dangerous for you and your family if you're caught helping me," Lexa replied, her fingers crooked as she made a tiny braid in Kellen's hair.

"And? Would you not do the same for me?"

Lexa's fingers continued their work even as she considered the question. After everything that she had been through there was little question in her mind that she would help if Kellen or Emi were to come to her like she had to Kellen. But before her family had been overthrown, she did not know if she would have been so ready to risk her position. "Of course I would," she said evenly, wondering if she was lying, even to herself.

Kellen's hair was quickly completed. With the proliferation of tiny braids woven throughout her free-falling locks, she looked somehow more complete, more imposing; every bit the woman of wealth that she was. Lexa caught a glimpse of herself in the mirror Kellen held up to examine her appearance, and wondered who the plain girl with the huge, dark eyes was. The beige and brown of her clothes was so drab in comparison to the beautiful bright green of Kellen's shirt. She missed wearing beautiful things and allowing her hair to fall freely about her face, but freefalling hair was for women of wealth, as were clothes of fine fabrics dyed in vibrant colours.

"You look as beautiful as ever," Lexa declared, swallowing her self-pity.

Kellen smiled at the compliment, her whole face lighting up. Then the smile quickly vanished and she took Lexa's hands in hers. Her eyes became sharp and focused, and anybody who might have thought she was a beautiful face would have been forced to reconsider. "Lexa, I know you do not want me to speak of it, but I cannot say nothing. Please be wary of Jaxen. I know that you trust him, and I'm sure that he has protected you, but he unveils himself in the company of women he does not know.

"Men who do not understand their place in our world are dangerous. They'll do anything for more freedom, more power. They're like a rabid animal. You must be careful." Fear made its way across Kellen's face as she spoke and the grip of her slim, white fingers around Lexa's hands was unexpectedly strong.

Lexa gently extricated her hands and pulled Kellen into an embrace. "I understand your concern. I am so fortunate to be gifted by Mawani with a friend such as you. I promise there is nothing to fear from Jaxen, though."

Kellen pulled back from Lexa and undid the buttons at the

side of her delicate top, pulling out a sheathed dagger that had been made so that it fitted flat to her side. "Here. Take this." She shoved the thin blade into Lexa's hands.

"Kellen!" Lexa was shocked at the fact that her friend carried a weapon, let alone wanted her to have one.

"I always have at least one knife on me. You never know when you might need it. It should fit easily under your vest. Just take it, and I know you'll at least have some way of defending yourself." Kellen's jaw was set; an unusually hard expression across her face.

"I hardly think I'm going to need this."

"Promise me you'll take it and be careful, Lexa." Kellen was all but begging.

"I promise," Lexa said, strapping the sheathed dagger to her side, more to assuage her friend's concern than anything else.

As the carriage rolled along the road to Ketter, Lexa realised with a guilty start that Jaxen had not enjoyed the same delicate breakfast that she had. Curled in a corner of the carriage, she watched him as he looked out the window at the land they passed. The hours should have been long, filled as they were with the same awkward silence that had descended upon the carriage the previous day, but Lexa found the time passed unnoticed as she observed Kellen and Jaxen and weighed their suspicions of each other against what she knew of them. Jaxen had grown up not trusting anybody he did not himself know, surrounded by people whose money compelled him to do as they pleased. Kellen had grown up being taught that even those she did know could betray her. Despite this, they were curiously similar, although she knew better than to voice that thought aloud.

Kellen read, the picture of absorbed serenity, but Lexa knew her friend better than that. She could see the tension in Kellen's shoulders and the clench of her jaw, in the same way that she could see the restless alertness in Jaxen despite his slumped pose. Had the price of betrayal not been so high, the mistrust of each other over her safety would have been almost comical.

They reached Ketter as the sun was setting. The clear early-winter sky gave them a stunning sight as they approached the port. Reds and oranges swirled magnificently together, mirrored in the waves that rolled in from the open sea. The sight of the red-tipped ocean was cut off as the carriage rounded a bend and entered the outskirts of the city, rumbling along the cobblestones with juddering efficiency. Kellen reached behind her and rapped sharply three times on the wall of the carriage. They pulled to a halt on the roadside.

"Here should be the easiest for you to make your way from," she told Lexa.

Lexa leaned across the space of the carriage to grip Kellen's hands. "Thank you for your help, Kel. You are a true friend."

It shocked her to see Kellen's eyes bright with tears. She was normally so composed. "We will see each other again," Lexa promised.

"Of course we will," Kellen replied, but her voice lacked conviction.

Lexa awkwardly hugged her friend then scrambled from the carriage. She turned to ask Jaxen where they should go, but he was in quiet conference with Kellen. The exchange lasted far longer than Lexa would have expected, before Jaxen gave a nod and exited the carriage, his hands at his face to ensure his veil was securely fastened. He wore a style of veil that looked almost like he had draped a blanket over his head. It was the style traditionally worn by men local to Ketter and its surrounding region.

"What were you talking about?" she asked, her curiosity piqued given Kellen's blatant mistrust of him.

The carriage pulled away with a rattle that made it impossible for him to say anything for a moment. The sound of the wheels on the cobblestones bounced off the buildings, even after the carriage was gone.

"Oh you know, she was threatening to harm me if I betrayed you," he said, amusement in his voice, presumably mirrored by the expression behind his veil.

"I'm sorry about that," Lexa said abashedly. "She means well. I think she's just overprotective given—"

Jaxen cut her off with a wave. "She's a good friend. People could do with more friends like her." There was a certain bitterness to his tone that left her curious as to what he meant by it, but this was not the time nor the place to pursue such questions.

"Come on." Jaxen set off in the direction that Kellen's carriage had taken, leaving behind him more questions about what exactly his comment meant. Lexa followed in his wake, taking in the experience of walking through Ketter's streets at night. Normally she had come in by carriage, conducted the necessary business, and left, only walking the streets when necessity dictated. Ketter was definitely not a beautiful city. Everything seemed to be built with purpose rather than form in mind. It was a grimier city than the Capital. The tall timber buildings crowded in on one another. Such invasiveness was probably due to the absence of any real houses of power locating themselves in the city. If the Capital was a place of industry, trade, and luxury, then Ketter was a town purely built to bring in or send off goods. Up on the bluffs there were a few beautiful houses, built by the few families whose trade interests meant that they came here often enough to want comforts of their own home, but the houses were at least twenty minutes' travel by carriage from even the outskirts of the city.

The walk was not particularly pleasant. As the tendrils of night began to softly hug the world, the cold of the day began to make itself known even more pointedly. Despite the cloak she wore – an ugly but effective garment – Lexa felt the tip of her nose begin to grow cold. It seemed inconceivable that it had been only the beginning of autumn when she had been driven to the Academy. Now, with winter encompassing the land, here she was walking on the street like a pauper, and had traversed half the country by foot, too.

Lexa followed Jaxen, trusting the knowledge that had gotten them through the rest of their journey safely to bring them once more to somewhere warm and safe, if not as luxurious as the *Dancing Sunset*. Eventually, the streets became more crowded. Most of those who were out were women coming home from work, chatting cheerfully with one another as they ambled along. The wider streets did have some appeal to them, although it was obvious that the blue or green paint which covered most of the buildings' facades was an afterthought to the oblong structures. Every so often, a huge sphere of captured lightning was placed inside a container high atop a pole, illuminating the street. The shadows of every person walking the street jumped around, giving a vaguely chaotic look to the street, but Lexa was glad for the light. Wandering around narrow alleys and backroads had not left her feeling particularly safe at all. For the briefest of moments, she had wondered to where exactly Jaxen was leading her and whether Kellen had somehow seen something in him that she had missed. Under the illumination of the light spheres, though, she felt ashamed for her lack of faith in Jaxen.

It took another ten minutes of reasonably fast walking to reach the dock area. The smell of brine, fish, and the sharp undertow of rot became stronger the closer they got. The creak of boats competed with the slap of waves and sound of voices calling to one another from afar. There was a familiarity to it all that left Lexa feeling disjointed. Normally when she heard such noises and smelled that salt-rot of the sea, she was stepping out of a carriage and being treated with deference and respect.

Jaxen turned off just before the docks and paused at an inn named the *Whale's Teat*. Lexa raised an eyebrow at the somewhat bawdy cartoon drawn on its shingle, then followed Jaxen inside.

She had never been in a less reputable establishment. She saw several men wearing veils so meagre they might as well have been absent, women who looked as though they would cheerfully stab anyone who approached them in the wrong manner, and at least one bloodstain on the floor. Jaxen walked confidently to a poorly upholstered booth, one of a line along one wall. After contemplating the unpalatable seat, Lexa slid opposite him with extreme reluctance. He leaned over the table to talk to her. There was one light sphere behind the bar. Everything else in the room was lit by the fireplace or candlelight, further adding to the inn's dingy atmosphere.

"I think this is my least favourite of the places we've been," she said.

She couldn't hear his soft laugh, but she could see it in the way his shoulders shook and his eyes crinkled. "We should eat," he said once he had recovered himself.

She gave him a look that she hoped perfectly conveyed her belief that any food that the kitchen of the *Whale's Teat* could offer might kill them, causing his shoulders to shake with laughter once more. When he resumed looking at her, she sighed and signalled to the man who was circling the room, clearing up dirty dishes, taking orders, or suffering several suggestive remarks.

Once she had ordered – the daily special, whatever that was – she watched as the server was slapped on the behind by a female patron to the uproarious laughter of her friends.

"Poor man," she murmured.

She realised Jaxen was watching her intently from the other side of the table. "But isn't it the lot of men to serve?" he asked, the question an uncomfortably pointed one.

"That doesn't mean that they should be treated like that." Lexa gestured to the leer that was being aimed at the server. "Nobody should be treated like that."

"Yet he's paraded around in clothing that clings to his figure to get a bit more coin from the patrons of this place."

The disgust in his voice made her look at him in frustration. "What do you want me to do?" she snapped.

He reached across the space between them and took her hand. His fingers gently kneaded her palm. They were delightfully warm, especially after the cold of the outside. "Nothing. The only thing anyone can do is look out for themselves. You know me, Lexa; I've told you before that I'll do anything to make sure I have my freedom."

There was a curious tenor to his voice. "Kellen didn't upset you too badly, did she?"

He shook his head. "She was just looking out for you."

She remained with her hand in his until their food came. Then, she withdrew it back to her side of the booth. The candle that flickered near them did not offer enough light to properly see what she was eating, something for which she suspected she should be quite grateful. The meal was so far from the delicate food she had consumed that morning in Kellen's room that it was almost laughable. She might have called it some form of pie, if she were being particularly generous. She could only get halfway through before she pushed the bowl away. Jaxen was cheerfully eating, rhythmically lifting mouthfuls underneath his veil. She noted the impediment of his veil, reflecting on his earlier inference that it was not right for men to be veiled and kept in the service of women. Certainly, she would never want to don any form of veil, especially not one that made a simple task such as eating so difficult.

Jaxen pushed his empty plate away and returned his focus to Lexa. "So, tomorrow morning we head to the crate manufacturers?"

She nodded. "I think it's a little away from the docks, near the packing area."

"You do know we could be walking into a trap?"

She nodded again. "I have to know, Jaxen. I have to at least try and find my mother."

"And if you don't?"

In honesty, she had barely considered such a possibility. But he was right to ask.

"I don't know," she admitted.

If he thought that was a poor response, he didn't say.

"And what about you once this is done, if my mother and brothers are there. What will you do?" she asked.

"I might board a ship. I think I could easily get passage to the Second Country. There are some vessels that go even beyond the Godskissed Continent; I'm sure I could get onto one of them, too." He sounded carefree, entirely unworried by the uncertainty of his future.

"You could stay, too," Lexa suggested hesitantly.

She could see just enough to notice him raising an eyebrow. "Stay?"

"Yes. With me." It felt so ridiculous that she was making such an offer to him in the middle of an establishment as disreputable as the *Whale's Teat*, but she wasn't certain when she would find the courage to ask again.

"And what would I be to you if I stay?" His voice was soft against the raucous din only a few spans away but she heard every word. There was a weight behind his words that made them easily carry across the distance which separated them.

"I don't know," she admitted. "But I know that I'd like you by my side." She reached across to take his hands.

"As your equal?" He let her hold his hand but did not return the pressure of her fingertips.

"As close to it as possible," she said. "I don't want you to get on a ship and never see you again."

Because she was looking into his eyes, she thought she saw a flash of something she could only call anger pass through them, but she couldn't know exactly what it was without seeing the rest of his face. Despite the fact that he then squeezed her fingers gently and suggested that they take a room in a tone that clearly indicated what he had in mind, Lexa couldn't help but feel she had said the wrong thing.

TWENTY

Lexa had expected the building which matched the address on the warehouse crates to look more as though it contained the secret cargo of her family, but it looked like the rest of the buildings that surrounded it: plain, worn-down, and built for a purpose rather than to look enticing.

The early-morning sun struggled against the clouds, losing the battle to break through the thick greyness that enveloped the sky. Lexa shivered and drew her cloak more tightly around her. As she did, her hand brushed the sheath of the knife Kellen had given her only the previous morning. She had heeded her friend's request and wore it. It fitted so snugly against her side that she almost couldn't feel it. When she had fastened it under her tunic that morning, she had not told Jaxen of the knife. His acrimony with Kellen was so prescient in her mind that she did not wish to bring up anything related to her friend, especially not something that so clearly spoke of Kellen's distrust of Jaxen.

As they walked along the chilly street, she wondered if her assumption that she could stroll in and be shown to her mother was wrong. Certainly, she had no prowess with a blade of any description. Such work had always been best left to the people who were paid to protect her. Or Jaxen. The brutal efficiency with which he had dispatched the guard at the warehouse in the Capital flitted through her mind. She wondered if she would see that side of Jaxen again. She had almost managed to forget what he had done.

She glanced at him. He still wore the local style of veil. A corner flapped in a breeze that rolled in off the bay and up the streets.

"Is that man following us?" Lexa asked, keeping her voice low amid the bustle of the street. Kellen's dagger against her side seemed to pulse as she contemplated the prospect that they were being followed. Now that they were so close, she couldn't stop herself from seeing assailants everywhere.

"Who?" Jaxen turned to look at the direction Lexa indicated with a slight nod of her head. He scrutinised the veiled man who was buying a bag of roasted nuts from a food cart that was almost certainly illegal.

"I don't think so," he said eventually.

"Perhaps I'm being paranoid, but I think a man with a veil of a similar colour left the Whale's Teat at the same time as us." She resisted the urge to reach under her tunic and check to see if she could pull out the knife with ease. This impulse to violence in the face of fear was why she wanted nothing to do with knives, either when Jaxen had procured one in the Capital, and why she had not wanted to take Kellen's knife.

Jaxen scratched his cheek through the fabric of his veil. "Perhaps. I wasn't really looking."

"It's hard to know. Veils make men seem terribly similar."

Rather than reply, Jaxen strode across the street in a gap between carriages. Lexa cast one last glance at the man who was devouring the nuts with apparent focus, and followed Jaxen. She almost lost sight of him amid a flurry of carriages that prevented her from crossing immediately, but when she reached the other side of the road, he was waiting for her.

"Are you ready?" he asked.

She glanced up at the building and ascended the small staircase before any of her doubts had time to crowd in on her.

The front office was lit by a light sphere that dispelled the gloom of the sunless morning. The lightning danced across the face of a woman sitting behind a desk. She was apparently focused entirely on the ledger in front of her. Her nose came to a sharp point, giving her a somewhat angular appearance, emphasised by the way her hair was tied back into a tight knot at the nape of her neck. At their entrance, she looked up.

"May I help you?"

Lexa found herself at a loss for words. She had not considered that she would go unrecognised. In her mind, all she had been required to do was go to the location indicated by her mother.

"Are you seeking something for your employer perhaps?" the woman offered. Her mouth puckered in apparent irritation at the interruption.

"Do you know what the secret to success is?" Lexa stammered out the first half of the Farwan motto. The woman did not answer but inclined her head with a birdlike curiosity.

"It's quality," Lexa finished, somewhat lamely.

"Would you like to see the workshop?" the woman asked. She did not wait for a response, but stood up, straightened her billowing skirt, and opened a door behind her.

Lexa cautiously walked past her and into the workshop, Jaxen following close behind. The door slammed shut behind them, trapping them in a room filled with sharp tools wielded by a number of individuals staring at them with distinctly unfriendly expressions.

"What did you do?" Jaxen breathed the question into her ear. He put an arm protectively around her as they stared at the craftspeople sizing them up.

"Mother always said that I could find my way into any Farwan trade house by asking them that question," she whispered back.

"Yes, but Lexa, what if this isn't a Farwan trading house?" Jaxen asked.

"Then we might be in trouble," she told him, her eyes not

leaving the silent craftspeople. Her hand crept to the hem of her tunic. She even had managed to get her hand to the handle of the knife, but she could only grasp it for comfort. Even she knew they were far too outnumbered for her lacklustre skills with a knife to be of any use.

For several seconds, everybody was completely still. Then one of the women put down the chisel she was holding and walked up to them, her steps cautious. Her copper-black locks were tied back tightly against her skill. "Lexa?" she said in a tone of wonder.

"Mother?" Lexa asked incredulously. She recognised her mother's voice, but not this diminutive, dirty woman in front of her.

Suddenly, she was caught up in a fierce embrace. She didn't remember her mother being the same height as her. "I thought you were dead," Tanita whispered, clutching her daughter even closer.

When she finally released Lexa, tears were conspicuously making their way down Tanita's face. That was almost more shocking than anything she had endured to get here. Lexa had never seen her mother even close to tears. The sight of her mother crying brought tears to her own eyes.

"And you found us." Tanita smiled and wiped her tears away with the back of her hand. "What's left of us," she added, the smile fading.

"Beji and Ket?" Lexa asked.

"Your brothers are here."

"And father?"

At the expression on her mother's face, Lexa felt her insides freeze. Despite her fear, she had clung to the idea that Tanita would have saved him, too. Tanita shook her head sadly. "I'm so sorry, Lexa. Our carriage was ambushed and I ran with your brothers. I saw him taken by a Kalabath woman. If I'd done anything to try to help him, I likely would have been killed, and your brothers with me. I had to leave him so that we could escape." A fresh sheen of tears entered her eyes. This was not the Tanita that Lexa had grown up terrified of, and terrified of failing to live up to.

"Mother..." Lexa said helplessly. "You can't be held responsible."

Her grief at the news that her father was dead hovered on the edge of her perception. It was almost worse knowing that she would be struck by its force at some later time than succumbing to it immediately. The prospect of her mother frantically running away from an ambush and leaving her first *elui* to die alone, Lexa's brothers scrambling by her side, was almost as horrible as the knowledge that she would never again see her father.

Tanita shook her head, some of her old composure returning to her. "Who is this with you?'" she asked, her gaze moving past Lexa to Jaxen.

"This is Jaxen. Without his help I never could have found you." Lexa stepped aside so Jaxen could more directly address her mother.

"It seems you have my gratitude for bringing my daughter to me safely." Tanita held out her hand to Jaxen – a gesture that normally was never offered to any but the most highborn of men. He stared at her proffered hand for a moment, then took it.

"I'm afraid if you did this for any kind of reward, I have very little to offer you," Tanita continued. Her gaze hardened as she met Jaxen's eyes behind his veil. Lexa knew that appraising gaze well. It reassured her to see that the woman she remembered as her mother was not gone.

Jaxen removed his veil with a quick movement, revealing a pleasant smile. While Lexa heard one or two gasps of surprise from the workers, Tanita did not seem to be perturbed by a man unveiling himself in the presence of strangers. She looked at Jaxen without her gaze wavering in the slightest.

"I only did it to help Lexa," Jaxen said.

Tanita's expression hardened into something far less friendly. "Where did you meet my daughter?"

"At the Academy," he replied. "I was one of Lexa's teachers, but then she got into trouble and I wanted to help."

"Why?" Tanita's voice now became sharp, almost rude.

"Mother, he protected my life more than once. You don't need to be suspicious of him." Lexa could not stay silent at the tone her mother was taking with the man who had been by her side as she made her way here. She could feel the eyes of everybody in the room on her, watching the exchange. Now that she looked properly, she could see two of her mother's *elui* among them, tools held at readiness. The clear willingness to commit violence unnerved her. She wondered what exactly her family had gone through to remain safe here.

"Not being sufficiently suspicious of people was what practically handed our land over to the Kalabath family and their allies," Tanita retorted. She had not taken her eyes from Jaxen, and the expression on her face was the one that might be used when regarding a potentially deadly animal.

"Mother, he delivered me here safely," Lexa said, frustration at her mother's paranoid interrogation of Jaxen's motives beginning to boil over.

"Or he's just delivered us all," Tanita retorted, suspicion tightening her features, making her eyes glitter.

"He's been more honest with me than you have. I found the forget-me-not." Lexa's accusation rang through the workshop, leaving in its wake a particularly startled stillness.

Tanita turned her head very slowly to regard her daughter. Suddenly she was the fearsome woman that Lexa had known her whole life, and the whole force of her personality was now being directed entirely at Lexa. "And?"

"How could you have turned our family into drug pedlars?" Lexa asked. Her voice slid from the accusatory tone into more of a dismayed whimper. She regretted that she had ever tried to stand up to her mother. She should have enjoyed being in her mother's presence after everything through which she had gone. But she could not allow Tanita to be so rude to Jaxen, after everything that he had done for her, and especially not with everything that she felt for him.

"Because it's what I needed to do to ensure that we were strong, Lexa. Importing forget-me-not gave us enough capital to make the Farwan traders the richest in the Fourth Country."

"So what happened?" Jaxen interjected. Lexa glanced at him. There was something almost sadistic about his smirk.

"What indeed." Tanita's head swung back to Jaxen. "Someone took me by surprise. But they don't know all my tricks." The ghost of a smile twisted her lips upwards for the briefest of moments. It was not a pleasant smile, either.

Lexa opened her mouth to ask her mother what exactly she was talking about when Jaxen pulled her closer to him and she felt the kiss of a cold metal edge on her throat.

"How did you know?" Jaxen asked her mother. It didn't sound like his voice. It sounded harder, more businesslike than she had ever heard before. She was still trying to understand what was happening, even as she knew that the metal against her neck was the same blade that Jaxen had used to slit the throat of the guard in the Capital. The room seemed to shift sideways. Lexa stayed completely still, terrified that moving may slice open her throat. Fire and ice coursed through her in those moments, and she felt this couldn't possibly be happening.

Jaxen held her against his chest like a shield against the force of Tanita's stare. "Jaxen, what are you doing?" Lexa whispered, feeling her throat ride the wickedly sharp edge of the blade with every word.

"He's been spying on you," Tanita said. Even though she answered her daughter's question, her eyes never left Jaxen's face.

"No." The denial sprang from her lips before she could stop

herself.

"I'm sorry," Jaxen said. His left arm was curled around her to stop her from leaving, almost like the way he had held her when they'd lain in bed together just that morning. He almost sounded sorry, too.

"Why?" Lexa wondered if she should be crying. Her eyes were completely dry, she was utterly still. Instead of betrayal or despair, she felt none of what was going on around her could be possibly real.

"Selling you to the Rewin family will give me enough money for passage away from here and a comfortable life wherever I go."

"Karra's family? But Kaitlen—"

"Was never spying on you. Her family's task was always to get your land. Karra's was to get the information on the Farwan traders. She found nothing when she searched your room."

"But, what happened between us..." She felt a prickle of self-consciousness that her exchange with him was being witnessed by a room full of people. But it was overridden by her desire to make sense of this mistake.

Jaxen's soft laugh held no malice. Somehow that made it sting even more. "I'm the master of seduction, Lexa. I've seduced so many of the Academy's students and sold their secrets that I've lost count."

"But Karra tried to seduce you," Lexa protested.

"She was in my room pushing me to hurry up and get what I could out of you. I must say, it was harder than I imagined. Although it wasn't hard for you to refrain from telling me anything of worth, given your mother trusted you with nothing of importance."

"He's buying time until the Rewin family comes to take us," Tanita said. She looked remarkably calm given that Jaxen had a knife to her daughter's throat.

The warmth of Jaxen's body against Lexa's back was so familiar, so intimate, that he could have been holding her in an embrace of tenderness. The sensation of the knife pushing against her throat was the only thing that felt wrong. "I was right. There was someone following us," she whispered.

"The Rewins will kill us when they come," Tanita said. She did not sound particularly scared.

"Your family has killed people, this is no different." Jaxen sounded so indifferent.

"Jaxen." Lexa breathed his name but was completely lost for what else she should say to this stranger who held her close. Each breath felt like shards of ice being driven through her body.

"I told you I'll do everything I must to remain free," Jaxen said, pulling her a little closer to him. The false intimacy of being so held like that, so close to him broke her heart.

Lexa looked at her mother's face and saw resignation written there. She squeezed her eyes closed as she realised that she had led those who would extract the secrets in Tanita's head right to her. She felt a burning shame wash over her as she realised just how foolish she had been. She should have been suspicious of Jaxen from the very beginning. Surely there was some way that she could fix this. But no matter what solution she conjured, there was no way out of the death promised to them. "You lied to me," she said, now fighting back tears.

"Not really. Remember what I taught you, Lexa. The best way to seduce someone is with the truth," Jaxen said.

Lexa ceased to care that her exchange with Jaxen was being watched. That was simply the final humiliation. "That's even worse," she said, turning her head slightly. She felt a tiny sting as the knife nicked her skin and the slick line as a trickle of blood made its way down her neck.

"You made me love you," she accused softly.

"I know, and I'm sorry," he said. He sounded genuinely regretful. He punctuated the apology with a gentle, absentminded kiss on the top of her head. It was a habit born from weeks of deception, and it was all she needed. She elbowed him in the stomach and pushed the knife away from her throat. Then she spun around, her hand flying under her tonic to the knife that Kellen had given her. She drew it in one motion, not hesitating for even a second as she plunged it up and into Jaxen's chest once, twice, three times. "I'm sorry," she whispered, looking into his surprised eyes. They were an almost green-grey, staring back at her as his hands feebly clutched at the wounds drawing out his lifeblood. He fell to the ground.

"Lexa!" Tanita's voice was like a whip, drawing Lexa's attention away from the dying man at her feet. "We have to run. Now."

TWENTY ONE

The flight from the factory was an exercise in organised chaos. Tanita snapped out instructions to the others in the workroom. Under the fierce urgency of her voice, the stillness that had descended on the workroom was broken. Tools fell with a clatter as obedient hands rushed to move Jaxen's body and open doors. People called to one another with instructions that spoke of a carefully prepared contingency plan.

Amid it all, Lexa stood still, not even moving when Jaxen's lifeless form was heaved aside and sawdust was thrown over the blood that had pooled on the floor. Disbelief that she had just taken not just a life but the life of Jaxen swirled around her. She felt that there had been some terrible mistake, some confusion that could be easily resolved if only everybody would stop moving about with such urgency.

"Lexa." Her mother was suddenly by her side, a hand on her shoulder.

"Jaxen?" Lexa said, her thoughts in disarray.

"We have to leave," Tanita said instead of answering her daughter's question.

Lexa did not reply, staring dully at the darkening sawdust soaking up the spilled blood.

"Lexa, those people he was working for are on their way. They might be here. We must go." Tanita's voice was filled with quiet urgency, but it did nothing to move Lexa whose limbs suddenly felt terribly heavy. She wanted more than anything to sit down and let her slippery thoughts settle.

Her mother's slap was a crack across her face, the stinging pain only making itself be known after a few seconds.

"We don't have time," Tanita all but shouted at her daughter.

The slap brought Lexa somewhat to her senses and she roused herself enough to follow her mother through the rows of workbenches and out into a yard behind the building.

"Lexa!" The excited voices of her brothers brought the pinprick of tears to her eyes. She had missed them so much.

"You can greet her later," Tanita snapped, her hand in a vicelike grip around Lexa's arm, propelling her daughter forward.

A small crowd of people were looking expectantly at Tanita. "Docks," was all she said, and they sprang into motion, the yard emptying in a matter of seconds.

"Docks?" Lexa repeated the word dreamily.

"Yes, I still have some captains who owe me favours. We were planning on leaving in a day-cycle's time, but today will have to do," Tanita replied grimly.

That comment further roused Lexa from the haze that had embraced her. "You were planning to leave? You said you thought I was dead."

"I did."

"But I wasn't. You would have left me behind?"

"Not now, Lexa," Tanita snapped, grabbing two large oiled capes from pegs that hung on the wall under the cover of an overhang. "Put this on."

Lexa did as she was bade, grimacing at the unpleasant texture of the oiled material under her fingers. Somewhere in the back of her mind were fluttering thoughts about Jaxen, but what her mother had just told her was easier to focus on, easier to think about. "I crossed the country to find you," she protested, following her mother around the yard as Tanita picked up a sack and heaved it over her shoulder.

"Nobody knew what had happened to you. I couldn't stay here with Beji and Ket just in case you were still alive," Tanita replied, handing her another sack. "Here, take this."

"What is it?" Lexa asked, a wounded stubbornness preventing her from following her mother's instructions without question.

"Just take it," Tanita snapped.

The bag was heavy, but the force of her mother's ire compelled Lexa to sling the bag over her shoulder, wincing as the strap cut into her.

The sound of shouting and crashes from inside the workshop turned Lexa's head.

"Come on," Tanita told her daughter as she headed out of the yard and into an alleyway.

Lexa followed her mother obediently. She was reminded of the desperate flight from the forgetting den with Jaxen. Despite the different circumstances, she couldn't help but feel that she had stepped back in time. But instead of Jaxen leading her down the alleyway at a frantic pace, it was her mother. She could see the others who had been in the workshop ahead of them, their strides nervous. Before she had properly considered it, Lexa almost called ahead to her mother to ask where Jaxen was. His absence was so strange. Without him nearby, she felt off-balance, like an arm was missing. As she hurried down the alleyway, she tried to tell herself that she would never see him again, but the prospect seemed so outrageously unreal that she couldn't quite accept it.

The alleyway led into a large street filled with people, carts, and hawkers. It had only been a few minutes since Lexa and Jaxen had entered the factory, since she had killed him, but it felt as though hours had passed. Certainly in those minutes more people had appeared on the streets, and the sun had even managed to break through the clouds and was now shining coldly down on Ketter.

Lexa spied the man she had thought was following her and Jaxen. She turned her face from him, hoping against hope that he wouldn't notice or recognise her, but she heard a shout and turned to see him pointing at her.

Her mother was aware they had been identified and called out an instruction for Lexa to hurry. Lexa shuffled her feet faster, focusing on the rasp of her breathing as she followed the russet glint of her mother's hair

The bag bounced with every step, painfully hitting Lexa's back, but she did not dare slow to adjust it. She fancied she could hear the sound of their pursuers, knocking people to the ground as they advanced on the Farwan group through the crowd.

The wharf area was even busier than the street. Negotiations, often escalating into arguments, between captains and merchants filled the area. Cargo was being loaded and unloaded, often in the least convenient of locations for everybody else. People criss-crossed in front of one another, pushing laden carts and trolleys, yet somehow managed to avoid collisions. It was a familiar scene to Lexa. She had been born and raised around the sound of trade. She slowed her step momentarily, and for a single second, she felt like the person she used to be. But that was broken by the weight of the bag across her shoulder, the coarseness of her clothes, and the urgency of being pursued.

"Dock Four, Lady Farwan." One of the women who Lexa thought had been in the workshop was waiting for them, her eyes wide with urgency.

Tanita nodded and turned left. She was panting, but she did not seem as out of breath as someone her age should be. Lexa caught up to her mother.

"Can you trust her?" Lexa asked. If Jaxen really had betrayed her, she couldn't understand how it was possible to trust anyone.

"I made sure that people I trusted were in that workshop. Their loyalty to me is unshakable," Tanita said as they wove their way   through   the   bustle   of   the   docks. The sound of agitated shouts followed in their wake. Lexa glanced back and saw several people scanning the wharves. She pulled the oiled cape around her with her free hand and tried to look as nonchalant as possible as she followed her mother.

"What happens when we're on the ship?" she asked, her voice fighting with the noise of the docks.

Tanita did not even break her stride. "We leave," she said, her words almost lost in the din.

Lexa glanced about. Shouts reached her ears that could have been the sound of people calling to seize her just as easily as they could be the normal business of the wharves.

She fought the urge to run, amazed that Tanita could look so carefree, walking with a near perfect imitation of the amble common to so many dock workers. They passed two berths, one empty, one with a ship whose contents were being disgorged. The ship berthed in the third dock came into her view, a looming behemoth of a vessel. Lexa amazed herself by wondering, despite the imminent threat, how much such a ship could hold, and if its size would slow down a quick passage. The ship was marked with brands which suggested it came from a place beyond the God-skissed Continent. Such places were considered primitive. Everybody knew that the Godskissed Continent was where human civilisation originated, where the veil between gods and people was first ripped asunder, then resurrected once more when the gods found the mortality of humans too painful to exist alongside. But how could such a primitive place produce such a massive vessel? It was not a question she did not have the time to ponder. Reluctantly, she dragged her eyes away from the huge ship and brought her mind back to the present and the danger it held.

Finally, they reached Dock Four, and Tanita all but charged up the gangplank onto the ship, Lexa in tow. Lexa could see her brothers along with some of the people who had been in the workshop at the far end of the deck, clutching an array of sacks.

The woman Lexa presumed to be the captain took Tanita's hand in greeting and began speaking to her in earnest. Lexa was too busy looking back onto the wharves from the extra height of the ship's deck to properly listen, but she heard fragments of the conversation. She heard the captain tell her mother that the ship was still waiting on a delivery of cloth the next day before they set sail, and they hadn't put in with the harbourmaster to leave until the following day. Tanita was asking for an immediate departure, but the captain was refusing until her ship was fully loaded and she had clearance from the harbour master to depart.

From her vantage, Lexa could see their pursuers searching for them, the way the women moved haphazardly amid the purposeful strides of the workers and traders.

She put down the sack and rested her hands on the ship's railing. The wood was bloated from years of exposure to the rough sea salt, and oddly cold underneath her hands. Jaxen's blood still was on her sleeves, had dried in dark flakes on her hands. She suddenly realised she didn't know what had become of the blade.

It was with a cold realisation of approaching danger than she realised one of the women was looking directly at her. For a moment, they were both locked in place, staring at one another, then the woman on the wharf began yelling to her companions.

"Mother," Lexa called, her voice urgent and imbued with fear.

"What's wrong?" Tanita was immediately at her daughter's side.

"We've been seen," Lexa said.

"They can't board the ship without Alyaine's permission," Tanita reassured her.

"Unless they've been paid enough to force the issue," the captain, Alyaine, Lexa presumed, said. She had come to join them, standing on Lexa's other side. Lexa glanced at the woman's lined features. She saw someone who was cynical enough about the world to survive a great many things. It was oddly comforting.

"Do you really think that's possible?" Lexa asked.

In response, the captain inclined her head toward the six women who were gathered around the hip's gangplank, menace promised by the way they held themselves. "I wouldn't, if I were you," she called to them. Lexa thought she heard the suggestion of an accent in the woman's voice. It was strange what her mind focused on amid the danger.

The group of mercenaries conferred among themselves while Lexa, Tanita, and Alyaine watched. It seemed an almost absurd moment of suspense. The pulse in Lexa's throat begin to accelerate, the fluttering uncertainty requiring her to force the breath past the beat of her heart. Finally, the thickly muscled women reached some kind of consensus and as one, charged up the gangplank.

"Oh dear," Alyaine muttered. She didn't sound overly concerned. Calmly, she stepped forward to greet the first of the assailants, an efficient thrust with her arm pushing the woman into the dirty water below. Lexa wondered with a dispassionate curiosity if the woman was able to swim. The second woman, closely following her comrade, did not give Alyaine time to swing again, bringing a cudgel to the captain's side that saw her crumpling to the ground. The five remaining women came at Lexa and Tanita. Lexa, who had stabbed Jaxen without hesitation, felt herself freeze. The women were so obviously comfortable with violence and death. It was terrifyingly intimidating. She prepared herself for the sting of their blows, but suddenly Tanita was between her and the attackers, the heavy sack still in her hands connecting with the head of the woman closest to her. The desperately elegance with which her mother wielded the sack amazed Lexa. Two more people fell at Tanita's hands. Lexa suspected that at least one of them would likely not get up again, judging by the angle of her head on the deck. However, Tanita's lawless technique, while offering her the advantage of surprise, did not match the obvious training of her remaining attackers. She was pulled into a hold that left her unable to move. Lexa watched all of this with a transfixed sense of horror, then realised the remaining two women were coming straight for her. Even though she knew they didn't want to kill her – whatever information she and Tanita possessed made them too valuable to kill outright – that did not ease her terror. She stumbled backward on the decking, her mind blank of any strategy that could save her. It seemed so unfair that she had come so far to be taken now.

The crew of the ship came to her rescue, running at the attackers. The invasion had seemingly frozen everybody with shock, but now that both the captain and Tanita overcome, the need to act pushed the onlooking crew into action. They ran sure-footed across the deck and crashed into the two women advancing on Lexa, fiercely defending the sovereignty of their ship. Tanita's captor was similarly taken, furious hands pulling her free.

The entire scuffle was over in a matter of seconds. Lexa looked at the scene which had shifted so quickly before her eyes. Tanita stumbled over to cast an appraising eye over her daughter to ensure her safety. A short distance from them, Alyaine was being helped to her feet. She was clutching her side and moving with obvious pain, but she otherwise seemed fine.

The attackers who were still conscious were being watched over by members of Alyaine's crew. Many of them held improvised weapons. Lexa would personally not have wanted to find out how a hook could be used as a weapon. She had no doubt that it would have a messy outcome.

"Captain?" one of the crew asked Alyaine. She straightened, her arm still slung around one of her people to hold herself upright.

"I think perhaps it's better if we leave right away, rather

than waiting for the extra cargo, or even the harbourmaster's permission," she said, her eyes sliding grimly to meet Tanita's. Several of the crew immediately moved to begin preparations to sail.

"As much as I'm not looking forward to paying the fine, and losing the cargo, we've got enough loaded that we'll still make a good profit," Alyaine added.

"What about them?" a crewman asked, jerking a thumb at the captives.

Alyaine once more shared a look with Tanita. Lexa saw a hard understanding pass between the women. She could understand why her mother trusted this captain.

"I think once we're out far enough they can swim back," Alyaine said, hobbling off to oversee the ship's departure.

TWENTY TWO

Four days passed at sea and Lexa spoke not one word in that time. Despite her joy a seeing her brothers again, every time she went to say something to them, she found herself unable to find the words to begin a conversation of any kind. They regarded her with an uncertainty whenever she approached that made her hesitate. She learned that they had been in the workshop and seen her stab Jaxen. She spared herself and them the difficulty of awkward exchanges by secluding herself, preferring to sit for hours at a time on the ship's deck despite the cold, gazing out first at the receding strip of land, then at the unending expanse of sea once the land disappeared from view. She found herself lost within the undulating waves. When it was overcast on the second day, the water became a grey that reminded her of Jaxen's eyes.

On the fourth day Tanita came to sit beside her. Huge sea birds swirled around in the distance, reassuring that land was not far away. Lexa had learned that from the idle chatter of the crew. They did not seem overly perturbed by the reclusive, silent behaviour of their passenger.

"I'm sorry," Tanita said eventually.

"For what?" Lexa's voice came out as a croak, stilted with disuse. She wondered whether her voice would fade away into nothingness if she simply stopped talking altogether. Perhaps then she would lose the words for the turbulent mess of grief and anger and deep hurt inside her, and then that would engulf her completely.

"For what you went through." The assurance with which Tanita offered the sentiment to her daughter was what Lexa had known her whole life. She was not sure if she hated her mother for the lack of any softness, or if she was grateful for it. She did not want to speak of what she had felt for Jaxen in poetic, emotional terms, or experience the great wave of confused feelings that she knew hid behind some wall inside her.

For a moment, Lexa contemplated asking her mother what had happened, how on earth they had managed to lose everything, but it ultimately did not matter. This truth was the one they were living, and to ruminate on the how and why would only send her into the seething well of emotion that she did not wish to feel.

"Are you all right with what you did to that man, Jaxen?" Tanita asked softly.

"I miss him," Lexa confessed. "I know he probably never cared for me, but I miss him all the same." That was a hard truth to admit aloud, yet it was the one thing she felt she could not contain. The shame of being deceived, the guilty horror that she had killed him, the grief for the fact that he was gone, they were all things she did not wish to allow to wash over her, but this truth, the fact that she kept looking for him, to make a comment, to reach out and touch, that was something into which she kept falling over and over again. His presence was a habit that she still had not unlearned.

"Did you care for him?" Tanita asked. Her voice held none of the gentleness offered to those who have undergone hardship, but there was a certain softness to the way she asked it that Lexa appreciated.

Lexa shrugged, her eyes still on the thin line where sky and sea merged. "I suppose."

Tanita was silent, but Lexa could feel her mother's stare on her.

"So what are we going to do to get our land back?" Lexa asked.

The tenor to Tanita's silence was disconcerting.

"Mother? What's your plan?"

"Right now, the plan is to stay safe."

"Stay safe?" Lexa echoed in disbelief.

"Yes."

The realisation was like a physical blow. "You don't have a plan, do you?"

"No. I had arranged passage with Alyaine to the First Country. All I had planned was for those of us who had gathered at the crate workshop to leave."

"You would have left without me?" The shock had worked its way through Lexa and now she was asking once more to confirm it for herself.

"I thought you were dead." Tania did not sound particularly appalled by the fact that had Lexa arrived only a few days later, she would have missed her family completely. It was a prospect that Lexa had turned over in her mind several times during her days of silence. She wondered what she would have done had she found nobody in the warehouse. She wondered what Jaxen would have done to her had their search been fruitless. Perhaps he would have turned her over to the people who were shadowing them.

Many times, she had gone back over their journey and found what she suspected were the points when he had communicated with the people for whom he worked. The brief times when he had left on some mysterious errand of his own, to buy a dagger, for instance, were obviously when he had appraised his employers of their progress. She chided herself for not having felt suspicious, for believing him when he told her that she had been a compelling reason to leave the Enclave. She chided herself for wanting to believe what he had told her. Kellen had been suspicious. She should have listened to her friend's caution, guarded her heart more carefully and thought more like the daughter of Tanita Farwan.

"You never told me anything about our family's business," Lexa's voice was so bitter that it sounded unfamiliar to her own ears.

"To protect you," Tanita said. Her voice was flat, uncompromising.

"If it were known that I knew nothing of importance, I would have been killed," Lexa refuted.

"Perhaps," Tanita said. "But there is always more than one way to protect someone," she added.

Lexa could not be bothered attempting to decipher her mother's cryptic comment. Instead, she was unwillingly reminded of Jaxen's comment the first night that they were away from the Enclave, that Mawani's husband had been named Elui. Hiding someone away to protect them. Hiding a whole gender away to protect them, and to protect the women who fell desperately in love with them and were hurt when they died. Or were betrayed by them.

"You can't keep things from me to protect me. It doesn't work," Lexa said. Something about the way she spoke sounded, to her own ears, like her mother's definite tone.

Tanita took a moment to reply. She rarely replied immediately. "I suppose it doesn't," she said.

Lexa was almost certain that they were both thinking of Jaxen who had been so desperate to escape the protection that was forced upon him.

"You know, if he had accompanied you without agenda, he would have been offered passage with us, perhaps even a place in our household," Tanita said.

Lexa nodded. It was a thought that had occurred to her among her many hours of solitude. "I don't think he ever would have stood to be in someone else's service." It was the conclusion at which she had arrived. Or perhaps it was the justification to which she clung.

Silence fell in waves between mother and daughter. Lexa had never realised how little conversation she and Tanita had that was unrelated to matters of business or trade strategy.

"Are we ever going back?" she asked eventually.

"I'm not certain." It was a remarkable response. Tanita was almost never uncertain. Her definitiveness was the compass by which Lexa understood the world.

Lexa considered the idea of never again setting foot upon the Fourth Country, never speaking with Kellen, or Emi, or even Serenah. Everything that was home, that she had known, felt distant, as though it belonged to another person's life. There was a bitter taste in her mouth too, at the realisation her mother believed there was no way for the Farwan lands to be retaken. What remained of the Farwan family was fleeing, not regrouping. What she had done to Jaxen seemed insignificant in comparison.

"I miss father," she said, more to herself than Tanita. Such discussions about the nature of loss, or the grief she felt for Jaxen that had yet to make itself truly known, would have been best had with her father in quiet moments, stolen from the gaze and world of purpose that Tanita occupied.

"So do I," Tanita said. Lexa glanced from the sea to her mother's face and saw tears swimming in her mother's eyes. "He might have been my *elui*, but I loved him dearly."

With anger, Lexa brushed away the tears that had gathered at her mother's admission. Her mother had never spoken or demonstrated any affection toward her father before. Now that she confessed she did love him, it only evoked a deep sadness within Lexa. She did not want to allow herself to miss her father in such a profound way. If she began to cry for her father, then she may never stop crying, for everything that had been lost, and for everything that had been done to her and her family. She hated herself for those tears that had leaked out.

"Where are we going?" she asked by way of moving to subjects that were less treacherous. She had paid not the slightest heed to any mention of their destination, nor had she bothered to ask. It had not seemed at all important.

"The First Country."

Lexa looked at her mother in surprise. The channel to the First Country was known only by a few ships and those who had been there spoke sparingly of what they saw when they docked there. There was some speculation that this was not by choice, but because it was impossible to remember much of the First Country, in the same way that finding it by land across the mountain pass had proven impossible in living memory.

"Where do you think forget-me-not comes from?" Tanita asked.

"I'd never thought about it," Lexa replied. "Do you know anything about what it's like there?"

"Not really. I know it's different. Men are viewed as equals, like in the Third Country. There's no fighting for land, like we have. It's a very peaceful place, I believe," Tanita said. "They're very careful about ensuring that everybody is treated properly, even the most lowly of individuals." From the way she spoke, it was clear that Tanita found this attitude bewildering.

Lexa could see why Jaxen had wanted to try to get to the First Country. It sounded like everything the Fourth Country was not. It seemed there was nothing of which she could think that she did not pair with Jaxen. It was as though guilt, or grief, or love, had like a persistent splinter, wedged itself into her.

"But they dislike foreigners, don't they? Will they let us stay?"

Tanita lifted a hand to capture a lock of hair that the breeze had blown across her eyes. "They've traded with me for long enough that I have some status there. We won't be accorded full citizenship, but they will extend to us every courtesy."

"Like the Katan family in the Fourth Country," Lexa said eventually.

Tanita nodded.

Lexa considered the prospect of being an exile. She silently tested the word on the tip of her tongue. It felt strange, but not humiliating as she once would have thought.

"I'm sorry I did not tell you about the forget-me-not," Tanita said.

"Why didn't you?" The boat crested a particularly large wave. A fine mist of salt spray came across the deck, gently settling onto Lexa and Tanita's hair. The droplets sparkled in the sunlight.

"I didn't think you were ready."

Lexa observed the frustration she felt at her mother's response as though from a distance. It was almost like she was smoking forget-me-not. But she did not use forget-me-not anymore. When she spoke, it was with measured calmness. "When would I have been ready?"

"When it would not have shocked you to learn that I did things that were not always good," Tanita said.

"I love you anyway," Lexa said simply.

"I know. Perhaps I wanted to protect you from that, too," Tanita admitted. "You were always so gentle."

Lexa couldn't tell if it was an observation or recrimination. "I'm sorry," she said anyway. She had prided herself on being Tanita Farwan's daughter, yet it seemed she had none of the hardness that her mother possessed. "Perhaps if I weren't like that, I wouldn't have believed Jaxen, or cared about him. Even now, I know he did bad things, but I still care about him," Lexa said. That admission in some ways was more shameful than the fact that Jaxen had fooled her so completely.

Tanita rested a hand on her daughter's shoulder. "I do not believe that the Fourth Country is a place where that sort of gentle heart is encouraged. I hoped that the Academy would teach you to harden it. I'm no longer so certain that it is what would have been good for you."

Despite the crisp sea breeze, the sun was warming, and Lexa felt the rays mix with her mother's words and sink into her skin, and she began to believe that she would be all right.

ACKNOWLEDGEMENTS

Once again, there are a great many people who deserve thanks which extends far beyond simply putting their name in this section. But to note them here is at least a start. By now, the list is looking quite familiar.

The most significant thanks must once more go first to my family. My mother and father have each in their own way assisted both through the provision of material support and emotional support in the production of Ruthless Land. Offering an eye to editing and formatting, as well as providing a sympathetic ear over many, many, many meals, both of them have listened to me worry and talk about my books with the love and (feigned?) interest that only a truly loving parent can possess.

Jason came on board again for the editing process and did another great job. I encourage any writers out there to very seriously consider taking on an editor to assist in the process of honing your work. Seeing through Jason's eyes has made me a better writer, both in this version of the text you have just read, and in future works.

In between various assignments and trip-planning, Marcus produced some of his best work for the cover, so I must thank him not only for his work, but for the fact that he did it amid a myriad of other demands on his time. Likewise Ellen, who did the illustrations for Queendom and King, and who graciously drew the map for the Fourth Country, absolutely outdid herself.

And of course, without Mitchell, I am not sure any of this

would have come to pass. His tireless love, and unflagging belief in the quality of my stories – even when I have doubted everything – makes pushing through those times of doubt and uncertainty that much easier.

Finally, I would like to that those first readers of Queendom and King who have loved it. My friends (old and new), students, fans, and everyone in between. I know this was a different type of book to Elen-ai and Gidyon's story, and Freya's story, which will follow, is a different type of book again. Thank you for your support, your appreciation, and your love. It means the world.

ABOUT THE AUTHOR

Alice Jane Boer-Endacott was born and raised in Melbourne, Australia. She does not have a pet kangaroo, and she certainly did not ride a kangaroo to school. She does have pet cats, but she has never ridden them to school, either. Queendom of the Seven Lakes, her debut novel, was written while playing Dragon Age Inquisition. King of the Seven Lakes was not written while playing any specific video game, although she does recommend Borderlands for some light relief when a scene isn't quite working. Ruthless Land was written while she was obsessively watching interviews with Stephen King. Read into that how you will...

You can visit her website to keep up to date with books releases, or to read more about the Second Country at:
www.abendacott.com
Alternatively, you can follow her on facebook (A B Endacott),
or Instagram (@alicejaneboere),
or Twitter (@ajendacott)

COMING LATE 2018

DARK INTENT

"you can either live in the world that surrounds you, or you can fight for the world you want."

Many years after the brutal Kade takeover of the Third Country, Freya Kuch, a healer, has succeeded when many Pious have failed: she is a perfect Kade citizen. However, this life of willing subjugation is torn apart when is caught in an attack perpetrated by the anarchic followers of the Dark Gods and assigned to care for Zarech, their captured leader. Contrary to her expectations, he is not a raving madman but charismatic and quite rational.

Over the long months of his treatment she unwillingly becomes close to Zarech and she begins to reconsider everything, especially as he reveals the supernatural abilities bestowed upon those with true piety. Her obedience to the strict Kade regime is further complicated by her attraction to Ashtyn, a member of the Pious Resistance movement. She tries to ignore her feelings knowing full well the brutal punishments for adultery and dissidence. But soon, she is forced to decide: will she maintain her life of careful safety, or give in to her heart's dark desires and join the fight against the Kade's regime?

READ ON FOR THE FIRST CHAPTER

ONE

The bells woke her.

As she did each morning, Freya rolled over and nudged Symon awake. He moaned softly in protest at the early awakening and moved further away from her.

"Wake up. We have to get to the square," she said when it became apparent he wasn't going to move. He sighed in resignation and after a moment longer, he got out of their bed. With the wordless accordance of long-established habit, they orbited one another as they quickly bathed and dressed. The first worship of the day was before the sun even rose, so the streets down which they hurried were cool and dark. People moved along with them to the square, the final vestiges of sleep still clinging to their movements.

The square was one of many placed every few streets so that worship was possible at any time. With the proliferation of squares across the city, nobody had an excuse to miss a single prayer. As she stood there alongside about seventy other people, their breath collectively rising in the grey predawn, Freya thought for a moment how brutal the sudden clear space was in contrast to the elegant buildings surrounding it. She couldn't quite remember, but she thought she recalled that this square had been created after the takeover by tearing a structure down to make room for it. Certainly, the ground was paved with the same smooth white stone as the city's streets rather than the more beautifully coloured stones that graced the floors of the city's older worship squares. With a glance at the trees that lined one side, she verified that this square was indeed a relatively recent addition to the city. The trees were only a few years old, nowhere near tall enough to provide the shade that people often enjoyed during moments of non-worship in the grander, older squares.

Wary habit had her observing the people around her. Guardians were in the crowd at nearly every worship in the Pious district, keeping an eye on them to make sure they were worshipping as the laws decreed. It was ironic. As a result of the measures, Pious were the ones who worshipped the Kade Gods the most dutifully. She wondered how many Kade across the city had left their beds that morning while it was still dark. Then again, they probably didn't have the same incentives as the Pious. The lives of Pious who didn't worship enough were inevitably made very difficult. They would suffer frequent checks by Guardians for any and all manner of things. Invariably, some inappropriate behaviour would be discovered, the punishment for which was the revoking of work licences, the requirement to retrain, or a restriction of movement...whatever was most inconvenient. Sometimes when a Pious was still particularly resistant to demonstrate how completely they had adopted the Kade way of life, the gas seams that supplied their houses with heat and light would ignite, without explanation, and the entire house and anybody who was unlucky enough not to get out was burnt to a charred wreck. Anybody who dared openly speak out against such things disappeared. Although, such occurrences were reasonably rare now. The citizens of Oranis had a long memory, and they remembered well what had happened to those Pious who had refused to accept the terms of the new regime when the Kade had taken control six years previously. Those individuals had been literally dragged through the streets, begging for mercy. Almost all of them had screamed that they would relent, to stop the torment. But, by the time that they offered their fealty it was too late, and they died within hours from the wounds inflicted by the unrelenting ground. Freya herself had watched as those people relinquished their beliefs while their skin was practically peeled away, and committed herself vigorously to the edicts of the Kade. For a second as she reflected upon such things, her mind filled with the image of Rohana, but she viciously clamped down on the memory, pushing it back into the space in her mind where such thoughts were safely buried.

As the square filled, Freya cleared her mind to commit her focus entirely on the ritual of the prayer. She'd heard it whispered that the Guardians and the Ordained could tell if you weren't fully focused on the rituals. Doubt weighed on her about the truth of such a claim; they were only people after all. That being said, caution guaranteed longevity. She emptied her mind of any thoughts which could be even vaguely deemed subversive and focused on the incantation. The Ordained began to move through the square as they spoke, waving smouldering arax root back and forth. The slightly acrid scent washed over the space, sending everybody into the trance-like state that facilitated focus on a single task or idea. Freya inhaled deeply. Occasionally, those who were perceived to not inhale enough arax root were questioned. She had no desire to give anyone any cause to question her, to doubt her loyalty. To be doubted was to ensure life became difficult, so she sucked in lungfuls of the smoky air. She felt her thoughts begin to slip and slide into what had become, over the years, a familiar state. The experience was almost akin to her memory of being drunk – intoxication was also not looked upon favourably by the Kade, and Freya had only ever been drunk once in her life, before the takeover when she had been a young girl. Now, she barely touched any fermented drink for fear of imbibing too much. She wanted neither to loosen her tongue to carelessness with the effects of alcohol nor to appear in any way counter to the ideals of Kade life.

The Ordained raised their voices in chant. The sound never ceased to be harsh to her ears, although she couldn't quite say why. The invocations today were mundane; for peace, fortune, for the Kade gods to evermore favour those who worshipped them, that Oranis would continue its prosperous reign over the Third Country. Her mind wandered into the dark, cavernous space that she went to when she prayed. Within it, her own mind and thoughts were contained only by her awareness of them. This was the place to which she had come in prayer from her earliest memory. Yet this space, while once comforting, was now somewhere she only went with reluctance. She assumed the reason she now found it so alien, so filled with an unfamiliar presence, was because she was here at the law's requirement rather than of her own desire. The act of praying which had once given her reprieve from her worries, and a sense of peace, now was a duty she undertook with a sense of dull intrusion.

She remained in the space of nothingness, of dark existence within her mind, and the words of prayer to the Kade gods filtered through her awareness. She was dimly aware of the Ordained as they moved through the rows of people in the square. The drone of the voices permeated everything as they repeated the prayers to their gods over and over. It was almost as though they were intoning the words into the ears of every individual who stood there with docile obedience procured by the law, and the promise of violent reprisal if they did not obey. Finally, the sun began to touch the rooftops, sending a pink glow down into the square as the walls reflected the light. As the effects of the arax root began to wane, the Ordained moved back to ascend the raised section at the front of the square, lining up on it and raising their arms. "Behold. They have blessed us with a new day!" Their voices rose as one before they fell silent. The crowd stirred, as though finally awakening. Freya looked to her left where Symon was. He was looking down, his face impassive but for a small frown. She wondered as she often did, what he was thinking. The crowd waited obediently until the arms of the Ordained fell – the signal of dismissal – before filing out of the square.

Freya and Symon walked back to their house, their feet falling into synchronised steps. It wasn't unusual for them to walk in silence but on that morning she perceived a difference to the tenor of Symon's quiet.

"Is everything alright?" she asked.

He reflexively glanced around before answering. "Do you ever think that their incantations are an attempt to control us?"

She glanced back at him, surprised by the boldness of his remark. Even now, years after the times of unrest, it was dangerous to say anything toward the Kade that could be construed as derogatory. "Of course," she replied casually. "Why else would they reinforce that peace and prosperity are achieved thanks to the Kade's governance?"

Symon dragged his feet as he walked, his footfalls tumbling out of step with hers. The sound grated on Freya's nerves. She didn't understand what he could possibly be kicking his feet against. The streets were paved with completely flat slabs of white stone that left no unevenness save the gutters that ran along their edges, yet he managed to produce the scuffing noise. "Do you think they're brainwashing us, Freya?" he asked abruptly.

She considered his question as they moved through the lightening streets. The glow of the rising sun seemed to breathe life into the city; Oranis was suddenly a symphony of tender pink, gold, and soft cream. She was as surprised by the suddenness of his questions as she was that he was sharing his thoughts with her. Symon was a self-contained, cautious man. "I hadn't really thought about it," she said noncommittally, trying to scan the shadows for any ears that may overhear their conversation. She liked her house. She didn't want it burnt down in an 'accident'. Especially if she was still inside it.

"Think about it, though," he pressed. "They drug us every morning and evening at the prayers, and while we're drugged, they tell us how wonderful the Kade is. Surely that's brainwashing?"

Nervous now at the lack of care he was displaying, Freya walked faster, practically running to their front door. "Symon, arax root clears the mind. It can't be used as a brainwashing tool," she said, opening the front door and stepping inside the relative safety of their house. She was profoundly glad to remove this particular conversation from the street where anybody could be listening.

"Are you sure?" he challenged as she closed the door firmly behind them.

"I'm a healer. I work in the Main Healing Centre. I have to know the properties of every herb in the Third Country. I would know if arax root could affect people like that," she said firmly. "What's brought this on, anyway?" she pursued, turning to actually look at him.

He made a half-shrugging motion. "Just something I overheard in the tailor's," he said vaguely.

"From a Kade official?" she asked, a sliver or curiosity aroused by this fact. Symon's skill as a tailor meant he made clothes for some of the Third Country's most powerful people. He often alluded to some of the things he overheard, but was normally quite tight-lipped about the specifics of what was said.

He made a noise of affirmation. "What did they say?" she asked.

"Perhaps I misheard," he replied.

"What did they say," she repeated, feeling a slight lick of irritation at his sudden reticence.

"Honestly, Freya, it's not that important," he replied.

Before she could inquire further, he walked into another room. The sounds of him readying himself for work told her that the conversation was concluded, and the likelihood that he would raise it once more was small. As far as she was concerned though, that was fine. She didn't want to engage any further in a discussion that could get them both sanctioned. Or worse.